A Version of Life

Daniel Lance Wright

ALL THINGS
THAT MATTER
PRESS

A Version of Life

ISBN 13: 9780999524343
Library of Congress Control Number: 2018932473
Cover Photos: Unsplash.com

Cover design © by All Things That Matter Press
Published in 2018 by All Things That Matter Press

This novel was an idea I privately kicked around for months. But it was a brain-storming session during a mere ten-minute drive with two members of my extended family that changed the dynamic of that privately held concept and kick-started the writing process. I began drafting A Version of Life a day later. I will be forever thankful to you, Bill Painter, for saying the right things at the right time.

Chapter 1 ~ The Love Story Begins

George Waller floated on his back in comfortably tepid water, arms to his sides, coursing under power not of his making. How he came to be here was unimportant. He didn't struggle and didn't want to. Where he traveled to and when it might end was equally unimportant. Going with it was the important consideration. Even without control, it was pleasant. His movement was guided—head above water looking into a sky that was not the blue of day nor the black of night but formless white that bore outlines of faces hinting familiarity. Current flowing by his face felt like cradling hands. He had no desire to do anything other than to be part of it.

An encroaching sensation that was not so pleasant layered thinly upon these easy feelings—a growing sensation of breathing difficulty. What was this simmering discomfort? he wondered. He fought desire to understand it—this unidentifiable yet disquieting awareness surging within him.

A sound came to him from a great distance. He wasn't certain he should care, indecipherable as it was. He wanted only to enjoy this peaceful river, distractions and sadness be damned. He forced breathing deep and deliberate, attempting to dispel the indefinable uneasiness bubbling inside him.

His throat tightened. It occurred to him that he mistook breathing difficulty for a billowing urge to cry. If this experience was as wonderful as he thought, he didn't know where an impulse to cry came from. There were no tears. But there was heaviness pressing his heart. Ragged breathing followed. Drifting into painless oblivion was apparently not to be, regardless of how desperately sought. Something, or someone, refused his wish.

What began as faint and distant grew louder—a human voice. Still, he couldn't determine if it was distant chatter, an imagined thing, or a sincere call to action. It contained the cadence of language, but indistinct. Flowing water enveloping him tugged at his ability to care about it, its source, or anything of humanity for that matter. The voice, if that is what it was, held equal distraction, reaching down from somewhere above, searching for attention. He became confused—torn between desires he couldn't define. He sensed longing, but he didn't know what for. Although the faraway sound of human speech came to him as competing multiple voices, one grew louder. The others withdrew. The white sky segued to limbo black. The faces that had been floating within the white swirling sky overhead vanished. He couldn't see beyond the black any better than he could the misty white. The change sparked a yearning.

The living river pressed into the side of his face, supporting it as warm loving hands might. His head moved side to side, while the blackness closed around him.

As awareness began to return, he realized those hands were not pushing, they were hitting. The slaps were painful and stung. The dominant voice that had been indistinct now came crashing into clarity.

"Hey, George! Wake up, buddy. Are you okay?"

Thirty-seven-year-old George Waller drew a quick panicked breath. He didn't know where he was or why someone would be striking him. The river he floated upon vanished. His head didn't float free as he thought, it lay heavily upon an uncomfortably cold and solid surface. He attempted opening his eyes but couldn't make it happen. He felt strong arms slip beneath him and lift.

"Come on back to me, George." The slaps reduced to a single hand patting one cheek.

He became aware of searing pain at the base of his skull. He groaned and felt for the point of misery on the back of his neck, uncertain why it hurt so. He wondered if he got hit or stabbed. He felt no wound.

The flat of a palm in the center of his back held him up. George fluttered his eyes open and looked into the face of a well-groomed young man, mid-thirties perhaps, tending to him. He wore a tuxedo and smelled of cologne. The man showed a frown of concern upon his face. In aggressive tone, he said, "Every time you do this, it scares hell out of me, George. You really need to get a handle on those headaches. If you don't, I'll hog tie you and force you to do something about it—and soon, too."

George examined the man's face. "Are you a doctor?"

The man's serious expression softened. He stared down at him quietly for a fat second, snicker, and then laughed. "Doctor? Hell, George, if you hadn't let me cheat off you I wouldn't have graduated from high school. But, thanks for thinking so. Honestly, those headaches of yours are odd little buggers, always starting with blinding neck pain, passing out—sometimes not, but always followed by these memory lapses. I know you've been ignoring them because they never last over a minute and the pain goes away as soon as your memory returns. Still, you ought to get checked out by a real doctor."

George continued massaging his neck. "So, I've known you for some time, huh?" He squinted up at the guy, noticing that he was a large man but not at all obese—six-four perhaps and well-muscled with thinning hair.

"All our lives." He sighed indulgently as if he had told this story many times before. "We grew up next door to one another and went through twelve years of school together, always in the same class. Just sit for a minute. It'll all come back to you shortly, always does."

The pain had not subsided and although there was familiarity to this guy, George could not yet pull a shared history from a slow returning memory. "Is your name Andrew or, maybe, your last name is Andrews?"

"Andrew? Where did you pull that name from?"

George bounced a quick shrug of the shoulders. "I don't know. It was the first thing that came to me and I thought I'd go with instinct." He rolled his head and again squinted up at the guy. "Besides, you look like an Andrew." He forced a thin smile. The pain abated. He continued rolling his head and stretching his neck side to side. And then, as if a flash bulb exploded in his face, it came to him. "Not Andrew but Alexander . . . you're Alex Burton."

George scanned the room. It was a study or a small library. He noticed movement and spotted a pair of cuddling white-wing doves. They were perched without worry on the limb of a sprawling and artfully gnarled live oak tree beyond a window with panes partitioned by leaded mullions behind a large highly polished desk. The birds cooed as if all were well with the world on a brilliant cloud-free day. The sky was a flawless crystalline blue while a faint breeze teased the leaves of the big tree. He looked to his legs splayed upon the floor. He wore black pants with satin stripes down the sides of the legs, realizing he wore a tuxedo. He gestured toward his pants. "I . . . uh . . ."

"That's right, my friend, you have a wedding to get to and we both will be late for it if I can't get you up and moving again."

George rolled over onto hands and knees. "Sorry about all this, Alex." He glanced up. "How come I get the feeling I tell you that a lot?"

"Because you do. This happens a couple of times a week and usually when I'm around. You say some truly goofy things before your memory snaps back."

"I hope nothing cruel."

"Nah, just odd stuff."

George rose to his feet but continued looking around, getting his bearings. He noticed the photo of a groundbreaking ceremony. In it was a sign next to a group of shovel-wielding men that read: Future Home of the First United Methodist Church. It set alone in a position of prominence on a bookshelf next to the desk. "So, I'm getting married today and this is a church. Right?"

"Yep, and you best not go out there until you remember your fiancé's name. Geez. How embarrassing would that be?" He chuckled.

"I can almost hear you now, 'I'd like you to meet my new wife, ol' What's-Her-Name.'"

George curled one side of his lip and frowned. "Not really funny," he said swaying slightly from side to side.

"Sorry. I couldn't resist." Alex pointed to one of two leather wingback chairs fronting that broad, ornately carved dark cherry wood desk with a slick glassy surface. "Why don't you sit for a short while? You're not a hundred-percent yet."

George felt the insistent pressure of Alex's hand push him toward the chair. "You're right. I need to take a minute. Just because I thought your little joke was inappropriate, that doesn't make it any less true." He acquiesced to Alex's urging and sat.

There was a knock at the door.

"Come in," Alex said, spinning around to face the door.

A man opened it a crack and craned his head around the edge of it. "Are you fellas about ready? I'm getting word from the bridesmaids that the guests are getting antsy and that Jennifer is ready to get married right now. Apparently, she's no less anxious."

Jennifer? George stared at the man's disembodied face that seemed suspended half way up the door and thought about the name. *Jennifer.*

Alex knelt beside his chair. "What about it? Are you ready?"

George felt ill at ease, still uncertain about everything that was going on. But, he couldn't disregard the man at the door that seemed to know him and the woman he was marrying or this guy Alex kneeling beside his chair waiting for an answer. His friend remained a foggy but familiar vision swimming in his reawakening mind that he intuitively felt comfortable believing. Pieces of the puzzle fell into place. "Well," he said, "I'm going to trust that this is what is supposed to happen." He rose from the chair hesitantly, by way of a two-handed assist on the front of the desk and then stepped over to a large wall mirror.

"Good," Alex replied. "I'm going to let history be my guide and encourage you to get on with it. These spells usually clear up entirely in less than a couple of minutes." He looked over his shoulder to the messenger at the door. "Yeah, we're ready." He then mumbled to George from the corner of his mouth, "We hope."

The man offered a beaming smile. "See you in the chapel," he said, as he closed the door, leaving them alone in the office again.

George stood before the mirror within a gilded frame and smoothed the front of his tuxedo jacket. Once he examined his face and straightened his dark hair, it occurred to him who Jennifer was, aside from being his fiancé. His hand froze in mid-stroke on the side of his head as he re-positioned a couple of errant hair strands. "Jennifer grew up with us and we went to school together, didn't we?"

"Now it's coming back to you."

"Brunette, dark eyes, five-seven, a-hundred-twenty-five pounds, or so?"

"Yep," Alex replied crisply. "But I think I'd say a-hundred-fifteen pounds, just to be on the safe side." He laughed. "She was one of our crew from the earliest days and, somewhere along the way you guys fell in love and voilà! Here we are. Come on, let's get this show on the road," he said as he opened the door with crisp confidence, ushering George into the hallway. "There's a chapel full of people down the hall that might find something better to do on a Saturday morning than sit through a wedding that's already a half hour late."

"Sure," George said, taking a final check of his appearance. His freshly cut dark hair left a narrow lighter skin color around his ears and neck where it had been trimmed above the tan line. Freshly scrubbed cheeks glowed above a cleanly shaven face. It was clear at a glance that he had spent time achieving the look. He turned and smoothed his tuxedo jacket one last time. He took tentative steps toward the door. "I suppose I'm ready." Suddenly nervous, George smiled weakly at Alex, adding, "Let's go see what I can do about re-inventing myself." *Re-inventing myself?* The phrase struck him as an odd thing to say, wondering if there were things he still couldn't remember, but should. As he and Alex marched down the hall, he finally recognized this as the church he had grown up attending but had been rebuilt on a nearby lot in nineteen-ninety-three. This explained the photo of a groundbreaking ceremony framed and in a place of prominence on that book shelf back in the office. Comfort level with his returning memory escalated quickly, but so did fluttery feelings over what was about to happen. He was getting married. He shuddered with the full force of realization of what that meant. Alex opened one side of the double doors into the chapel. A mélange of smells went up George's nose from inside the chapel—various perfumes, colognes, and the sweet smell of freshly cut blossoms.

"Wait 'til I take the best man position on stage," Alex said, "and then come on up."

George leaned sideways into his friend and nodded. "Yeah, it's all coming back to me now. Thanks for being patient. I must be a real pain-in-the-ass to you."

Alex stifled a laugh. "Yeah, you are." He gave George a friendly slap on the shoulder. "But that's okay, I'm used to it. No more piddlin' around, let's do this thing. And don't worry. You'll do fine. See you up there." He gave George a final reassuring pat on the back and left him standing.

While George waited for his friend to walk up the center aisle to the front of the chapel and assume his place next to the altar, he scanned the chapel—up, down, and to both sides. The high and heavily beamed cathedral ceiling rose to a peak about twenty feet above his head. Behind the podium and the stepped choir risers, a beautiful stained-glass arch extended down about half-way to the floor from the ceiling peak. Below the glistening stained glass was a large window looking out onto a meticulously manicured garden with a fountain flowing into a pond from a pot held by the statue of a winged angel. The stained glass captured rays of the sun and transformed them into a marvelous mix of reds, blues, greens and yellows—bathing all attendees in a rich array of colors. The chapel was full. There were a couple hundred people seated and waiting. Once they saw Alex walking swiftly toward the front, a few heads turned to see if he was about to follow. Some even looked again. *They're all looking at me as if surprised I showed up. Would they have reason to wonder?*

As Alex took his place on the platform and turned, George moved swiftly up the central aisle between row after row of filled pews—everyone smiling. Reaching the front, he stepped up onto the platform before the altar. He shook Alex's hand and whispered, "Ready or not, here we go." He turned to face the closed double doors into the chapel.

A pastor holding a bible rose from his chair and stepped to the altar, nodding to a lady sitting at the organ behind Alex near the edge of the stage. She took the cue and began playing the wedding march. Without further prompt, the congregation followed protocol by rising and facing the door into the chapel. Two young ushers simultaneously opened each side of the double doors revealing the love of his life standing in a full glittering white wedding gown with a veiled face standing next to a man that he instinctively knew as her father. An odd thought struck him. George couldn't remember ever having seen the man and wondered where he had come from to be here. But all it took was a glance back to Jennifer to erase concern about the incongruity. An emotion-filled swirl of memories raced through his mind of this woman walking toward him that he was about to marry. Snapshots over twenty-plus years told an indelible story of how they had grown so close and how the inevitability of this moment could be nothing less than carved deeply in his psyche. His bride-to-be walked in time with the music toward the front. George's heart swelled. *This time it's going to happen.* The random thought stuttered his heart and sent a tingle coursing through him. His dreamy smile stopped growing and lost a bit of gloss when it occurred to him how strange it was to think such a thing. He discounted it as a residual memory lapse from the fainting spell less than five minutes ago. The earnestness of his smile returned. He waited for Jennifer to join him.

The wedding vows and responses came and went. Facing Jennifer, holding her hands, George stared into the gauzy haze of her veiled face—the woman who would be his lawfully wedded wife in a few more seconds. Jennifer Louise Harvey was about to become Missus Jennifer Waller—his Sweet Jen—forevermore.

The pastor ended in traditional form, "I now pronounce you husband and wife." He looked to George. "You may kiss the bride."

George lifted the veil and lay it as gently as a drifting rose petal over the back of her hair, careful not to muss the perfectly coiffed arrangement. When he did, memories of their shared history swarmed over and warmed him. He shuddered with joy. George Waller and Jennifer Harvey had been part of a larger group of kids near the same age growing up in a small rural farming town situated on the edge of the Caprock in northwest Texas. There was little to do in Smithtown and the kids depended on one another for entertainment. The crew, as they called themselves, went to school together, played together, laughed together, got into trouble together, and spent all their formative years within sight of one another. No one of them was ever far from the others. They had become more than friends. They were extended family. Unlike most of the other kids in town, the *crew* had various family problems that pulled them together in the beginning. Shared circumstances created lifetime bonds and strong friendships. For George, Jennifer was beyond even that. When the dating years began, they were the closest of confidants, sharing intimate details of dates with other people—always comfortable holding one another's secrets. As age and maturity crept up on them, they realized what a rare thing they shared. Love flourished. It grew to be deep and abiding. They eventually became exclusive.

Jennifer's smile dazzled as he leaned in and pressed his lips to hers. The organist let that be her cue to begin playing. The entire assemblage within the chapel stood and applauded. Whistles and whoops went up across the room. George followed those sounds and saw they came from the rest of his crew, Lenny Poe and his dad, Buck. Next to Lenny stood Bubba Leal, his wife and two young children. The youngsters were scrubbed shiny and dressed for church. George was proud of Bubba. He had grown into the man that George always knew he'd be. He waved appreciation at Bubba and his family, and then each of the others of his crew in turn.

As he looked across the crowd of applauding and smiling people, his roving eyes suddenly stopped. A pretty woman stood next to a young teenage girl, thirteen perhaps, both seemed to be stalking him with their eyes, expressions neutral. The two were dressed much more casually than others around them, even dowdy. It appeared they may have just returned from a camping trip and came straight to the church. Although not objectionable, the woman and girl he assumed to be her daughter stood out from the crowd. The woman was beautiful. She was Latino, or at least appeared so—voluminous dark hair cascading down over her shoulders with gorgeous exotic eyes. She wore an oversized man's blue plaid flannel shirt with cuffs rolled up to the elbows over faded blue jeans. The young girl next to her was dressed in similar fashion and as tall as the woman but much slighter built with no womanly curves. As he and Jennifer walked by, the image of the pair lingered in George's mind. There was familiarity that he couldn't place. Perhaps they were friends or family of Jennifer's side that he may have seen somewhere before, he thought. He did feel as though he should know them, but couldn't put them in any context as he passed by them.

The newlyweds stepped into the brilliant sunny summer morning in Smithtown, Texas. They paused long enough to wave at the gathering crowd at the bottom of the steps. George took the opportunity to kiss his Sweet Jen again, much to the raucous glee of the crowd. They walked down among the tight gauntlet of waiting people and picked up the pace toward the car painted liberally with well wishes as rice rained down upon them. George stopped next to the car and opened the back door. Jennifer, with her back still to the crowd, tossed the bouquet in the general direction of a gaggle of laughing girls. They reached for the bound flowers, but only one came away with them. She squealed with delight as his friend and best man, Alex, hurried around to the driver's side preparing to chauffer them away.

George laughed and waved goodbye to the girls now gathering around the one that caught the bouquet. In a sweeping gesture he then waved to the crowd at large. As his eyes swept across the gathering, the scan stopped abruptly. There, standing together, were that woman and young girl holding hands as they had been doing inside the chapel. They didn't look happy, but not sad, either. Both returned his wave but did so slowly, methodically, unlike the cheerfully boisterous well-wishers crowding around them. There might as well have been a spotlight on the pair. Their appearance coupled with bland expressions and mechanical movements set them apart. As a lifelong resident of Smithtown, he knew that they didn't live here—never did. Their paths must have crossed his at another time and place—Lubbock or Abilene, perhaps. He ushered Jennifer into the backseat and slid in next to her, but was compelled to take another examining look at the woman and the girl.

A hand cupped his chin and pulled his face around. "That's enough attention to all of those people. They're all wonderful but, hey, it's all about us now," Jennifer said as she pecked him on the lips.

He smiled. "Yes, it is, Missus Waller."

"Missus Waller . . . I like the sound of that." She bit his lower lip.

"Ow."

She giggled when he recoiled, hitting the back of his head on the window.

The shock morphed into a grin. "Sweet Jen, you've always been the prankster. I don't suppose marriage is going to change that. Will it?"

"No way, bucko. The only thing that's going to change is that I will not be going home when the joking is done. I'll already be there."

The easy banter between them had been forged over decades, beginning long before sexual passion had reached the horizon of their lives. Jennifer pressed her hip into his and pulled him back in close. This time she kissed him slowly and deeply as her tongue sought his. When she pulled away, her breathing had quickened, expression mellowing to something less mischievous and more erotic. "I know that we can figure out ways to continue enjoying ourselves when the joking is done. Don't you?"

George nodded. "Always." He traced the contours of her face with his eyes. "I know I've told you many times, but it bears repeating. I've loved you since we were six and you pushed me out of the swing because you thought I'd hogged it long enough."

She pouted. "Well, it was my turn." She dipped her head and grinned.

He laughed. "I know, but now you understand why I always found reasons to provoke you. It was my way of staying close. During those years I simply thought you were pretty darn cool."

"Still am."

His grin grew to match hers, dimples crowding the corners of his mouth. "Yes, you are. Any reason I could find to hang out with you I did. That has never changed." He slapped Alex on the shoulder up front in the driver's seat. "Hey, buddy, crank this machine up and take us home to change clothes."

"Aye, Cap'n," Alex replied as he started the car.

"We have a honeymoon that needs to get underway."

Jennifer bit his earlobe. "Yes, we do—in the worst way." She snuggled her cheek onto his shoulder and sighed. "Love ya, baby."

"Love you, too, Sweet Jen," George replied. He glanced a final time at the woman and young girl on the church steps as Alex pulled away from the curb.

Chapter 2 ~ Good News, Bad News

The first six months of marriage was a blur. George's only living parent, his mom, passed away in late autumn of that same year. The stress of that sensitive time played negatively upon the increased frequency of his odd head aches and occasional fainting spells. Jennifer attempted forcing the issue of seeking medical attention. He resisted, citing how his commission based job at the John Deere dealership in Smithtown required he keep selling to keep earning. Base salaries were reserved for older, more experienced sales people. Taking the job under such circumstances proved necessary. Employment in an isolated farming community such as Smithtown was challenging. His only other employment choices at the time were seasonal farm labor, night clerk at the convenience store at the intersection of the only traffic light in town, or a stocker at the only grocery store in town. Still, the first months on the job indicated that it might have been the best decision even if more choices had been available. George sold two tractors and assorted machinery and implements during his initial weeks on the job, bringing in enough commission to justify the job by the standards of the company and his own. Winter months, though, were tough on this type of agricultural sales, even for the more experienced salespeople.

If fainting spells and slow sales were not stressful enough, George dealt with another problem. He had the house he grew up in to deal with since his mother's passing. He had a notion of what to do about it, if Jennifer agreed. Beyond these sticking points, there happened to be an added element to his resistance to learn the source of the spells. Yet, he couldn't pin down what that was. All he knew was that a thrumming cadence in the back of his mind spoke to him, chanting a murmured caution not to delve into it. It didn't need to come to him in spoken language. All it had to do was continue that doleful hum. The seemingly dire but indecipherable warning didn't matter so much because there were plenty of other reasons to procrastinate without needing to understand a vague negative hum in the background of his thoughts. Besides, the spells hadn't gotten worse—zoning out for a few seconds followed by a pounding headache and confusion, up to the worst of the episodes—faint, wake up with a shooting pain in his neck, a few minutes of interrupted memory, and then on with his day. Even the worst spells never lasted long enough to require an aspirin. Although he wasn't worried about the episodes, Jennifer was concerned. A confrontation with her was inevitable. When that might be was the only variable. Sidestepping the issue was becoming more difficult as time went on. He loved Sweet Jen so much that acquiescing to her insistence might happen whether he wanted to see a doctor or not.

It was the first Friday in December—cold and blustery with snow flurries in the forecast. The winter weather made for a drag on time. His hours of work at the tractor and implement dealership seemed to multiply as biting wind, portending change on this dreary day, swept across the South Plains of Texas. Farmers stayed away—cozy near heaters and fireplaces, waiting for warmer and sunnier weather to begin preparation for spring planting. Traffic on the street fronting the building, visible through the large display window of his office, was sparse. The vehicles he saw zipped by, all heading someplace other than the John Deere dealership. He figured that even those few motorists would not be away from home and hearth if there were not emergencies, minor or otherwise. It was a chin-cradling finger-drumming clock-watching kind of day, he thought. Enthusiasm for his job that had been seeping out now poured, and his reservoir was near bone dry.

Even his friend, Lennie Poe's dad, Buck, had locked down all the bay doors and sent the mechanics home. He was the senior supervising technician back in the shop. When it came to fixing tractors, or any other kind of farm equipment, Buck was a consummate professional that had been doing the job for several decades. This place was lucky to have him. George sat alone but obligated to keep the doors open until closing time in the hopes of picking up a few parts sales before dark.

Large snowflakes appeared outside through the big window, flying by at a sharp angle, pushed by gusting wind. It wasn't a blizzard, but certainly did not contribute positively to his mood.

When five o'clock finally came, he could not be readier to get away from this place to begin a weekend. As eager as he was to be anywhere but at work, eagerness to go home was tempered by a promise he made Jennifer earlier about having that dreaded conversation over his spells. On the drive toward home, he thought of avoiding the situation a while longer—maybe drop by Alex's house or Lenny's for a beer, or something like that. In the final analysis, he groaned and sighed deeply, keeping the car heater on high and pointed in the direction of home. If the subject of his spells came up, he'd deal with it. But, he certainly had no intention of bringing it up.

George stood on the front porch of the small house that he and Jennifer rented on the north edge of town—likely built in the thirties. The old house was not in good condition. The word "dilapidated" could be used when referring to it and not be a far-fetched exaggeration. White paint hung in peels from the original shiplap siding and a few shingles stood erect on the roof from the gusty north wind. The wire mesh of the front screen door had torn loose and flapped in two places. He pulled the handle. Rusty hinges squawked. He cringed and pulled it no wider, not yet wanting to be heard. His coat collar fluttered from the wind at his back. He reached past the rickety screen door and wrapped a gloved hand around the door knob, but hesitated. He wasn't ready to go inside. A snowflake as large as a piece of torn tissue paper hit his bare neck, delivering a shiver. The red mercury of a thermometer mounted on the molding trim of the door registered twenty-eight degrees. It had not fluctuated over a degree or two since first checking it at daybreak on his way out to go to work. The cold, the wind, and the snow were not enough to rush him. He needed this moment to collect his thoughts should a debate be coming in the next few minutes. If he planned on successfully arguing with Jennifer over medical tests that they could ill afford anyhow, he needed his head in the right place. They had no health insurance. Medical tests would not fit any better in the household budget than insurance premiums bypassed due to lack of funds. Costly testing and medical procedures were out of the question. He wondered if he should simply submit to her wishes without arguing his point. When the day began, just before leaving the house, he promised her a conversation about his episodes. At the time, it was an expeditious way to get out the door without having to engage her on the subject. He figured she'd have had her own hectic day and wouldn't want serious discussions of any kind, much less a contentious subject like recurring fainting spells. If procrastination had worked before, why wouldn't it work this time, too? he asked himself. Although, he had sensed something different in her tone, and her insistence more pointed, when she wrenched the promise from him before he left the house this morning.

His ears were numbing. Gloved fingertips, nestled snuggly in the rabbit fur-lining, now felt the pinch of the cold as well. The longer he stood in the buffeting wind and thought about it, reasons to resist going to a doctor obscured with dwindling resolve to remain in the icy cold and engage in this mental game of badminton. Maybe the freezing weather rushed the changing opinion. He couldn't be sure, but he did know that the disposition of his mother's vacant house had to take precedence. A plan on that had to be put into place first before thinking about anything else, and that included a trip to the doctor.

George drew a long breath and sighed, blowing a white cloud of frosty air that spirited away in the wind. He forced a smile and went on in the house. "Hey, Sweet Jen, I'm home." When the warm air from inside the house hit him in the face, it carried great smells of something cooking. "What's for dinner?"

Jennifer appeared around the edge of the door from the kitchen wiping her hands on a towel. She flashed a grin followed by signature acerbic wit. "You're a Texas boy, you tell me what goes with cold weather."

"Chicken fried steak smothered in cream gravy and mashed potatoes."

"Good for you. You got it on the first guess." She disappeared back into the kitchen. "Wash up and come on in, Babe. It's about ready."

Her sense of humor and easy manner was one of the things he appreciated most about her—always had—even back to their earliest days in elementary school. For example, a couple of months ago Jennifer took her hairstyle to an extreme, cutting those long-burnt umber tresses to a short, almost boyish, style. Her dark eyes, hair color, and high pronounced cheekbones mirrored the Comanche blood in her line. That heritage dated back to her great-great grandmother who broke from tribal tradition to marry a German settler in the nineteenth century.

Jen loved athletic pursuits—tennis and jogging mostly. George enjoyed joining her in those activities. Lately, she had attempted opening conversations on taking golf lessons at the little country club on the highway north of town. But, George cut those conversations off every time. He couldn't wrap his mind around spending a half day or more chasing a little white ball around a manicured pasture with a fancy bag of sticks. Although, George thought, driving a golf cart around the course might be fun.

As he walked into the kitchen heading for the small table against the wall, he had to turn sideways behind Jennifer who stood before the free-standing range. She was bent at the waist and with mitted hands over the yawning mouth of the oven and retrieved a cookie sheet from inside it. "I thought you might like biscuits, too."

He paused behind her. "Good heavens, yes." He slapped her playfully on her jean clad butt."

"Hey, watch it . . . unless you want a face full of hot biscuits." She straightened, faced him, and then forced him away with the edge of the hot pan.

He backed away a single step, coming in contact with a chair. He tossed his hands into the air. "Okay, okay. I give up." He leaned over the pan and kissed her quickly on the lips. He looked down at the chair behind him. "This house is too small."

She set the tray on top of the range and plucked out hot biscuits, juggling each awkwardly, placing them one at a time on a plate. "If you think it's too small now, just wait."

"I was thinking Jen, instead of selling or renting out Mom's house, we ought to do some remodeling on it while we're still in this one and then move in to it. Just today we mailed the rent on this place for December, so we have a full month to get it ship-shape. Barring any unforeseen financial woes, I believe I can muster enough money for a meager amount of paint and materials. So, the timing couldn't be better to give it a minor cosmetic facelift while it's vacant. It's over twice as big as this one, and then all we would have to pay are taxes and insurance, no more rent. What do you think of that idea?" He saw an incredulous look on her face. "What?" he asked. "Why are you looking at me like that? Do you have a problem with what I said? I thought you'd be excited about getting out of this old, drafty, and cramped place and make a home in a better house."

She laughed. "Sometimes, you can be so dense."

"I don't understand." He inclined his head. "Don't you think it's a good idea?"

She placed the plate of biscuits next to a platter of chicken fried steak on the table. She poked her forefingers in the belt loops at each side of his pant waist and yanked him toward her. "Think about it, Hon. What did I say right after you said, 'This house is too small'?"

"Something about agreeing that this house was too small."

"Well, yeah, but remember it the way I said it."

"You said 'just wait', but what does that . . ." He suddenly tingled as if cold water had been tossed into his face. "My sweet, Sweet Jen," he drawled her name, "are you saying what I think you're saying?"

Her grin remained fixed. "You're a might slow on the uptake but, maybe, you're not so dense after all. You know that family we've talked about starting? According to that stick I peed on this morning, I think the process is underway."

"Oh my," he muttered, his head suddenly spun out worries that included lack of health insurance, housing concerns, family finances, sporadic and mostly inadequate income, plus many other things—large and small. And then, something snapped.

Abruptly, as if his head became trapped in a swirling vortex, he felt as though his body spun one way as Jennifer, the kitchen, and smells of food spiraled the other into the distance. Blackness dropped over his universe and absorbed him. He became conscious of the now familiar perception of floating on his back with only his face above pleasantly warm water in a fast-flowing river. Darkness gave way to a sky of white. Familiar faces swirled above him like white-on-white shadowy specters. Some he could put names to, some not, but all were familiar. He instinctively knew them as players on the stage of his life. He wondered why names of some came to him quickly while others didn't, or not at all. He thought he knew them all equally well.

Once again, a distant sound came to him. It was far too vague to distinguish, or its source, although he now understood that it would likely turn out to be a human voice. He felt safe and protected—no worries. He didn't want this experience to end. The sound indeed became understandable as a voice. "George, sweetheart, are you all right?" The voice strengthened and became clearer fast. The comforting water of the flowing river vanished.

Who is this George that she's talking about? And . . . who is she? A sharp pain bit into his neck just below the base of his skull as if hit by a baseball bat. "Crap that hurts." He opened his eyes to see a beautiful young woman on her knees next to him. The joy of seeing such a beautiful face replaced the pain as the most important thing to his awakening mind. Quizzically, he examined her face while massaging the ache in his neck that had already begun to subside. "Do I know you?"

She shook her head with an expression that he couldn't identify. It might have been anger, but it also could have been fear.

"I sure hope I do," he continued. "You're beautiful."

The knit in her brow remained, but a smile grew. Her head wilted forward. "These episodes—if that's what you want to call them—may not mean much to you, but they're scarin' hell out of me."

"Episodes?"

"Yeah, episodes, spells, headaches—I don't care what you call them. You've got to get a handle on this. For Christ's sake, George! What if it's a brain tumor? What if it's a *malignant* brain tumor?"

Memories began coming back in a linear stream. "Oh yeah, the spells." It dawned on him that he had worked hard, scant minutes ago, at figuring out a way to not let this issue come up. Now, here he lay on the floor having suffered another one, meaning there would be no getting around it this time. "I, uh, probably should see a doctor."

Jennifer's frustration bubbled higher, along with the pitch of her voice. "How can you be so lackadaisical about this? It's your life we're talking about, for God's sake! It's not like we're arguing over who's going to mow the lawn. And another thing, you are out of your freakin' mind if you think I'm going to raise this baby alone without a father." Tears rose in those beautiful dark eyes until the eyelids could no longer contain them, spilling out onto her cheeks. Her lip quivered. She drew a ragged breath. "You idiot. I love you," she said, her voice trailing down to a whisper. "I want you around for many years to come so that our child can have a father to love, a conscious father. I don't think that's asking too much."

"Jen, I'm so sorry." He sat up.

She rubbed away a final escaping tear. "Are you okay now?"

"I'm fine." He rolled to his side and came to his feet.

She kept her hands thrust out, as if he might collapse again. "Take it slow."

"Really, I'm fine. It's over." He pulled a chair out from the table and sat. "It's not that I'm taking my condition lightly. It's just that . . . well, there are things that need to be done and so little time and money. I'm feeling pressure to take care of all that other stuff before I think about myself. And, now, with a baby coming, the notion of getting us moved into a larger house is more than simply an interesting thought. It has become necessary."

Jennifer lifted his chin with her fingertips and bent at the waist to look him in the eye. "Don't feel the pressure, hon . . ." She offered a soft smile as her eyes drifted dreamily over his face. "Feel the love," she said, tilting her face toward his.

George let it happen and returned the affectionate kiss as his eyes closed to enjoy the moment with his Sweet Jen. Although, once his eyes shut, his mind went to that place where a white on white image of a woman's face appeared above him while in the throes of his fainting episode moments ago. It was not Jennifer's.

Jen pulled away and stared into his eyes a moment longer, presumably making sure he was not about to go out again. She then smiled. "If you think you can sit upright without assistance," she quipped, "I'll finish putting dinner on the table. I'm eating for two now and very hungry."

George smiled at her humor. But when Jennifer turned her back to him, the joy faded. He held his hands open, looking at the backs of them and then turned them to examine the palms. The thought attached to the move was philosophical. *What is existence? Is it a result of personal affirmation? Does the simple act of consciousness prove existentialism? Or, must it be external forces that validate existence? What makes that place I go to every time I pass out be any less real than what I am right now? Can I exist in more than one place at a time?* He shuddered when a concluding thought crossed his mind: *because that world, whatever the hell it is, doesn't feel any less real than this one.*

Chapter 3 ~ A New Friend

"Howdy neighbor," came a voice straining to impersonate a Texas drawl, from down in the front yard.

George looked up from the chore of replacing a few scarred and worn composition shingles on the roof of his mother's one-story ranch style house. Although vacant, it would soon be his and Jennifer's home. He saw a tall slender man a few years past his prime, hair silver and thin on top, but evenly so, and neatly combed. He was pale, but not necessarily in an unhealthy way. He just appeared to care more for indoor pursuits than being outdoors getting tans. There was familiarity in the old guy's appearance and demeanor, but George realized there could be no way he would know this man—probably just looked like someone he once knew in passing. The gentleman seemed sophisticated—quite the striking figure. "Well, howdy to you, too," George replied. Unlike the old gentleman standing down in the yard, George's Lone Star accent was genuine.

"I'm Doctor Levine—Edward Levine."

"Nice to meet you. I'm George Waller. Although you're trying hard to sound like a friendly Texan, I get the feeling you're not from around here."

"Not originally. I'm a New Jersey boy. But I've been a Texas resident for quite a number of years now. I just can't seem to shake the last vestiges of that northeastern accent."

"You're a doctor, huh?"

"Retired from a psychiatric practice in Lubbock a couple of months ago. I did that for thirty years. I thought I'd try something different, like nothing." He chuckled.

"Smithtown is a great place to retire and do that very thing. No doubt about it. Set apart from the hustle and bustle of big city life, or Lubbock." He grinned then added, "If *big city* can describe Lubbock." George used the hammer in his hand like a pointer toward Levine's house. "I have a lot of memories associated with that place you bought next door."

"Oh?"

"One of my best friends grew up there. Alex Burton. I'm sure you'll meet him sooner or later. Smithtown is too small to remain incognito for long. His mother was an incorrigible alcoholic that hardly ever left the house, whereas his father was a carousing prick that couldn't keep his pants zipped up. He didn't hang around home much. Pardon my language."

The old man nodded and shrugged in an accepting way. "Not a problem. You're just saying what you feel."

"It's just that I remember so distinctly Alex coming over to our house with bruises on his face after his old man had beat him. Sometimes, it wasn't physical abuse but mental. The old sonofabitch would belittle Alex until he ran from the house crying. And, it wasn't just once or twice. It was at least a once a week thing, sometimes more. I'm amazed that Alex grew into the great guy that he is. He and I are still the best of friends—the best man at my wedding as a matter of fact. My home life was a little more stable, so he was over at our house a lot when we were growing up. My dad left my mom when I was a baby and he never came back, so I never knew him."

"Sorry to hear," Levine said.

"It's okay. Mom raised me, and pretty darned well . . . I think." George chuckled. "The point is Alex and I, along with a couple of other friends, had atypical family experiences and we are like family. That house you're living in now has as much sentimental attachment for me as this house under me."

"I'll take good care of it. I promise."

"Oh, I already know you will. Believe me, Doctor Levine, it looks a heap better now than it did in those years and that was over twenty years ago. In fact, I may have to work extra hard to keep my house up to your standards, not the other way around."

Levine shielded his eyes from the sun and scoped the roofline that George stood on. "Anything I can do to help?"

"Nah, I've got it. But thanks for the offer." George mopped trickles of sweat from his brow and came out of a crouch to stand on the gently angled roof. "I'm just patching it—can't afford a whole new roof—tight budget, you know, baby on the way and all things related." He looked across the sky to the horizon, squinting against the harsh glare of the sun. "Beautiful day, considering it's the dead of winter, certainly better than that cold blustery spell last—" Suddenly, he felt faint, knees weak. *Oh crap. Not here. Not now*, he thought.

"Son, are you okay?"

George recognized it as a spell coming on, but something remarkably different was happening. It was not the usual way an episode began. Foremost, he was not stressed. Secondly, he didn't pass out and collapse. He distinctly saw and heard the doctor's concerned question. As he stared down at his neighbor, the hodgepodge of familiar faces etched in a white void was superimposed over the world as it was now. *I need to sit before I fall.* He only had time to think it. As the disembodied faces remained floating and visible, consciousness faded. *Oh shit. Oh—*

Swallowed by blackness, things quickly changed into the familiar white as he floated in the comforting water. Once again, on his back staring up into the faces that followed him from consciousness to this. Whatever *this* was.

As he emerged to rejoin the world, the shooting neck pain was accompanied by another kind of discomfort, intense stinging sensations on his face and a few other places over his body. Even before his eyes opened, he lifted an arm to check the source of new and indeterminate pains. And then he heard, "Don't move around yet, son." George opened his eyes and saw an elderly man kneeling at his side. He wondered who the guy was. This time memories tumbled into place quickly. He remembered the events that had occurred mere moments ago.

"Aside from the scratches, are you in pain anywhere else?" Doctor Levine asked.

"Just the usual neck pain."

"Usual? Do fainting spells followed by neck pain happen often?"

"Afraid so."

"How long?"

"A long time. It has been happening since . . ." His voice trailed off, as it abruptly occurred to him that he couldn't remember an episode, any episode, prior to waking up in the church before his wedding. It was Alex that had told him how often the spells occurred, but he couldn't personally remember a single one before the wedding. "How odd. I can't seem to remember when they started." The doctor had inadvertently given him a bothersome conundrum: when did all this begin?

"That's okay. Don't attempt to think on it too hard right now. You're addled from the fall."

"The fall?"

"If it had not been for that shoulder-high euonymus bush against the house slowing your descent, we might be concerned with issues much more important than not remembering a few details. We could have been racing to get paramedics over here for broken bones. I'm surprised you didn't gouge an eye since you rolled off the roof face-first into the top of the bush. You are a lucky boy."

George looked away from the doctor and lifted his eyes to the bush which grew to a height about three feet below the edge of the roof. Two of its larger limbs had snapped and hung down by its sinewy bark, leaving a gap in the otherwise even foliage. "That explains the stinging scratches."

"That bush may have prevented you from breaking your neck but it exacted payment for saving you from more serious injury." The old man smiled. "It seems you're intact though." He put a hand beneath George's head and coaxed him to sit up.

He winced at the pressure on his back, realizing scratches were not confined to his arms and face. As he came to a sitting position, legs splayed on the grass, he saw Jennifer pulling up to the curb in their aging Toyota. She threw open the door, got out, and sprinted. As she approached, she called out frantically, "Are you okay?"

"I'm fine."

"Did you have another one of those spells?"

He nodded. Wanting to deflect the inevitable conversation that would surly follow, he blurted, "Meet our neighbor, Doctor Edward Levine. He's a psychiatrist, retired."

"I think you need a psychiatrist sometimes." She shook Levine's hand. "Jennifer Waller. I wish we could've met under different circumstances. If you're a doctor, then surely you'll agree that George is being an idiot for not having it checked out."

The old guy looked down at George, pursed his lips, shrugged his shoulders, and nodded agreement. "I don't know you. So, I can't agree to the 'idiot' part. Otherwise, I'd have to say she's right. Things like this might become life threatening even if the spells are not. What if this should happen when you're behind the steering wheel zipping down the highway at seventy miles per hour?" He thrust his chin toward Jennifer. "Let's take that scenario a step further. What if she happens to be in the car with you? Or, what if that bush hadn't broken your fall? Worse yet, what if that roof you were just standing on had been two-stories up and not just one? Sorry, George, but I can go on and on with potentially deadly situations from blackouts like yours. Even if they aren't, otherwise, all that dangerous to your physical health."

George massaged the back of his neck. "You're right. I know. You're both right. Unfortunately, we have no insurance and precious little money. I can't afford it right now."

Jennifer became frustrated and clenched her teeth. "That argument is growing really thin. We have great friends in Smithtown that would help, if it came to that."

The doctor stroked his freshly shaven neck beneath his chin. "George, let me make you an offer. This is backwards to the way things are usually done, and should be done, but let me help you eliminate psychological causes first. It's preferable to rule out physical problems before considering psychological abnormalities, but I understand your situation. If neither your wife nor I can convince you to see an MD, let me do what I can for you. It may have been a few years, but I've been where you are and know your dilemma well, first hand. There was a time that a simple package of Ramen Noodles would have been welcomed, but I couldn't even afford that while I was still in school. I certainly know and understand lean hungry times. So, please allow me to do what I can for you."

"You're very nice for offering, but I can't pay you, even in Ramen Noodles." George grinned.

Doctor Levine laughed. "I'm not asking for payment of any type, my boy. Let's just say that I may have retired but it's hard to abruptly stop what I've done for three decades. Plus, it's the neighborly thing to do. This will ease me into retirement. It will be as therapeutic for me as it might be helpful to you."

George looked to Jennifer who was already nodding enthusiastically. "I don't suppose it would hurt to talk it over with you, Doctor Levine," he replied.

"Good," Levine said. "We'll arrange a time to get together soon. For now, it looks as though you and your wife may need a moment alone." He turned and walked toward his house.

"Thanks, Doc," George said, as he fell back to lay on the winter brown front lawn and stare at the sky.

Levine continued walking away but called out over his shoulder, "Since we're neighbors now, call me Edward. We'll talk more later."

Jennifer sank to her knees beside him. "Although, it was terribly kind of Doctor Levine to offer his help, I still think you need to rule out tumors or other ghastly problems first." She sighed at his lack of response, resigning as usual to his hard-headedness. "Are you hurting?"

"I'll probably be sore tomorrow but right now all I feel are stinging scratches from that bush." He sighed and looked away from the brilliant unfettered blue of the winter sky into Jen's eyes. The sun radiated warmth, but the breeze was cool. He stroked her cheek with the flat of his palm. "Please don't be angry. I love you so much that the mere thought of us not being together knots my gut."

"Why would that cross your mind . . . ever?"

"I-I don't know. But since that spell I had at the church on our wedding day I've been stricken with sporadic fear of losing you. I can't say why. But, when it does come over me, it's frightening."

Jennifer placed a hand over the left side of his chest. "My heart, my dear heart, we have only begun our lives together. There is nothing on this spinning planet or in the heavens above that would cause me to leave you." She lifted his hand and placed it over her own heart. "We are one, now and forever." She lowered her face to his, nuzzled her cheek against his, and then kissed him lightly on the lips. As their lips parted, "I'm going to ask you a question and I want a truthful answer," she whispered.

After hesitating, he slowly nodded agreement, uncertain where she was going with her question.

In a soft but serious manner, she asked, "Is it possible that your resistance to seeing a doctor about your condition has more to do with fear than money? Could that be the reason for your separation anxiety?"

He smiled. "That's two questions."

She slapped him on the chest. "That's not funny and I'm not kidding." She sat back on her heels and tightly crossed her arms over her chest, pouting.

He lifted his torso to sit upright. "I'm sorry—just trying to lighten the mood." He felt a trickle and dabbed his temple with a finger to see a blood streak on his fingertip. He rubbed it away on the dry dead grass giving it no further consideration. "Every time I think about going to a doctor for tests, or whenever you and I talk about it, I get an overwhelming feeling that I'll find out more than I want to and my life, or our lives together, may be altered in an irretrievable way." He touched her pregnant belly. "And I certainly cannot allow anything like that to happen."

"I love you beyond words, but that's silly—nothing but paranoia, for God's sake."

George offered an apologetic head tilt. "I don't think it is."

"A doctor might be able to fix the problem. Are you afraid it might be life threatening? Is that it?"

"Amazingly, no. In fact, I feel certain deep inside that the problem is not life threatening at all, unless of course something happens like what Doctor Levine was talking about. I view these fainting episodes as potential life-changers, if I go searching for answers."

She kissed him again. "Always remember, I believe in you, George Waller. I believe in you." She poked him on the chest with a stiffened finger. "I believe … *in … you.*"

The words of his Sweet Jen didn't fit the conversation and seemed to echo inside his head. It was only a flash, but her face softened out of focus, replaced by the shadowy glimpse of another woman. Jennifer's face then snapped back into sharp focus, causing George to blurt, "I'm not going anywhere, ever. I love you too much."

Chapter 4 ~ The Intervention

Seasons changed from winter, to spring, and then on into summer. It was extraordinarily hot and dry, even for Texas. Jennifer's heat tolerance clicked downward everyday closer to the birth day. The baby, almost at full-term, continued growing. She suffered, complaining of breathing difficulty when outside on sunny afternoons. Discomforts like this were normal at this stage. Her pregnancy progressed nicely. She succumbed often to fits of anger and frustration—argumentative over unimportant things—as she entered her ninth month during the hottest part of summer. July was about to roll into August and this day, like all other recent days, promised only sunshine and sweltering heat. By mid-afternoon, clouds of any size might be difficult to find in the heat hazed sky. Since the middle of June, afternoon temperatures hovered around a hundred.

Jennifer hurried from the bathroom to the living room while pulling on a wristwatch. She walked with back arched, protruding belly, and without much knee action. Being in a rush added a comical air to this picture. That athletically charged, lithe frame she could always boast had to be put on hold for a while longer. "George, I'm going downtown to pick up the cleaning and stop by Wimberly's to buy a few groceries. I want to get these chores done before it gets hot. It'll be in the nineties by ten o'clock. I'm sure of it. I want to be home and back in air-conditioned comfort before that happens."

George smiled and nodded, then bolted up from his recliner. "Look, Jen, why don't I blow off this golf trip with Alex and the boys and help you out. I don't think it'll be much fun anyhow."

"No," she snapped. "I *want* you to go and see how much fun it can be. After the baby comes, I want to start playing. It'll help get the baby weight off. We can play together." She turned and headed for the front door.

He smirked. "So you say."

She spun back around. "Don't be a wiseass. Learn well and then teach me."

"Sorry." He paused and sighed. "Okay. I'll do it for you. I will learn the game of golf."

She smiled. "Get over here and kiss me."

George did a fast shuffle toward her, stopping only when the growing baby stopped him a bit short. He put his hands on her shoulders. "Either our daughter has suddenly gotten larger or my arms are getting shorter."

"Shut up." She craned her neck to reach his lips.

He put his hand behind her neck, refusing to allow her to pull away. He traced her mouth in a circle with his lips, nibbling. "I sure do love you," he sighed into her mouth. "I don't know what I'd have done if you hadn't been in my life."

"Go crazy probably." She snickered. Her smile faded to a dreamy look. "Although, that's something I can never hear too much of." She kissed him again, and then, quite abruptly, pushed him away. "I don't want you aroused. For heaven's sake, George, the guys will be here at any moment. Besides," she said, patting her protruded belly, "do you really think I'd be in any mood for that . . . or physical condition for it?"

He sighed. "I guess not. Excuse me for being a guy." The sound of brakes squealing beyond the front yard captured their attention.

"Never apologize for being a man. I need one around to fix things."

"Sweet Jen, you *do* have a romantic way with words." He stepped away from her and looked through the open front door to see their friend, Alex Burton, stop against the curb in front of the house.

She kissed him quickly a final time. "Now go forth, my child, and learn the game of golf so you can teach me in a couple of months, because we certainly won't be able to afford lessons with a new baby." She shoved him back.

Alex stepped out of the car and looked over the top of it toward the house. "Come on George, hurry up. The morning is getting away from us. Our reserved tee-time was scheduled for ten minutes from now. And, you know how long it takes to drive to the course?"

"Let me guess, ten minutes? How'd I do?"

Alex smiled indulgently. "Well, aren't you quick with the quips this morning?" Come on wiseass, get a move on."

He and Jennifer stepped outside. She headed for her car. "See you this afternoon," he called out, and then waited to make sure she got into the car without problems. Fitting behind the steering wheel while still able to reach the brake and accelerator had become difficult with the growing girl inside her. From the moment that the sonogram showed a girl, they both knew and blurted the name Rachael Irissa simultaneously. The name for their future daughter began as a joke long before they were teens, playing house as prepubescent friends. It stuck, and certainly no joke now.

After she backed out and pulled away, he hurried to Alex's car, the front passenger seat left vacant for him. In the backseat sat two other lifelong buddies, Bubba Leal, whose mother was still alive and made the best tamales in Smithtown. Next to Bubba sat Lenny Poe. Bubba was married with two children, but Lenny was single and still living with his father. Lenny's mother had lost a battle with breast cancer before they had graduated from middle school. George figured Lenny, unwittingly and continually, sabotaged his own chances at marriage for his father's sake, so Buck wouldn't have to live alone. George knew Lenny's father, Buck, quite well. The old guy worked as a tractor mechanic at the John Deere dealership where he sold tractors and implements. He opened the car door and dropped into the seat. "Hey guys. Everybody doin' okay?"

"Hell no," Bubba said. "I have to work tomorrow. Old man Turnbow decided he wanted to break out that forty-acre pasture on the back side of his farm. So, I guess my butt'll be occupying a tractor seat on the Sabbath, communing with nature."

"I hear ya. It's no fun workin' on a Sunday," George replied, turning to Lenny. "How about you, Len?"

I'm fine. Although, I'm worried about Dad."

"Why?"

"He's a lonely ol' cuss and I can't get him to do anything about it. He goes to work and comes home, nothing outside that framework . . . ever."

"When you get home, tell him not to bring lunch Monday. I'll fry up extra chicken tomorrow and share it with him. Jen can't stay on her feet long enough to cook these days. So, I'm doing the cooking. She hasn't missed a day this week telling me how much she craves fried chicken. Maybe I can talk to Buck over chicken and potato salad and encourage him to get out and make some new friends."

Lenny reached over the backrest and patted George on the shoulder. "Thanks, buddy. I really appreciate that. It'll mean more coming from someone other than me," Lenny said.

"Not a problem, Len," George replied.

"Are you ready to learn all about the wonderful game of golf?" Alex asked.

George sighed. "I guess."

Alex snickered. "Don't get too excited. I'm afraid you might pass out again."

"Ha . . . ha."

"Sorry, but someone needs to keep prodding you to see a doctor."

"My Sweet Jen's got that covered."

"Is it working?"

"Uh, well, I've got a psychiatrist next door that offered to help."

"Have you let him?"

"No. But I will. Someday." George saw all three of his friends exchange quick glances. "What?" George added.

"Nothing, George," Alex said. "It was just us affirming that you're going to do what you want to do, come hell or high water."

George smirked. "Just drive."

Alex, Bubba, and Lenny were reasonably proficient at golf and all pitched in to give George tips on his swing and other nuances of the game. Much to George's surprise, he was having a good time, but it had more to do with hanging out with friends on a Saturday morning than the game.

As they were about to tee off to begin the back nine, Alex commented on a small but menacingly black cloud that seemed to appear from nowhere, its top billowing very high. "I didn't think it was supposed to rain today," he said.

"That's what you get for believing a television weatherman," Bubba said.

Lenny turned a full circle. "Judging by the rest of the sky, the weatherman was *mostly* right. I don't see another cloud like that one anywhere."

"In that case, all I can say is that George must be bad luck," Alex offered.

Bubba nodded agreement. "Sounds reasonable."

Lenny grinned. "Yeah, George. What the hell, man?"

The three burst into laughter.

"Okay, okay, let's get on with this silly game," George said, as he pushed a tee into the grass with a golf ball balanced atop it. "Are you sure you still don't mind me borrowing your clubs, Alex?"

"Nah." He handed George a one-wood. "Give it your best shot. No pressure, but, if you break it you bought it."

George lined up on the ball and wasted no time. He smacked it very high and hooked it into an oak tree off the fairway about seventy-five yards down the slope from the tee box."

His three friends snickered. Alex took the club from him and joked, "Interesting strategy. Someday, you'll have to share it with me, but not now. I don't need to be laughing when I'm trying to keep my ball in the center of the fairway."

"Funny . . . real funny."

Alex handed him a seven-iron. "Here, this should get you back on the fairway and a few yards closer to the green. Don't forget. Follow through," he said, offering a swinging arm gesture.

George snatched the club from Alex's hand and took out walking. As he strode down the slope toward the rough to the left, he heard snickering banter fading behind him from his three buddies. He made it to the huge old oak tree and stood beneath it. He saw that the small thunderhead had moved close enough that a rain shaft appeared within a quarter mile or so.

Suddenly, a bright flash exploded in his face. His next awareness was of bobbing in that flowing river on his back, as if someone, or something, had disturbed the water around him, temporarily disrupting the flow. Aside from that deviation, there was something else different and disturbing about it. The ethereal white-on-white faces he normally saw suspended in a bright misty white sky above him were there as usual, but one was in vivid color, swooping down at him and growing larger, bearing an expression of curiosity, as if examining him. It was Doctor Edward Levine, his neighbor.

Before he could question what he witnessed, the face spiraled upward into the white sky and returned to being a phantom figure like the others, and then a quick fade to black.

He opened his eyes and saw the world as it should be, the gnarled limbs of an oak tree with a thunderhead encroaching on a blue sky. Three faces appeared and stared down at him. "Buddy, you okay," one said.

Buddy?

"Did you get struck by lightning?" another asked.

Lightning?

He felt three sets of hands probing his body for damage, and then he looked to his right and saw a golf club in his hand. It all began to come back him. The faces were of his friends. "I don't think so. If lightning had hit me, I'd expect to be in a lot more pain than just a neck ache."

Alex sprang to his feet. "It must have been the concussive blast from the lightning bolt striking the tree that knocked you down."

George looked in the direction Alex had thrust his chin and saw a smoldering broken limb.

Alex narrowed his eyes. "Or, did you have another one of those stinking fainting spells?"

"I-I'm not sure. There was something really weird about it."

"Lightning or episode doesn't matter. It's time you get checked out by a doctor."

"Yeah, man. You're nuts for letting this thing go on as long as you have," Bubba added.

Lenny nodded agreement. "Sorry, bud, but we're going to gang up on you and make it happen."

George sat up. "Hang on a minute, y'all. Let me get with Doctor Levine first. That was the plan anyhow."

"Fine," Alex said. "But, you've put that off, too. If you don't talk to Levine by Tuesday, the boys and I will be banging on your door with handcuffs. We *will* haul your butt in to a doctor of our choosing in Lubbock, willingly or not."

"Okay, okay. You've made your point."

Lenny looked to Alex and then to Bubba. "I'll check with Jennifer Tuesday evening to make sure ol' George here has kept his promise. How's that for a plan?"

Alex nodded approval. "Good idea."

"Yeah," Bubba added.

George rolled onto hands and knees. His friends helped him up. Annoyed by the impromptu intervention, he shrugged the helping hands off and then waved them away. "I'm all right. You guys just go on back and tee off." As his three friends walked away, he had time to ponder his experience and thought, *Why the hell was Edward Levine in my hallucination? I haven't thought about him much at all lately. Why did I see him in vivid detail but no one else?* And then a large raindrop splattered between his eyes.

Chapter 5 ~ Doctor Levine

George's distraction was near complete. He couldn't think of, or about anything else the remainder of Saturday and woke up Sunday morning with that vivid image of Doctor Levine's face inches above his own. It was eerie and disturbing. He chose not to share the golf course experience with Jen. She would find out soon enough if he failed to follow through on his promise to the guys to seek help from his neighbor, the same guy who currently was haunting him, Doctor Levine.

George sat reading the Lubbock Avalanche Journal newspaper working his way to the comics, having to re-read the occasional paragraph when his mind drifted. Playing low in the background was his favorite smooth jazz singer, Diana Krall. It was difficult to concentrate on the articles. It was that mental image of Levine's face flying out of the cosmos at him yesterday. If it had not been for that disturbing vision, this would have been just another quiet Sunday morning at the Waller house—typical.

"I think you're a good guy for promising Lenny that you'd fry chicken today and share it with his dad tomorrow," Jennifer said.

George dropped the newspaper into his lap to reveal Jen standing in front of his chair licking her lips. He chuckled. "That hint was not at all subtle, ya know."

"Sorry. Can't help the cravings."

"Well then, hint received. I'll get off my butt and get busy. That chicken isn't going to fry itself."

"I've been looking forward to this Sunday dinner for several days. But, hey, no pressure."

George's eyebrow went up. "Yeah, right. I assume you want the full meal deal: mashed potatoes, cream gravy, and some kind of good green veggie to go with your extra crispy bird."

"What a dumb question. Of course. Now, quit talking and get to frying. See if you can make that chicken dance for me."

George folded the section of newspaper in his hands and tossed it onto a pile next to his chair on the floor. As he pushed to the edge of his seat, Jennifer stepped toward him, blocking his ascent. He put a hand on her distended belly. "How's our girl doing?"

"Kicking the crap out of me."

"Well . . . yeah. She wants out of there."

"Just another week, or so, and she's welcome to do just that." She stepped back, smile fading. "I'm getting a little scared, hon. I'm not sure I can handle the pain," she said.

He rose and put his arms around her. He kissed her on the forehead. "I'll be there the whole time. You won't have to endure it alone." He began to sway, moving with the mellow music and lilting voice coming from the CD player. Jen allowed him to lead. She went with his gentle motion. After a quiet romantic couple of minutes, he added, "I've heard that labor pains are almost totally forgotten once a mother sees the baby for the first time." He pulled his head back and with a gentle touch tilted her chin upward. He kissed her lightly on the lips, allowing it to linger. "I'll have to trust you to tell me if that's true," he said, "once Rachael Irissa Waller makes her debut into the world." He gave her another quick peck on the lips. "But right now, I hear a chicken calling my name." He patted her belly and spun on his heels, heading for the kitchen.

Jen took the cliché, 'eating for two,' to heart. She devoured two large pieces of chicken, a hefty pile of mashed potatoes smothered in gravy, and ate an adequate amount of broccoli, which she did not really like. She sprinkled it with lemon juice and melted enough butter over it to make it palatable. Aside from the baby belly, surprisingly, she hadn't gained a large amount of weight, even eating like that for the past month. She was his Sweet Jen and gorgeous—always worth a stare. That super short hairstyle suited her perfectly, especially above those high cheekbones and dark brown exotic eyes. If the baby was lucky enough to have Jen's thick dark hair, eyes, and cheekbones, the child was destined to be beautiful. She still had enough Native American blood flowing in her veins to give their child a most beautiful blend of different races. George was eager to meet that child.

* * *

Monday was typical for the time of year at the John Deere dealership. Cotton farmers pressed for quick equipment or tractor repairs and replacements to maintain still young and tender cotton plants. Those farmers with new wheat income in their pockets from the June harvest were looking to buy tractors or other equipment. It was after eleven o'clock. George's thoughts turned to food when his stomach growled. He finished with a customer and looked around. It appeared everyone had already knocked off for lunch, leaving him the only one up front—not unexpectedly. Monday was his day to watch the store at lunch time while others left for the hour, the break was usually more like two hours. But he was as guilty as any when it came to long lunches on his days to be out with the guys during the midday break. That was simply small town living and taken for granted. No one punched a time clock, but employees inherently knew that whatever time was necessary to get a job done or make a customer happy was what was done. The clock on the wall be damned. Work days were normally over the standard eight hours. There were never complaints about the occasional long work day, nor lengthy lunch breaks. It all averaged out.

George's duty as shop caretaker during lunch was the specific reason he chose this day to invite Buck Poe to share fried chicken with him and have that promised conversation with the old guy. As a friend of Lenny's, George felt responsible for helping out and gently pushing Buck Poe into a life that did not always only include his job as head mechanic and his son. Lenny needed to feel free to pursue a relationship. It was worth a try.

He looked at the brown bag he had just retrieved from the break room refrigerator and set on top of his desk. The wonderful aroma as it attained room temperature was enticing. Even the sight of grease spots on the bottom of the brown paper sack watered his mouth, thinking it might be nice to have some of that chicken and those potatoes now—right now.

He snatched up the bag and headed for the break room. He removed the food and put it in the microwave and then stepped lively out into the parts room, down between rows of shelves loaded with bolts, nuts, steel pins, brackets, and plows of all sorts toward the service bay in back. It was cool with a musty smell laced with dust in the darkened parts area. He threw open one side of the swinging double doors into the shop—greeted with the strong odor of diesel and oil, plus a sudden rise in temperature. He saw Buck Poe talking to one of the other mechanics standing beside an old tractor that had been literally split in half suspended by a chain hoist. Oil dripped from the point of separation into a pan on the dirty concrete floor. "Hey, Buck. Ya ready for some of that fried chicken?" George called out over the noise of a pneumatic impact wrench at the far end of the service bays.

"Sure am. Be there in a minute," Buck yelled.

George spun around and headed back inside, walking toward the front.

Suddenly, a man stepped from between two narrow rows of bins and shelves in the poorly lighted area, blocking his path.

Startled, George stopped too quickly, forcing a stutter step to regain balance. He recomposed and stared for a fraction of a second, quickly determining that he didn't know the guy. "You scared the crap out of me," he said with a smile and a hand over his heart. He added, "I'm sorry, sir, but this is an employee-only area. Is there something I can help you with?"

The man acted strange, fidgeting with a hand behind his back. Light coming through the windows in the top of the double doors toward the front glistened on the man's sweat covered face. "I want all the cash in your register."

All semblance of George's pleasant demeanor vanished in the timespan of a single heartbeat. His stomach knotted. "Uh, there's only a couple of hundred dollars in it, certainly not worth the trouble it will bring down on you for stealing it."

"Just do it," the guy yelled, as the hand that he had been holding behind his back slid forward to hang at his side. Clutched in the man's fist was a semi-automatic pistol—the move was clearly meant as a not-so-subtle threat. The man may have had a drug or alcohol problem and appeared as though he was in a desperate state of withdrawal, probably needing a drink or a drug fix.

George tossed up his hands defensively. "Okay, okay. Don't get violent. I'll go get it." He turned sideways to step past the man and then walked up the narrow aisle between the tall shelves, never taking his eyes off the gun.

The doors to the service bay swung open with ample force. "All right, George, let's do it," Buck called out enthusiastically with a loud clap of hands.

Startled, the intruder spun around and raised the pistol at Buck.

George saw in a blink that the crazed man had panicked over Buck's abrupt and raucous entry into the parts area. "Don't shoot," George shouted. The guy jerked off a shot anyhow as the plea was still spilling from his mouth.

The bullet hit Buck high on the right side of his chest. He whirled around from the impact and off his feet to the concrete floor.

George lunged at the man and grabbed the wrist of his gun hand, shoving it up and away.

The man had surprising strength, forcing his arm back down. George was unable to resist the aggressive push backwards, pinning him against the wall. He fought for control of the gun, but losing the battle.

Despite George's best effort, the man hunkered forward for increased leverage and managed to lower the muzzle of the pistol. He shoved it into George's stomach.

Buck appeared over the man's shoulder swinging a length of pipe at the man's head with his left hand. His right arm hung limp at his side.

George heard a thudding crack as the piece of pipe glanced across skin and bone of the man's skull, causing him to squeeze off a round.

George flinched.

The would-be robber inadvertently tossed the pistol. It skated across the slick concrete floor, as he crumpled down, plainly unconscious.

George held that part of his abdomen where the muzzle of the gun had been. There was no pain and no blood. He yanked his shirt open and saw no wound. *What the hell . . .?*

Buck tossed the length of pipe. It clanked across the floor. He grimaced at the pain in his shoulder and then pressed the point of impact to stanch the bleeding. Forgetting his own pain, he stepped in for a closer look at George's belly. "How could he possibly have missed you?" the old man asked, face awash in amazement.

"I-I don't know." George then stepped away from the wall to reveal a calendar from a cotton seed company. The picture of a bikini-clad model sitting provocatively on a pile of seed bags had a neat bullet hole through her neck, directly behind where George's lower back had been pinned against the wall.

* * *

"Maybe when you saw Mister Poe swinging the pipe at the assailant's head you flinched sideways at just the right time," Edward Levine said.

"Couldn't happen, Doc. I would have had to end up perfectly perpendicular to the guy at the instant of the blast. I wasn't. I was pinned flat against the wall . . . before and after he squeezed the trigger."

Levine's expression remained neutral, as any good psychiatrist should. "Then something else is going on that we need to explore, because it makes no sense that a bullet hole magically appeared behind you, unless it was coincidentally already there."

"Even if the hole was already there, it doesn't explain what happened to the round that the crazy guy squeezed off. There was only one hole in the wall behind me."

Levine nodded. "You're right. It's a mystery."

"Now you know why I finally gave in and took you up on your offer to talk it over. I can't seem to make sense of things in my life these days—*many* things. And it's been going on for the past year and a half. The fainting spells, the memory lapses and now, bizarre bullshit like this. Not to mention odd déjà vu-like familiarities with almost everyone in my life, including people I've known my whole life, for Christ's sake."

"Calm down, George. We'll work together to find answers. And we will. We simply need to examine clues and follow them. It's the same technique for solving any mystery. So, stay calm and objective. We'll get there . . . together." He finally smiled. "Don't forget. In the end there's always an answer."

In the end there is always an answer. George thought about that comment. The simple and direct statement hit him with another one of those strangely familiar feelings. It contained a strong ring of having heard it before, at a different time, in a different place. But from where and from when? he asked himself. Regardless, it was a comforting thought. George sighed in relief. "Thanks. I need someone that is neither friend nor relative that I can trust will hold our talks in confidence and be discreet. I love my wife deeply and I care for my friends, but you're what I need for this, not the Smithtown version of the Keystone Kops."

"Don't be too hard on them. They're concerned for you. That's all."

George sighed. "I know."

Doctor Levine talked about an agenda to adhere to for their discussions and what he thought George should contribute.

This was the first time George had been inside this house since Alex Burton lived in it when they were teenagers. Although next door to where he and Jennifer lived and similar on the outside, the interior was much richer in appearance than their place and only distantly reminiscent of the house that Alex had grown up in. It was obvious that the man had made his money and retired well-heeled. He was a widower and had no housekeeper, but the man was clearly no stranger to house cleaning. The place was immaculate, everything in its place and spotless. George felt a twinge of regret for not helping Jennifer more around the house, especially in the final days of pregnancy. Levine was thin. He appeared tall, always walking straight with a proud, gliding gait, but he was shorter than Jennifer, five-eight perhaps. His silver hair had thinned on top and his pallor indicated he spent very little time in the sun, but there was sophistication about him and an innate trustworthiness that George had taken to. That made him wonder why he did trust the guy to the extent that he did. George really didn't know him—not very well, anyhow. As that thought crossed his mind, it piled upon other incongruities. Things simply didn't add up. He struggled to understand and asked himself, What the heck was so mysterious about his life? What was he so afraid of all the time? He knew he was lucky enough to marry his hometown sweetheart, had a baby on the way, and lived isolated in a small farming town on the Texas high plains— mundane stuff really—nothing to fear except occasional boredom.

So, George . . . George?"

"Uh, yeah, sorry, mind drifted."

The old guy smiled indulgently. "We'll talk about that, too, but another day. Any other mysteries we need to be exploring in the days and weeks ahead?"

"There are other things that don't feel right."

"At home? At work? With friends? Where?"

"Not with any one of them, but all of them—life in general. It seems that . . ."

"Seems that what?"

"Forget it. Never mind. I shouldn't have thrown out such a vague concern that I cannot explain in a concise way. I don't want to get sidetracked, not yet. Let's concentrate on the spells and that episode on the golf course Saturday. I've already explained everything I experience during them except for one important detail of Saturday's event."

"Oh?"

"Your face appeared above me in disturbing detail, not ghostlike, but in vivid natural color. It was not all dreamlike—instead, quite real and in the moment. You seemed to be examining my face at extremely close range. It didn't at all feel as though your face was an imagining." His voice rose an octave. "I was looking at you in real time . . . or so it seemed." Realizing that he was allowing frustration to ratchet up, he sighed and relaxed his stiffening body. "When I regained consciousness, you were nowhere around, of course," he mumbled.

Levine pressed his lips into a tight thin line, thought processes plainly in overdrive. "These talks you and I are embarking on contain the elements of a fascinating journey, looking for the answers you seek. I hope the trip isn't too bumpy for you, but I'm obligated to warn you that it might stretch your ability to cope, depending on the direction our journey takes."

"Bumpy or not, Doc, I have to know. Something is just not right."

Chapter 6 ~ Rachael Irissa Waller

George, glancing toward Jennifer, chewed nervously on the inside of his cheek. He put a hand on her distended belly as they sped northward up the highway toward Lubbock. "Have you had any more pains?"

She sat with her head tilted against the headrest. Unmoving, she looked sideways at him. "I'm fine. Slow down." She continued breathing deep and even through rounded lips and then added, "We should've planned on having this baby in the county hospital so we wouldn't have to race to Lubbock. Planning it this way was not at all necessary."

Before she had finished the statement, George was already giving her a definitive nod to the contrary. "Oh yes it was. I want the best care we can get. If all goes well—great. If all does not go so well, then we'll be among the better hospitals and doctors." He wrung his hands repeatedly over the top of the steering wheel. "If it's a trouble-free birth, then we can argue about the wisdom of it later. But if anything should go wrong . . ." he bounced a quick smile, ". . . I can say I told you so."

Still breathing slowly, deeply, and evenly, her only response was a roll of the eyes. She attempted to lean forward, reaching for the air conditioning control. She couldn't reach it, finally giving up and falling back against the seat. "Would you turn it up for me?" She fanned her face with both hands. "It sure seems hot in here."

"Sure." He flipped the fan switch to a faster speed.

Jennifer took a deep cleansing breath. "Thanks." She rolled her head to face him. "I hope you realize how expensive this could become if all doesn't go as planned, doing it this way. It could be a budget buster."

He offered a grin. "Now you understand why I wasn't so keen on going to a doctor right away about my problem." He placed a hand on her belly. "I want to make sure if we're destined to have uninsured medical expenses it's to make darn certain we have a healthy, beautiful child."

Jennifer stared. Her eyes moistened. "I love you so much." She let out a breathy moan.

George moved his hand from her belly to her shoulder. "Are you okay?"

"Just happy beyond words and getting emotional." She kissed the air between them.

He stroked the side of her face with the backs of his fingers. "I love you, too, Jen."

She groaned and jerked forward, holding that position, face reddening, for several long seconds. "Damn that hurts!" she blurted, forcing the words from between clenched teeth. Once again, she fell back against the seat and resumed breathing deep and evenly through rounded lips.

"Only a couple more miles to Lubbock and then a short drive across town to the Women's Center. Can you hang on?"

She drew a breath. "I think so. The pains are still far apart. That doesn't make them any less painful when they hit." She patted his knee. "Slow down. Your foot is getting heavy on the gas again."

George knew better, but it took a force of will to keep lighter foot pressure on the accelerator as he drove across Lubbock. His eyes darted right to left continuously, looking for a telltale black and white car. Being pulled over for speeding wouldn't help matters at all. Still, he couldn't help himself, cheating the speed limit five to ten miles per hour the whole way. He finally wheeled under the portico at the Women's Center just as another pain pitched Jennifer forward—contractions now only minutes apart.

He raced inside and returned with a young orderly pushing a wheelchair. Once in the chair, the young man hurried her inside to other waiting personnel that took over. George was breathless but refused to lag. He marched along beside the chair, holding Jennifer's hand as they took her directly to a birthing room, put her in a gown, and situated her in the special chair, legs elevated and apart. "She's fully dilated," said one of the two attending professionals. The nurse smiled at Jennifer and then to George. "It won't be long. You arrived just in time."

George resumed his position as husband and coach, slipping his hand into Jennifer's hand and squeezed it.

Jennifer perspired heavily. Pains had become so close together as to become indistinguishable one from the other. She squealed.

"Can't you give her something for pain?" George asked the doctor.

"Not at this point," the doctor said as she withdrew her head from beneath Jennifer's gown. "Take a look."

George stepped around behind the doctor seated on a stool between Jennifer's legs and saw the baby crowning. "Oh." He looked over the sheet covering his wife's raised knees. "Just a matter of minutes, Hon." He moved back around to stand at his wife's side. He grabbed her hand just as an intense pain hit. She squeezed so tightly that a couple of his knuckles popped. He grimaced.

"It's coming!" Jennifer growled loudly, clearly attempting to muffle a full-blown eruptive scream.

"Push," the doctor ordered.

Jennifer lifted her torso as high as possible and complied.

It all happened so quickly. The baby came gushing into the world with a clear and healthy sounding cry. The doctor cut the cord, clipped it, and then swaddled the unwashed infant and handed the baby to him. He nervously took the infant and turned to face Jennifer. She lay back exhausted but smiling. George leaned over and presented a good view of the newborn to her. "Jen, I'd like you to meet our daughter, Rachael Irissa." He gave Jennifer a moment to catch her breath and then carefully placed the baby into his wife's waiting arms.

With two fingers, she peeled back the blanket flap to reveal a bright-eyed and observant little girl in need of cleaning.

George leaned over and kissed Jennifer on the forehead.

A radiant smile graced Jennifer's sweaty face. "She's beautiful. She looks just like you, George. Can you see me in her face?"

He pulled his face away to an appropriate distance for a better view and his first good look at his daughter. He saw strong similarities to himself but not to Jennifer. He didn't know how to respond. He finally said, "You're right. She's so very beautiful."

Chapter 7 ~ What now, Doc?

"That little girl is a marvelous addition to your family," Doctor Levine said, standing between George and Jennifer looking down into the infant's crib in the couple's home. The old guy held an appreciative smile.

Jennifer, mesmerized, stared down at the sleeping infant. "Yes, she is," she replied. Maintaining that gaze, she added, "I see a wonderful future—Christmases, Easter egg hunts, all holidays, school, and all things child related. It's going to be a blessed journey."

"I couldn't agree more. Right, George?" Levine asked.

George met their next-door neighbor's interested eyes, but the smile he offered his elderly friend was inadvertently reserved.

"I have to go get her bottle ready," Jennifer said as she turned toward the bedroom door. "Might as well have it for when she wakes. That should be any moment now."

George glimpsed Levine examining his face, craning his neck slightly, attempting to look directly into his eyes. The scrutiny made him uncomfortable and finally met the doctor's gaze head-on. "See something interesting, Doc?" he quipped.

"Something odd for sure. I see confusion."

George nodded affirmation. "You *are* really good at this psychiatry thing. You know that?" He glanced toward the open bedroom door. "You're right, but I don't want to talk about it here."

"Let's walk over to my house. I'll brew us some coffee."

George hesitated, but then nodded agreement. "Okay." He allowed Levine to lead the way. "Jen," he called out, "the doctor and I are going over to his house for a cup of coffee."

From another room he heard, "Go ahead. While you're gone, I'll feed Rachael."

As Levine crossed the threshold into his house, he said, "We're alone now. What's bothering you?"

"When Rachael was born I thought she looked like me and not at all like Jennifer."

Levine pushed out his lower lip and shrugged his shoulders. "That's not uncommon." The doctor opened a cabinet door and retrieved a can of coffee. "Children often reflect the dominate traits of only one of the parents, not so unusual."

George began filling a carafe with water from the tap. "Maybe not. But what would you say if I told you that I wasn't surprised at all? In fact, expected it, and felt there was a deeper meaning to the child's appearance, something I couldn't understand or retrieve, yet deep in my bones I knew was real, but nothing I was capable of explaining?"

The doctor's hands came to an abrupt halt just as he was about to place a filter in the coffee maker's basket. "Okay, you have my attention. Let's start with the child's natural favoritism. If you thought the baby didn't resemble Jennifer, who did you think the child looked like—other than yourself, of course?"

"That's just it, Doc. I don't know. I saw something familiar in the baby's face. But I couldn't figure out why I thought that. It was another one of those damn feelings that there was—is—something I should know but don't." He set the water filled carafe down hard onto the countertop, sloshing some out. He waved his hands spastically. It's maddening!"

"Calm down, son."

George paused and took a breath. "This feeling gnaws at me all the time. I chew antacids like candy treats. My stomach roils day and night. Answers are barely beyond my fingertips, yet I can't reach them—like veiled secrets are in an easily opened box, if only I could reach the damn box. Doctor, something in my life is out of whack. Or, is it simply a cranial misfire of some sort?"

Doctor Levine gently pulled the carafe from George's hand. "Maybe I should take this." He smiled. "I don't have another one."

"Sorry, Doc. I guess I was becoming a bit too involved in my explanation."

Levine poured it through the top of the coffee maker. He hit the on-button to begin the drip. "Come on, let's go back into the den."

As George followed, "I don't know what to do," he said.

"Are you afraid?" Levine asked as he lowered himself into a chair facing the sofa.

"I guess I am." George sat on the sofa across from him.

"Of what?"

"I fear knowing the answer. Yet, I equally fear not finding it. It's twisting me into knots."

The doctor shrugged his shoulders. "Sounds like you have a reasonable handle on your feelings. I just need to help you find out where those feelings are coming from, and what it is you fear that you might discover."

"The longer I know you," George said, "the more I believe, somehow, that *you* are the key. Believe it or not, even that scares me."

"No matter how you resist it, this perceived pall must eventually be peeled back. Otherwise, it will always hang in your psyche as a clouded awareness that no matter how hard you strain to find it, will always remain just out of sight or just beyond your reach. You do realize that, don't you?"

George closed his eyes and nodded rapid agreement. "Yeah, I do. Still, I can't help but believe when that day comes I might not survive the shock of knowing."

"I understand. On the other hand, you might die of bleeding ulcers or pass out and fall off a tall building if you keep it bottled up like that. Based on what I've seen so far, either scenario is quite possible."

"I know." George puffed his cheeks full of air, held it a second, and then expelled it in a huff. He held up two hands side by side. "Some days, I feel like the unstoppable force barreling toward the immovable object." He emphasized by slamming his palms together in a thunderous clap. "Today is one of those days. It's wearing me down. I'm almost to a point of tiredness that I'll never be able to sleep away."

"We'll work at resolving at least one of those things, the force or the object."

"I'm thankful for you, Doc. I like having someone to talk to about it. Someone that knows what they're doing. I love my wife and my friends—think the world of them actually—but talking to them is not at all the same. Deep in my gut, I'm confident I can get there with your help."

"What you tell me stays between us, always. That's vital to penetrating the bubble you find yourself in and cannot seem to get out of. I don't want you to ever feel guarded around me. It's the only way to get you to where you need to be. You have a beautiful wife and child that deserve a husband and father that functions at a hundred per cent."

"That's a comfort. Thanks," George said as he sat back on the sofa, much more relaxed.

"Have you had any more of those spells?"

"Not since the golf course."

"That's a good thing. I'm feeling more confident that it is a problem I can help with and not a physical one."

"I'm certainly no doctor, but I've never believed that it was physical." He gave the doctor a wan smile. "I'm a wuss. If I had an inkling that it was a brain tumor or something like that, I'd run screaming to an emergency room."

"You're right. You're not a doctor. So, what makes you so certain?"

"I hate being so vague all the time, but it's another one of those mysterious feelings. Oddly, I'm extremely confident that it's a mind thing only. Of course, Jennifer and my buddies wouldn't agree. So, I haven't tried to convince them of my conviction. But, you're different. I want—no that's not right—I *need* you to believe me."

Levine put a thoughtful finger to his lips. "Tell me, if we dig into your past using standard therapy practices and find nothing, would you consider regression therapy?"

"Are you talking about hypnosis?"

"Yes."

Suddenly, George fidgeted and squirmed. Breathing became difficult, as if a weight had abruptly dropped onto his chest. His eyes darted around the room, fearing another episode.

Levine slid quickly to the edge of his chair. "George . . . George, look at me."

George panted in short bursts. Levine's order finally registered. He forced his eyes down to meet the doctor's, but floating disembodied and free in front of Levine was the vision of a woman's face, not sad, but not smiling.

"You're experiencing a panic attack. Focus on my eyes. As I count, take a single breath with each number."

George nodded affirmation in jerky fashion as his eyes traced the female form between them."

Levine began to count, "Thousand-one . . . thousand-two . . . thousand-three . . ."

Levine's methodical and monotonous tone had a relaxing quality that began getting through. George's breathing leveled out. The woman's face faded to reveal the snapshot of a young teen girl's face that lasted for only a second and then both evaporated, disappearing entirely. The spell was over.

". . . thousand-nine . . . and a thousand-ten." Levine stopped counting, leaned forward, and searched George's eyes.

George took a final cleansing breath. "I think I'm okay now."

"You were seeing something, and it wasn't me," Levine said. "What did you see? What were you looking at?"

"The face of a woman and a young girl, thirteen—fourteen perhaps."

"Who were they?"

The question agitated him. "I should know, but I don't!" His voice choked off, stifling an urge to cry.

"Calm down. Together, we'll find out, just not today."

George closed his eyes and drew a deep needed breath. "Sorry. Didn't mean to snap at you."

"No need to apologize, but that level of frustration does suggest that you do, indeed, know them, but can't recall from where or when."

George nodded agreement and let his head wilt forward.

"That episode began right after my suggestion of hypnosis. Coincidence?" Levine asked.

"I don't think it's coincidental at all. For some reason, the thought of going into a hypnotic trance scares hell out of me. I-I instantly felt as though I was being shoved forcefully toward a cliff's edge."

"Fearful of what we might discover, you think?"

"Exactly."

"We can put the hypnosis suggestion on the back burner for now. There are other avenues we can explore first. Just remember, in the end there is always an answer. Still committed to taking this journey with me—wherever it may lead?"

The question was simple. The answer was not. George finally said the only thing he could say, "I think so. Yes."

"Good." Levine rose and turned toward the kitchen. "I'll get us a cup of coffee. I think we both need one."

Chapter 8 ~ Family Life

"Get a move on, George," Jennifer said as she scurried by the open bathroom door while slipping an earring into her pierced ear. "We're supposed to be at the elementary school by nine. Can't be late getting Rachael registered for first grade. It's a big day and . . ." George heard her stop cold. She back-stepped and looked in at him. ". . . and for you and me, too." She smiled.

"I'm almost finished." George said. He saw in her smile the knowledge that this was one more step in a stream of family milestones and, clearly, quite pleased with this one. He stood before the mirror, noticing a few more gray hairs at his temple. He turned his head one way then the other. *What the heck am I doing? he* thought. *It's not going to magically become any less gray because I'm staring at it.* He snickered at the absurdity of his vanity. The graying temples were one thing, but deepening crow's feet wrinkles at the corners of his eyes ended his snickering. He checked his wristwatch—eight-forty-five. "Oh well." He sighed and then slipped his shirt on.

"Hurry, George," came Jennifer's voice from the other end of the house. "Even Rachael beat you getting dressed."

George exited the back hallway, tucking his shirt tail into his pants to see mother and daughter waiting by the door. "Don't worry so much. It's only a five-minute drive," he said.

"I know, but it's a special day."

George smiled and dropped to a knee in front of six-year-old Rachael. He smoothed an errant strand of hair back away from her face to join others that ended in a ponytail to the middle of her back. Over the past few years, Rachael was indeed growing to resemble Jennifer. "Are you as excited as your mother about starting first grade?" He glanced up at Sweet Jen.

The youngster bounced on her toes. "Oh, yes, Daddy," the youngster replied, eyes sparkling.

He hugged her and then kissed her on the forehead. "In that case we'd better get you there." He looked up at Jennifer with his best mock expression of seriousness. "Why are we still here?" The look melted away. He laughed.

She rolled her eyes. "Oh hush."

As he drove them to the elementary school across town, he felt blessed. He had endured a few of those odd spells over the past six years but most had been brief periods of zoning out with visions of faces, but seldom more serious than that. Whenever he felt stressed and on the verge of creating a situation that might induce one, all it took was a calm conversation with Doctor Levine to put things right. Living next door, Levine had become a convenient friend and trusted confidant. It helped immeasurably that he was a professional in the field that George needed. The old guy was another blessing—one he didn't take for granted. George had even become jaded over the familiarity of those faces in his visions, having grown inured to them—accustomed to but not comfortable with. They were part of his life now and he reluctantly accepted that. Someday, he might even come to know the owners of those ethereal faces that floated above him during those fainting spells. Although something invariably would pull him back whenever curiosity pushed him to uncover the mystery. That, unto itself, was the larger enigma.

George pulled into a rapidly filling parking lot across the street from the school, found a slot, and steered into it. "Are we ready for this?" he asked but expected no answer, as he bounded out of the car.

He may not have waited for an answer, but it didn't matter. Jennifer and Rachael beat him out of the vehicle. That was answer enough.

Rachael pulled her mother along by the hand. George followed closely behind.

When they turned the corner into the appropriate classroom, the young girl was suddenly fearful. The room was crowded with parents and children—every desk full. The overflow of adults and children at their sides lined up against the back wall. "It's okay, honey. The crowd is just a little intimidating, that's all. After today, it'll just be you, the other kids, and the teacher," Jennifer told her.

Rachael pouted. "I don't know what 'timidatin' means, but if it's a bad thing, I agree."

George stifled a laugh. "Let's go stand over there." He walked by, taking Jennifer's hand. They created a two-and-a-half-person caravan to the back of the room. He and Jen greeted other parents and excused themselves as they necessarily slipped by the line of adults in close quarters. The room was like all classrooms—rows of desks with the teacher's desk centered at the front and a broad blackboard behind it. Above the board was a row of green cards with white lettering, featuring the alphabet in both block and cursive. It crossed George's mind how cursive writing was rapidly becoming a thing of previous generations, including his own.

Rachael noticed friends from kindergarten. The child's smile bounced back.

The registration process completed in an orderly fashion. After a half hour, the teacher welcomed the children to first grade and then dismissed the assemblage. The room suddenly began to separate like cream from milk as all the children congregated away from the parents. "Mama, can we stay a while? I want to go out to the playground with Cindy and Sara."

As Jennifer gave approval, George looked through the windows that lined the playground side of the classroom. There was an adequate view of the area, the swings, and all the apparatus geared toward a good time for children. He saw no harm in it. He and Jennifer quickly became engaged in a circle of parents chatting about children, school, summer vacations, and all things related.

After a time, George casually glanced out the window to see, what he thought to be, Rachael standing precariously atop a geodesic climbing contraption, or so he believed. She was indeed standing atop it. But his breathing quickened. Heat rose in his face. He experienced that uncomfortable and unwelcome tightness in his chest, foretelling an episode coming on. His face flushed with fear. He suddenly felt the overpowering need to get her down. That piece of playground equipment grew in his mind as dangerously high, threatening the life of one of the two most precious things in his life. He must go to her and quickly. *I must save her—I have to save her—I have to save her.* The mantra pounded inside his head.

"What's the matter, George?" Jennifer asked. She clutched his arm with both hands, clearly realizing he was fidgeting and about to bolt, or pass out.

He panted, becoming frantic. "It's Rachael . . ."

Jennifer looked through the window and spotted the child. "So? She's playing. What's the problem?"

"She's gonna fall, gotta save her." He ripped his arm from her grasp and, with eyes fixed on his daughter through the window, navigated the maze of desks to the other side of the room. Paying his footing little mind, he kicked one of the desks and nearly fell, but continued stumbling toward the exit. All talk in the room ceased. All the parents reacted to the noise and watched George's manic exit from the classroom. He was so focused on what he believed that he needed to do that he had not noticed the room had gone silent.

"George, wait!"

The mantra rolled in a circle: *gotta save her—gotta save her—gotta save her.*

As he threw open the side door of the building and sprinted across the playground, he caught sight of his daughter sitting atop the dome meant for climbing. It was only six-foot high at the center. A playmate sat directly in front of Rachael. They were talking and laughing.

His mind's-eye was abruptly assaulted with a vision of two people sitting in an open vehicle, panicked and screaming.

Oh God no! That was his last thought as blackness swallowed him whole.

* * *

"When you saw that image of the two people," Levine asked, "what were you thinking?"

George rubbed the area between his eyebrows, frustrated. "I was thinking that I couldn't let it happen again."

"Let what happen again?"

"I can't say."

"Can't or won't?"

"Seriously, I don't know. I *can't* say."

"Did you recognize them?"

George shook his head, but slowly and hesitantly. "That's another strangeness. I was thinking that I knew them but, no, I didn't get a clear look at them. I couldn't even determine what gender they were. There was no visual recognition of the pair. It was as if there was a force obscuring their faces so that I wouldn't see them clearly. I'm getting so tired of this—this crap!"

"Sit back and take a breath. Relax. The harder you try and more frustrated you become, it tightens that lock on your memory. It's counter-productive."

Levine's advice was sound. George felt himself on the verge of losing control and, if history held true, that would lead to things he really didn't want to experience right now—or ever again. He pushed backward from the edge of his seat and slid down until he could press the back of his head into the cushion behind him. "You've been a tremendous friend, Doctor Levine. You've put up with my craziness and, frankly have become my anchor. You keep me grounded."

"It's my pleasure . . . the neighborly thing to do. Speaking of neighborly, I wish you'd stop calling me Doctor Levine. My name is Edward. Call me that, or Ed would be fine, too. I know you think of this as formal therapy. To an extent it is, I suppose. But, it's also just another impromptu chat between friends."

George lifted his head off the cushion somewhat surprised by Levine's sudden display of affection. "Edward it is." He let his head fall back and sighed. "We've had a lot of good chats over the past few years. Have I ever given you enough information to draw any conclusions? Or, have all our talks simply been chats between friends?"

Edward leaned back in his chair and crossed his legs, the wheels of his mind detectable in his expression as he formulated a response. Did he plan on skirting the truth, figuring a way to do that without lying?

He finally said, "George, I came to a strong conclusion several years ago. I know exactly what your problem is."

George sat bolt upright. "You do?"

"Yes, I do. But, here is my conundrum: I don't know why. And, that's the reason I've never shared it with you. I was hoping to have a full answer for you and then lay out a curative plan."

"Tell me, please."

Levine again hesitated.

"Come on, Edward. Maybe I can do something with the information—maybe even get to a reason faster if I have a handle on what it's doing to me." Even as he spoke, George felt that familiar tug pulling him in the opposite direction of full understanding. He sought answers that, in the end, he might regret learning.

"Okay, George, here it is. You are extremely happy with your life—with Jennifer, with Rachael, with your friends, and life in general here in Smithtown. In fact, you like it so much that there is nothing you wouldn't do to keep it just the way it is."

George reared his head back, confused. "So? Isn't that what happiness is all about?"

"Sure it is. But, you see, you are also mortified by it—extreme guilt feelings intense enough to become physically debilitating."

"Are you serious?"

"Very."

"How can that be possible?"

"The only thing I can tell you by way of an answer is that there is a paradigm, possibly a mind-altering and shocking event, in your past that planted a seed in extremely fertile soil, your receptive mind. For some reason, at that point in time, whenever that was, you had a strong need to capture happiness, like lightning in a bottle, and you did. Unfortunate to our understanding is the fact you are repressing the catalyst for that need."

"Are you saying that my happiness is a sham?"

"No, no. Not at all. It is as genuine as genuine can be. All I'm saying is that you think it's undeserved. In fact, it's more than a thought. It's a deeply embedded truth to you, just locked away in that head of yours."

George rubbed his face vigorously. "I've got to figure out why."

"Right. You already know how to make that happen." Levine smiled indulgently.

Suddenly, Levine's front door whooshed open. Jennifer poked her head inside. "Hey George, why don't you come out and enjoy some of this beautiful day? Besides, Doctor Levine may have other things to do besides visit with you all afternoon."

"George checked his wristwatch. "I hadn't realized I had been here so long. On my way," he told her. He sprang up from the sofa and then turned back to Levine and whispered, "I suppose you were referring to hypnosis."

The old man nodded. "Yes."

George adamantly shook his head. "Sorry, still not interested."

Levine rose and offered a friendly hand. He smiled as he shook George's hand. "I know you're not at all amenable to the idea. But, my boy, a day will come that you will be. Don't wait too long. I'm not that young anymore." He flipped a dismissive hand toward George. "For now, go on and get out of here. Go outside and play with your wife and that marvelous little girl of yours."

George walked out into the afternoon sunshine. The warmth bathed him and felt nice, but his mind was in overdrive. He wondered why did hypnosis scare him so badly? What was in his past that he was drawn to seek but afraid to know? And, what about the unfounded panic over Rachael atop playground equipment, or the gunshot that should have struck him but did not? What about all the other anomalous things that have happened beginning on his wedding day?

These questions remained unchanged over the years, although he remained compelled to ask them over and over. They invariably led to no answer, just a final question. Do I really want to know?

From out of nowhere, he suddenly had a terrible headache at the base of his skull.

Chapter 9 ~ Rachael's First Date

"Hey, old man, mind if I get another beer?" Alex Burton asked, pointing down at the ice and beverage-filled cooler.

George grinned wryly at his friend. "Go ahead. And, who the heck are you calling old man, baldy?" With a hand on his hip, he waved away rising smoke from the grill with the spatula in his other hand and then flipped a hamburger patty. "If you haven't noticed, I still have all my hair. I don't care what color it is."

"That's cold-blooded." Alex twisted the cap off a beer bottle and tossed it into a nearby trash can. "Besides, is that sag developing under your chin meant to complement gray sideburns?"

"All right, guys, that's enough talk about getting old," a paunchy Bubba Leal said as he came away from the picnic table toward them, leaving his wife sitting alone. Bubba had his own middle-aged woes, evidenced by the flabby roll over the waistline of his jeans.

"Yeah," Lenny Poe chimed in. "I'm still trying to convince Anna that I'm in really great shape for a guy my age." He kissed the air toward his latest girlfriend sitting next to him at the picnic table. She reciprocated by kissing the tip of her finger and pointing at Lenny. And then, with a little girl smile, she shyly dropped her chin to near her chest and looked away as a flush of embarrassment lit her cheeks.

Jennifer came out onto the patio carrying a large round aluminum pizza pan, doubling as a tray, and piled high with cut vegetables and assorted condiments.

Alex held his beer bottle toward her as she approached. "Now, there's a woman that cannot be accused of showing her age."

George stopped pushing patties around on the grill and watched his Sweet Jen. "You're right about that, as beautiful today as she was on our wedding day sixteen years ago."

Jennifer set the tray on the picnic table. "That's nice to hear, considering it's coming from two guys who tickled me until I cried in the second grade."

"Hey, I was there too," Lenny said.

"Yeah, but you and Bubba were standing back cheerleading. In fact, if you remember, Lenny, you tried to make me feel better when I started to cry."

Jennifer winked at Lenny and then nodded toward his girlfriend.

"Oh, yeah, I guess I did," Lenny said, suddenly realizing that Jennifer tossed out the compliment specifically for his new girlfriend to hear. It apparently worked. Anna sidled closer to him. Lenny took the cue. "I'm really a sensitive guy," he murmured, "and that goes back a long way."

Anna sighed dreamily. "I'm learning that you may not exaggerate as much as I thought you did." She threaded her arm through his and caressed his shoulder with the side of her head.

It was clear to George that, judging by the broad smile on Jen's face, that what she intended to do for Lenny had been a rousing success. George scanned all the other faces—smiles on all, but no one commented, allowing Lenny his moment. Maybe this woman, Anna, would finally be the one. She fit like a puzzle piece into their crew and had been welcomed from the first group gathering she attended nearly four months ago. The length of time she and Lenny had been exclusive was, unto itself, a record for Len. The unspoken consensus was that no one wanted to scuttle their chance as a couple by stupidly making a crude joke or some other comment that might break the spell.

As George quietly enjoyed the moment on this late summer afternoon with lifelong friends, a thought trespassed on his good mood, flattening his smile. Rachael—his sweet little Rachael Irissa—was to have her first date tonight. Sure, there had been plenty of occasions that she met boys at the Dairy Queen or sat next to them at football and basketball games, but this was the first time a boy would be picking her up and taking her out for the evening, out into the world beyond the range of her parent's protective view. She had turned fifteen earlier in the summer and he couldn't deny her this rite of passage afforded to all teenage girls. Still, he worried, wanting to keep her close and safe. He wondered if his shielding nature transcended normal parental boundaries. There was something unnatural about the depth of his concern for her safety. This led to a re-awakening of fears that had lain dormant for months.

Suddenly, George had a problem relaxing and enjoying the afternoon. He sensed foreboding. Dread he couldn't define began weaseling in. As misfortune would have it, the thought was not a passing one. A smile abruptly became difficult to raise and short-lived when successful. Laughter by Jennifer and the others dimmed into the background. There was a definite and disturbing correlation between his sinking mood and the transition from dusk to dark on this calm clear summer evening in north Texas.

* * *

"Thanks for coming," Jennifer told Alex as he ambled from their front door up the sidewalk toward his car. He was the last of the friends to leave. "Tell Patricia that George and I are sorry she wasn't in town so she could join us."

"I will," he replied without looking back. She'll be back from visiting her mother in a couple of days and we'll get together then."

"Sounds like a plan," George called out from behind Jennifer, looking over her shoulder to Alex. He pulled Jen back into him and then wrapped her up at the waist with both arms, holding tight. "But for now," he whispered with a weak grin, "I'm glad they're gone."

Jennifer pulled away from his encircling arms and faced him. She backhanded him on the chest. "George! That wasn't nice. What in the world made you say such a snippy thing?"

"Sorry, the party sort of lost its mojo for me a couple of hours ago. What time did Rachael and that David Willey kid leave?"

"You talk about him like he's a stranger. The Willeys are our friends."

"I know. I'm sorry." George stepped toward her, eliminating the gap she had created. He put his arms around her and took a moment to enjoy her. "I wasn't overstating earlier. You are as beautiful today as you were the day we married." He kissed her lightly on the cheek then more passionately on the lips. "Time seems to be more of a friend to you than it is to me. You wear fifty-one years extremely well. You know that?"

"Okay, now, you and I made a deal. Remember? You would never mention my age aloud and wouldn't raise your eyebrows when I tell strangers I'm forty."

He grinned and nodded. "You're right. I did. Your secret is safe. But I can't speak for our friends. They know exactly how old you are."

"I'll grant you that. Let's get back to you. What soured your mood?"

"Rachael."

She reared her head. "Really? She's a beautiful, well-adjusted young lady. "What would make you think otherwise?"

"Oh, I know she's a good kid. That's not the issue. I'm the problem. This date she's on has set my nerves on edge to an unnatural degree. I don't know why. I'm so frightened of her being out there alone."

"She's not alone, sweetheart. She's with a really nice young man from a great family that we've known our whole lives."

"That's just it. I know that. So, why do I have such deep misgivings about her being where I can't look after her and protect her?"

"Because, dear heart, you're a good father that loves his family to a strangely possessive degree. But it's sweet." She kissed him, then again.

George felt her breathing quicken as their lips remained passionately engaged. It was wonderful. He didn't want it to end, running his fingers through her short hair and cupping the back of her head.

Without pulling her lips from his, she said, "Let's go to the bedroom. I have the cure for tension—relaxation guaranteed."

* * *

George woke startled, not realizing why. He lay on his stomach, his arm draped over the edge of the bed. He and Jennifer were nude beneath a single sheet.

The phone rang again.

He glanced to the digital alarm clock—12:01 in the morning. A brilliant moon beyond the window washed out the dimmer stars, angling a downward beam of silver-blue light over them.

He licked moisture back into his dry mouth and awkwardly snatched the phone from its charging cradle. "Hello."

"George?" came the reply.

"Yeah, this is George Waller."

"Sheriff Ratliff here, George."

In a fast and smooth maneuver, he threw the sheet off and swung around to sit on the edge of the bed. "What's wrong Dewey? What's happened?"

"Now, don't get all bent out of shape, George. It's nothing serious. David Willey and your daughter were involved in a little fender-bender. They're both fine, but David's car had to be towed and they need a ride home since Bill and Mary Beth Willey are out of town for the evening."

Sheriff Dewey Ratliff's calming words had no effect. Terror shot through George. "Oh my God, Oh my God!"

Hearing him, Jennifer rolled over and pressed against his back trying to hear the other side of the conversation.

"Where are they, Dewey? Where?" he asked almost yelling into the phone.

"Stay cool, George," Dewey said. "They're both here at the Sheriff's Office. Neither one of them has so much as a bruise or a scratch. Honestly, I'm not shading the truth for your benefit. They're fine . . . really."

"Okay," he replied, and then took a ragged breath.

"Not only that, it wasn't David's fault. An old man that had a bit too much to drink ran a stop sign and clipped the front of David's car. Damage was minimal, but it collapsed the left front fender into the tire. As a result, he can't drive it home."

"All right, I'll put some clothes on and be there in less than ten minutes." His hand shook as he clumsily placed the phone back in its cradle.

"It's not serious, is it?" Jennifer asked.

"No."

"Then why are you shaking all over and acting like you're about to hyperventilate?"

He heard the question, but didn't have a chance to answer as he fought for a deeper draw of air that didn't complete. He fainted. The last thing he remembered was a drop of sweat tickling the side of his head until he opened his eyes to the featureless sky above him. All familiar elements in place—floating prone in a fast-flowing tepid river and those faces—all those translucent and colorless faces floating free and randomly in that bright white sky, some remaining unnamed, even after all the years since these episodes began. As was usually the case, he felt that this was where he belonged, what he deserved, and at peace with wherever the river should take him.

The easy feeling was short-lived as a disturbing scene materialized in the mist overhead—a vision of Jennifer and Rachael falling, screaming in terror, while he watched in horror. As mother and daughter tumbled and rolled in nothingness, the faces he saw transformed, becoming two others. They were not those of his Sweet Jen and Rachael Irissa.

Chapter 10 ~ Levine's Impassioned Plea

The week following Rachael's and David Willey's car accident passed agonizingly slow for George. Visions and imaginings of what might have happened if things had been only slightly different dogged him relentlessly. He went through the motions of living. Going to work, coming home, doing whatever household chores needed attention and other mundane and forgettable things, all the while consumed by dark negativism. Friday, he stopped by Wimberly's Grocery and Market. Jennifer had called him at work and asked him to stop and pick up a few items before coming home.

He hadn't talked to Levine about Saturday's midnight episode and harbored a twinge of guilt for not sharing it with such a trusted friend and confidant. For many years the man had listened patiently to George's fears, even inviting him to keep up the visits and the discussions. He was interested in this case to an unusual degree, George thought. George couldn't help but believe the good doctor knew more about what was going on than the old guy ever shared. That last episode was different, though, and he wasn't prepared to hear Levine's recommendation of hypnosis yet again. The reason was simple. Regression therapy hypnosis was on his mind and had been all week. His resolve to prevent it was dwindling. Three times this week, while giving hypnosis serious consideration, he hyperventilated and perspired at the mere thought. Considering hypnosis a viable tool to find the truth might prevent falling down a flight of stairs, crashing the car with his family inside, or any other disaster brought on by loss of consciousness. But even as he moved toward acceptance, he was not there yet and summarily discarded the notion.

He steered into the paved lot fronting Wimberly's and parked across from an aging Cadillac that he recognized as Edward Levine's. He contemplated not going inside the store just yet, maybe drive around the block a few times and wait for the old guy to get his shopping done and leave. He drummed the top of the steering wheel with his thumbs and thought about that.

Becoming disgusted with the evasive line of thought, he muttered to himself, "George Waller, you have turned into a grade-A wuss. He's your friend, for God's sake. What is it? Are you scared he might actually help you? Or, scared that he won't?" Taking his own implied advice, he threw open the car door and bounded out to complete the promised chore for Jennifer.

He marched through the store's automatic sliding door with no hesitation and walked directly for the stack of hand baskets and grabbed one. He pulled the scribbled and partially wadded note from his shirt pocket and refreshed his memory on the half dozen items needed and shoved it back into his pocket. The hunt was on.

After getting everything except the pasta, he stood in the aisle before the broad array of spaghetti, linguini, macaroni, and fettuccine, wondering about the type Jennifer had wanted. He suddenly felt the presence of a shopping cart. Without looking away, he stepped in closer to the shelves. "Sorry. Didn't mean to block the aisle."

"Not at all. I meant to stop."

George looked in the direction of the familiar voice. "Edward, I didn't know you were a Friday grocery shopper."

The old man smiled. "Nor I you."

George grinned and blushed. "I'm embarrassed to say that I hardly ever do grocery shopping. I'm merely picking up a few things to fill in gaps until Jen's regular shopping day."

Levine's smile faded. "George, Jennifer told me about that spell you had last weekend. I understand it went to a more intense level."

George sighed. "Yeah, that's putting it mildly. I should have ...." He hesitated to take the statement to its conclusion. The words trailed to silence. It became awkward as George stared at the floor.

Levine smiled and shook his head. "It's okay. I know your mind must be reeling from it." He paused and put a contemplative finger to his lips. "I've told you many times over the years that in the end, there's always an answer. I can help if you'll allow me to move our conversations to the next level. Especially since your spells have gone to a new level as well."

"Hypnosis, right?"

Levine nodded and leaned closer to George. "You do remember that I was sixty-two and retired when we met and that was sixteen years ago. I'm not getting any younger, George," he whispered in a kindly way. "I'm honestly not sure how much longer I'll be able to keep that promise open for you. Please believe me when I say I'm not telling you this as a pressure tactic. It's just that I'm feeling the onset of declining health."

George had not taken stock in the difference in Doctor Levine's physical deterioration since their first meeting. The old man now walked with a decided stoop—his face pale and drawn, eyes sunken, appearing emaciated. He suddenly understood Levine's concern. He pursed his lips and nodded confirmation of the Doctor's personal health concerns. "The simple fact that you're keeping that option open means the world to me. You have become so much more than a neighbor, you're my friend and as important and welcome in my life as anyone. And I do mean *anyone*.

"My friend," Levine said, his voice moving into an impassioned range, "I know I have said it so often that it seems like a platitude, but it's not. It is a solemn promise. You *will* remember what it was that put you on the path to this point in your life, if you allow me to take you back to its root. Hypnosis is the only way to tear down that impenetrable wall your mind has thrown up."

George drew a breath, held it a moment, and then sighed. "Tomorrow afternoon—your house?"

Levine began pushing his cart past George. "I'll be expecting you." He rolled the cart to the end of the aisle, turned the corner, and then moved out of sight.

George thought about the depth of his quickly offered commitment. His breathing became shallow and fast. He raced for the nearest checkout line. His face dampened with perspiration. *I've got to get out of the store before this thing takes hold and squeezes consciousness right out of me.*

* * *

Saturday afternoon after lunch George guided Jennifer out onto the patio at the rear of the house he had inherited from his mother. Every spare cent they earned went into making it a lifetime home where good memories could be made. Throughout lunch and even now, she chattered on and on about remodeling projects, furniture shopping, landscaping needs and other domestic concerns. He didn't mind at all. He preferred it. She carried the conversation almost entirely. His head was elsewhere and feigned interest with short non-committal responses.

Jennifer, still talking, sat sideways on a heavily padded chaise lounge in the shade of the patio awning.

George sat next to her, close enough that their bodies touched. He interrupted her rambling. "Jen, you know that I love you, right?"

She pulled her eyes down to a suspicious squint, and replied slowly, "Yes, I do. And every time you say that you love me in that tone of voice, I get the feeling that the next thing out of your mouth is bad news. What's going on?"

"Not necessarily bad news," he said.

"Then what?"

"How about I create a scenario and let you answer your own question?"

She smiled, as if about to be included in a game. "Go for it."

"Let's say, for example, that the John Deere Company chose me, out of hundreds of other salesmen across the country, to fly overseas and negotiate a big deal with foreign buyers."

Her eyes widened. "Have they?"

He bounced a fast grin. "Afraid not, just wanted to use an example that gave me a temporary ego boost."

"Oh. Go ahead."

"Somewhere, far from any mainland, the plane goes down, but I escape alive and make it to an uncharted island. In the meantime, the crash is widely reported in all the media that all crew and passengers are presumed dead."

"This is getting morbid."

"I don't mean for it to be. What I want to determine, if humanly possible, is the power of our love and the strength of your intuition."

"Where are you going with this?"

"Do you think you would be able to sense that I'm alive, that I love you with all my heart, and that I'm doing everything I can to find my way back to you?"

"What an odd question."

"Maybe. But I need an answer."

"This is turning into a really odd conversation," she said, and then sat quietly, thinking about his question for a couple of seconds. "I've always believed I could sense what's on your mind, George. I have known you far too long to think otherwise. I don't see why I wouldn't be sensitive to those things you speak of and, who knows, maybe into a perceptive extra-sensory range. So . . . yeah. I think it's possible that I'd know you were still alive in that scenario you cooked up." She smiled. "I'd feel your living energy in my heart."

He sighed relief. "Great answer and good to know."

She raised a suspicious eyebrow. "You've decided to let Doctor Levine hypnotize you. Haven't you?"

"You really are sensitive to what's on my mind."

She nodded. "About you? Oh yes. I'm glad you've finally decided to go through with it. It may give us the answers that have eluded you all these years. Regardless how you view it, you are not about to be fired off into space on a one-way journey, as you obviously believe. Or, deserted helplessly on an island."

"Then why do I have the feeling that is exactly what will happen?"

She fully faced him and draped her arms on his shoulders. She laced her fingers together behind his head, pulling him in, kissing him slowly, warmly. Before pulling away, she allowed her lips to brush a light circle over his lips. Every doubt he ever had about the strength of their love took flight. She whispered, "I've known you since kindergarten. What the heck could possibly be in your past that I don't know about?"

George shrugged his shoulders. He had no answer. Still, it did not allay the fear that his life was about to change unalterably.

* * *

George knocked on Levine's front door. After a moment, it opened slowly, as one might expect from a frail older man. "Hey, Edward, you doing okay today?"

The old man snickered once and said, "That's the first time you've knocked and waited for a response in years. Usually, you knock and stick your head in and shout my name, all at the same time. You know what that tells me?"

"I have a feeling you're about to tell me."

"It tells me you're not totally onboard with taking your journey to the next level. The obvious moment of hesitation on my porch gives you one final out, one last moment to back out of a plan that you, clearly, are not all that committed to yet. If I would have taken any longer getting to the door, your burst of courage would've evaporated. You'd have turned and scampered away. How'd I do?"

"You're amazing. You know that?"

"Nice of you to say. Come on in."

"You were right-on with the first part and now that you put it on my mind, I guess I *was* prepared to turn and run."

"You didn't though. That's a good thing. An amazing amount of progress can be interpreted by your willingness to wait for me to open the door."

As soon as George sat in his usual spot on the sofa across from Levine's overstuffed chair facing him, the Doctor handed him a pill and a small glass of water.

"What's this for?"

"It is a mild tranquilizer. I know you've had a problem with hyperventilation lately. And watching you cross the room just now, I'd say you're heading in that direction as we speak. Your movements are stiff, as if you have a couple of two-by-fours shoved down your pants."

As nervous as he was, George chuckled at the comparison. He took the pill from Levine's open palm and popped it into his mouth, washing it down with the water from the juice glass in his other hand.

"Good," Levine said. "Now, I want you to drink this." The old man poured hot water into a cup over a tea bag from a dainty teapot with roses and gilded trim. "I've not had the opportunity to use my late wife's tea set in years," he mused, and then handed the steaming cup to George.

"Now, what are you having me pour down my gullet?"

"Chamomile tea. A bit of added insurance that you'll relax. Tell me, now, how are Jennifer and that darling daughter of yours doing?"

It was clear that Doctor Levine intended on keeping his mind off the hypnosis, at least until the tranquilizer and the tea had accomplished what they were intended for. George fully appreciated how the good doctor was, thus far, handling a truly unnerving situation. He took a deep breath, forcing his body to relax. He began, "I've known Jennifer for nearly half a century and I can honestly say that my love for her deepens by the day. She takes care of me with a beautiful gentle side." He chuckled. "But she certainly has the capacity for sassiness when called for. Unfortunately, I give her cause far too often to let that side show." He paused and thought about that. A smile crept across his face and remained. "As for Rachael, that girl is my light. I see the best of Jen and me in her. I love them both so much that sometimes I can't stop tears when I think about the depth of that love. I look forward to growing old with Jen and watching Rachael grow into the woman and mother I know she'll be someday." He stopped talking. His mind took flight into thoughts of his family and happy times shared over the years. The prospect of many more good years warmed him.

"George, look at me," Doctor Levine said, his voice low and monotone. He held what appeared to be a large shiny golden lollipop on a stick. He rolled the stick back and forth between his fingers, causing the golden disk to wobble rhythmically, picking up natural light in the room that flickered in George's face. "I want you to relax beginning with your feet," Levine said. "Think about all the tension in them draining out onto the carpet. Now, your calves, thighs, and hips. Let all the muscles in them have a well-deserved rest. You have nowhere to go and nowhere to be . . . except right here . . . calm and relaxed. Sink deep and comfortably into the cushion beneath you."

All of George's focus narrowed to that wobbling and flickering golden disk. Back and forth—back and forth—back and forth. The room and even Levine dimmed into the background as the small flashing reflection took center stage.

Why was I so scared of this? The question flit through his mind, as if on butterfly wings. *It's actually quite wonderful.* His eyelids became heavy.

Levine kept his voice low, even, and soothing—inviting to listen to. "George, you and I are going on a journey, traveling into your past to your wedding day."

George remained aware of Doctor Levine's presence but nothing else, until his wedding day was mentioned. Suddenly, his heart filled with love and happiness.

"It was a glorious day for you, wasn't it, George?"

"Oh yes," he mumbled. "As if my life started on that day."

"Do you feel as though everything else in your life was only a rehearsal for that day?"

"I-I guess."

"Tell me about your life leading up to that blissful day."

George searched his memory. But, even in this open state of mind, he couldn't conjure memories before the wedding. "I can't." He fidgeted.

"Stay relaxed and continue traveling back along the highway of your mind, George."

Soothing words had their effect. He calmed.

"Think back. Think all the way back to the last memory you have before the day of your wedding," Levine said. His voice was void of stressful intonation—low and constant.

George sat quietly trying desperately to remember, but it was like trying to see into a boiling black fog. Abruptly, a scene popped into his mind so clearly that he could've been reliving it. "I'm sitting on the steps of the high school with Jennifer. It is the day after graduation. The last time we'll see one another for a while. Jennifer is getting emotional. I don't know how to handle it."

"Why will you be separating, and why so emotional?"

"I'm leaving to take summer courses at the University of Houston and will be gone all summer. We're sitting very close to one another, talking about getting married. It'll be the first time apart for over a week since we were six. She's sad. So am I—so very sad."

"Tell me about that summer."

"Busy. Meeting lots of new kids. Staying confused and homesick."

"Did it get better?"

"Oh yes. I met someone. A girl."

"Tell me about her."

"She was . . ." George couldn't pull a clear memory of her.

"What was her name?"

"I-I don't know. I can't remember." He became agitated.

"What bothers you so about the girl?"

He jerked his head side to side as snippets of memories, happy memories, attempted to penetrate the obscurity swirling about the girl, but he couldn't put them together in any logical sense.

"George, what are you seeing right now?"

"Nothing—just a feeling that I'm falling in love. How can I not see her face if I'm falling in love with her?" He white-knuckled the sofa cushion. "Damn it! Why can't I see her?" he said barely below a shout.

"It's all right, George," Levine said in that soothing monotone. "Let's travel forward in time. We can revisit that later."

George felt stress leaving him.

"Did you come home to Smithtown at the end of that summer?"

"Yes." A smile came up. "Jen is waiting for me." The scenario playing out is suddenly not what he expected. His smile abruptly vanished. "We're arguing."

"What about?"

"I'm making a mistake. I'm telling her about the feelings I developed for the girl in Houston. She's crying and screaming at me. I cry, too. I shouldn't have told her. All it did was hurt her. I don't want Jen to hurt. I screwed up. I screwed up in a big way." George felt Levine's hands come to rest on the points of his knees.

"Shh. It's okay, son. You may have said something that you shouldn't have, but it all worked out in the end."

George felt the weight of sadness slathered over with a thickening layer of anger he had never known. His lip quivered as he moved to the brink of meltdown. Words spilled from his jumbled brain into the back of his throat, building explosively with nowhere to go but out. "No, God damn it, it didn't work out. It ended!" He wailed. Tears pushed from between tightened eyelids. His voice squeezed down into a hoarse whine. "It all ended. Can't you understand that?" He felt Levine's hands on his knees squeeze tighter.

"George, listen to me. George?" The crescendo of Levine's voice competed with the horrendous memory breaking through. "George, always remember; in the end there is always an answer."

"I don't want the answer." George reanimated violently and thrashed about. "No! I don't want to remember."

The hands on his knees became tighter and then he felt another pair of hands on his shoulders and yet a third pair at his feet. It abruptly occurred to him he was no longer sitting but lying flat on his back. Levine's decade-long refrain, 'In the end there is always an answer," repeated over and over in his head. He tried a third time to shout that he didn't want to remember but no sound came out, just a raspy push of air. His voice was little more than a morose murmur.

"It was my fault, all my fault," he managed to whisper.

George opened his eyes to see Levine's face above him, but what he was looking at was very wrong. The old psychiatrist's face was about twenty years younger than the one he closed his eyes to minutes ago. It was the same face that he saw after the lightning episode on the golf course many years ago—and about the same age as then. *What the hell?*

Chapter 11 ~ A World Away

George looked about frantically at an ultra-sterile environment. Hands of people that had not been in the living room when his eyes closed in response to the disk now surrounded him, confining his thrashing body at the ankles, waist, and shoulders. Confusion doggedly refused to abate. *Who are these people? Where did they come from?* After long seconds of violently struggling against confinement, a more analytical side finally kicked in. Although still in a state of utter confusion, agitation subsided. He felt tight grips on his body easing. Why he was in this place came to him in a flash and then disappeared as quickly, thoughts decaying rapidly. His sight darted around the room trying desperately to interpret the situation. *Who are these people? What is this place?* Even as these questions raced through his mind, George, somehow, felt as though he knew where he was, but couldn't pull it from memory. George put words to his thoughts, "Where am I?" His voice oddly weak, tears thoroughly wet both cheeks.

A voice said in low monotone, "You're in Covenant Hospital in Lubbock. You've been in a coma. Something happened while you were under that apparently traumatized you to a wakeful state—probably a painful memory as you were emerging."

George opened his eyes and saw Edward Levine's face. "I don't understand." He strained to make his words audible. He coughed a couple of times and swallowed, attempting to remedy it. It apparently didn't work. "How did I . . . how did we get here, Doctor Levine? Did hypnosis fail in a big way—a psychotic disconnect of some sort? And, why do you look young again?"

The doctor looked at him curiously. I'm sorry, Mister Waller, but the name is Doctor Levenson, not Levine. I'm a neurologist that has been keeping an eye on you since the accident last week, not a hypnotist. You must have heard my name while you were under and it registered in your subconscious as Levine."

Neurologist? Accident? George's confused mind spun out snippets of visions but nothing that told a story of why he was on his back in a hospital bed. A gentle flow of oxygen hissed into his nostrils from a tube. He looked to his arm where an I-V needle was taped down and the clip on his finger monitored pulse. A heart monitor beeped rapidly and rhythmically, an audible demonstration of his confusion. The pain in the back of his neck and skull refused him deep contemplation of this collage of contradictions.

The doctor turned his attention to a nurse that had been holding his waist. "Call his next of kin. Let them know he's awake."

Apparently unaware she whispered so loudly, she said into the doctor's ear, "He has no living family." She quickly added, "How about his friend that was here a couple of days ago. I think his name is Alex. He left contact info? I believe that I heard him say he was staying in Lubbock a while longer."

"What do you mean 'no living family'? Call Jennifer Waller, my wife." His voice strengthened with each utterance. She's probably with Alex and his wife, Patricia somewhere." He groaned and swallowed hard. "I need water. Throat's dry."

The nurse and the doctor stared at one another for an awkward second. "I'll get him water," the nurse said, and then the doctor told him, "Call the one you have contact info on." The doctor returned his attention to George. "Are you experiencing pain or discomfort?"

"I have a helluva headache."

"Understandable, considering the thumping you took when you flew into that tree."

"Why did you tell the nurse to call Alex and not Jennifer?"

"Mister Waller, your friend will likely be here shortly. When he arrives, we'll have a discussion. For now, I want you to rest," he said as he inserted a hypodermic needle into the diaphragm port in the I-V tube and pushed the plunger.

"What's that?"

"A mild tranquilizer to relax you."

"The last time you gave me a mild tranquilizer, I woke up here."

The doctor smiled indulgently. "Just relax." He looked to a stocky young Latino man in scrubs at the foot of the bed. "Stay with him and monitor him closely." He looked back to George. "If you need anything, ask Antonio. He's a nurse. I'll be back to check on you shortly."

As the nurse checked and tweaked monitor dials and recorded the numbers on a computer pad, George glanced toward the square-built male nurse, his mind filled with answerless questions. His head throbbed. *I don't understand any of this. This unbearable pain has got to go.* As he grappled with the throbbing ache in his head and trying to cope, he thought, *I may not understand it now, but 'in the end there is always an answer.'* His thought process became less focused as the tranquilizer coursed through his bloodstream. Levine's words rolled through his mind, *always an answer—always an answer.* Sleep took him.

* * *

"Hey, buddy?" came the question in gentle tone.

George opened his eyes. It took effort to get that done, realizing he had dozed. The pain in his head had lessened to an uncomfortable but not unbearable throb. Lifelong friend, Alex Burton, stood bedside. He moaned, cleared his throat and replied, "Hey to you, too." A smile began to come up, but then disappeared.

"What the hell? You have a full head of hair." George studied his friend's youthful face and physique.

Alex frowned, choosing not to address the comment immediately — a statement that even George knew had to have sounded absurd to his friend. "The doctor told me that it may be a few days before your mind settles and events fall into place as they should," Alex said. "Your rehab will be both psychological and physical." He paused and took a step back, and then added, "By what you just said, it would seem you have an odd form of amnesia."

"What happened? How did I get here?"

Alex's face went somber. "You aren't aware of any of it, are you?" He made a series of shy and retiring gestures. He didn't know how much to share, if anything. "I'm not sure we should get into all that right now."

"Bullshit," George rasped. "Tell me."

"I'll try." Alex thought for a moment. "What is the last thing you remember?"

"Going next door to Doctor Levine's house to let him hypnotize me."

"Huh?" Alex tilted his head, confused. "Who's Doctor Levine?"

"You ought to know. You hounded me for years to get a handle on the fainting spells and memory lapses. So did Jen." He closed his eyes and attempted stretching the pain out of his neck. "Doctor Levine was trying to help me find the root cause for those episodes. Even Lenny and Bubba were on my case about it."

"Bubba?" Alex asked. Obviously, he couldn't grasp what George was telling him, but then suddenly, the light of recognition unlocked his expression. "Are you talking about Bubba Leal? He's the only guy by the name of Bubba that I've ever known."

"Of course. He and Lenny bugged the crap out of me."

As George responded, Alex shook his head slowly. "George," Alex said, drawing out the name, becoming overly cautious. "Bubba Leal was—"

"Where's my Sweet Jen?" George interrupted. He massaged his throbbing neck. "Let her explain it to you."

"George, I'm sorry, but I don't have any idea what you're talking about. Jen who?"

George's irritation became tinged with apprehension. "What game are you playing? Where is Jennifer?"

"Are you talking about Jennifer Andrews?"

"Andrews? I don't know a Jennifer Andrews."

"Of course you do. We grew up with her in Smithtown."

George's head began a slow spiral.

"Although back then it was Jennifer Harvey. How could you forget the girl you walked away from the day before your wedding when we were nineteen?"

That slow spiral now had begun to rob George of breath as it sped to dizzying speed. Breathing became shallow and fast. "I didn't leave her. I married her. She's my Sweet Jen, my wife!" The beep of the heart monitor escalated rapidly.

Antonio, the nurse, came back into the room, responding to the abrupt change in the otherwise monotonous beep.

Alex put a hand on George's shoulder. "Your wife's name was Marie. I'm sorry to be the one to tell you, but she didn't survive the accident." Alex's lip quivered. "It pains me almost beyond words," he took a breath, "to tell you that your daughter, Louisa, didn't survive either."

From somewhere deep inside a primal scream coursed upward and erupted from George. A kaleidoscopic array of colors and strobing white lights exploded in his mind when the world, as it was, dropped on him with brutal clarity and crushing force.

Chapter 12 ~ George Remembers

George poked at the campfire with a smoldering stick, pushing red coals closer to the base of the substantial tin coffee pot, blackened around its bottom by soot curling up from the coals. High wispy clouds painted the dawn in hues of pink and orange—a beautiful calm and cool autumn morning in New Mexico's Sangre de Cristo Mountains. Wife, Marie, stood a few feet away cradling a steaming cup of coffee. She was enjoying a panoramic view of the aspen and pine filled valley from this high vantage point. George eyed the Latina beauty admiringly, lingering over his own personal view of things that had nothing to do with the mountainous landscape. The floppy red plaid flannel shirt with sleeves rolled up to the elbows over snug jeans, the long plait of nearly black hair extending down to the center of her back, made her all the more appealing. He always liked dark-haired beauties the best. He rose from the campfire and dusted his hands. "You think we ought to wake Louisa?" he asked.

Marie did not look away from the view, spanning a valley that must have been over five miles wide. "Let's let her sleep a while longer. It's her vacation, too, ya know." She glanced back and smiled. "She didn't complain about coming along on this trip. I think we owe her for that." She snickered. "How many fifteen-year-olds do you know who will spend three days away from friends with parents *willingly*?"

"Good point." George stepped next to her and circled her waist with his arm. He breathed deep the perfumed air. "Magnificent." He looked down at the exotic beauty whose head was just below the level of his shoulder.

She sighed and looked up at him, returning his gaze. "It certainly is magnificent." She sipped her coffee, and then leaned in to him.

George kissed Marie on top of the head. "Sort of a spiritual thing, I'd say. Times like this remind me just how much I love you." He gently hooked a finger beneath her chin and pulled her face around and tilted her head back. He kissed her lightly on the lips and then, while enjoying her warm breath on his face, added, "Sorry. Didn't mean to interrupt your enjoyment of the view. I was compelled."

Her pleasant smile didn't waver. She searched his face with roving eyes. "That's okay. The view I have right now isn't so bad."

"The twists and turns our lives have taken brought us to this point and let me tell you, girl, you are as beautiful today as you were the day I met you in Houston." He kissed her again.

"Back then my head was into getting my degree and having a good time and not much else." The luster of Marie's smile faded. "I think often and shudder each time I remember how close I came to losing you when that summer ended." She flicked a glance toward him. "You know, when I discovered I was pregnant with Louisa. I was so scared to call and tell you. I almost waited too long."

George maintained a pleasant but neutral expression. Her comment took him to thoughts he didn't want to recall. But there it was, a mental display playing out in fine detail. His life took a hard-fast turn the day Marie called with the shocking news sixteen years ago, less than a day before marrying lifelong friend and sweetheart, Jennifer Harvey. Had his mother not lived in Smithtown, George often thought that he might not have ever returned to his hometown after marrying Marie, for fear of running into Jennifer. What he did to that girl, on that day, all those years ago, was unfair and cruel. It never stopped stalking him with nagging questions. What would have happened if Marie hadn't been pregnant? How differently would my life have turned out? What would life have been like with Jennifer? These questions would forever be locked away unanswered and unspoken.

"Hey, y'all, what time is it?" Louisa asked as she exited the tent, rubbing red sleepy eyes. The girl had gotten her mother's beauty but George's height. Louisa was already taller than her mother but still a shapeless young teen.

"Time to get up. How's that for an answer, sleepyhead," Marie said, turning to face the young girl.

"Yeah," George added, "we're on vacation. Who cares what time it is?"

Louisa came to her father and leaned her head into his chest, snuggling as if it were a pillow. "You're not going to try and cook breakfast again this morning, are you? Please—*please* say you aren't."

"What? You didn't like my cooking yesterday?"

Within a yawn, she replied, "Sorry. No."

"It's a gorgeous morning. How about we put the top down on the Jeep and drive down into Taos for breakfast?" Marie asked.

George nodded and turned his attention to his daughter. "How about that idea, Punkin?"

Louisa suddenly became fully alert. "That's a great idea."

"Hey, remember that nice lady from Dalhart we met at the convenience store in Plainview on the drive up? When she found out we were driving through Taos, she recommended a place called Michael's Kitchen. How about we go and see if her recommendation will live up to our ridiculously high standards?"

The answer to that question came in the form of three people hurriedly securing the campsite for a short road trip. George put the top down on the Jeep. "Come on guys, let's get a move on. I want to get there before they run out of pancake batter."

As they pulled away from the campsite and eased up the park road toward the winding and steeply descending highway, George saw the building that housed the restrooms near the park's main gate. "I have to make a pit stop before we leave." He wheeled into the small parking area, unfastened his seatbelt, and leaped out.

"Don't waste time," Louisa called out to his back. "I'm starving. If we mess around much longer, we'll be needing lunch menus."

George glanced back at her with a look that could only be construed as asking the silent question, "Are you serious?" He continued walking toward the restroom but pointed at the sun, just now fully above the horizon for Louisa's benefit.

"I don't care. I'm hungry. Hurry," she shouted, as he disappeared into the public restroom.

George came out and jogged back to the Jeep. "Wow, that didn't take long," Louisa said.

"Well, us guys don't take quite as long, ya know. Let's hit the road." He cranked the Jeep and they were on their way.

Heading down the mountain, George kept the vehicle in a lower gear to prevent it from free-wheeling down the steeper stretches. The mood was light and happy. Laughter came frequently and even George's stupid jokes brought on shrill laughter from the girls. "We should be able to see the valley floor and Taos once we get around that curve up ahead."

"I don't want to see it. I want to be there," Louisa said from the backseat. "Do we have to go this slow?"

He pressed the accelerator and steered into the outside curve and glanced over his shoulder at her and grinned. "How's that?"

Marie screamed.

George snapped his head back around to see an impatient driver attempting to pass on the blind curve. He reacted, jerking the steering wheel toward the cliff's edge.

The open Jeep hit rocks on the shoulder of the blacktop.

It bucked high on the front and then higher at the rear when the back tires hit the same rocks.

George flew from the driver's seat high into the air and the Jeep went on without him.

Time slowed.

Shrill screams came from Marie and Louisa still strapped in their seats as the Jeep went over the edge.

George tumbled through the air, striking his head as he came down against the trunk of a short stout evergreen.

The last thing he remembered were terrified screams fading in the distance far below him.

Chapter 13 ~ Alex Turns to Jennifer

"Jennifer?"

"Yes."

"Jennifer Harv . . . I mean Andrews?"

"This is she. Who am I speaking with?"

"Your ol' buddy, Alex Burton." He stepped to a near corner of the visitor's area of Covenant Hospital in Lubbock—phone to his ear, head down, facing the wall, trying not to disturb others with his conversation.

"Alex! This is wonderful. I haven't heard from you since . . . well, since the funeral."

"Are you okay? How are you holding up? Coping, I hope."

"I'm not going to gloss it for you, Alex. Losing Sean to a curable type of cancer like prostate at such a young age has been hard. I know it's been almost two years, but I occasionally still grind my teeth when I remember that we could've done something about it, if only we would've caught it sooner. How are Patricia and the boys?"

"The boys are getting meaner and Patricia is a gem for putting up with me and all my craziness. How about you? Are you getting on with life?"

"I've had a few dates and have cool friends here in Abilene that have helped me along the way. Are you still in Smithtown? How's our crew doing?"

Alex went silent, taking a moment to frame his answer.

"Is everyone okay?" Jennifer asked.

He heard the alarmed concern in her voice. "Sort of, yeah."

"You're worrying me. What's going on?"

"I'm calling from Covenant Hospital in Lubbock."

"Oh my God! Who? What?"

"Calm down," Alex said in a low consoling way. "It's George. He was in an auto accident a little over a week ago. He's going to be okay, but he lost his wife Marie and his daughter Louisa."

"Oh, God, no. I'm so sorry."

"Jennifer, that's only a small part of a larger story and for lack of a better word—creepy. Here's the kicker: it involves you."

"Me? How? I don't understand."

"I'm not sure I do either. He was in a coma for seven days and believes that he was married to you for sixteen years—all during that short seven-day period. His delusional life and memories of it are ridiculously detailed. Frankly, I don't know what to think, except that, to George, that sixteen-year marriage to you is equally real in his mind as his marriage to Marie."

"Wow. I want to know more."

"Can you get away from Abilene for a day or two and drive up to Lubbock?"

"I've accumulated some personal days at work. This is a good reason to use them. Besides, things here at work are a little creepy lately, too. I need a breather away from my boss. I'll be on the road north right after five."

* * *

Jennifer should be arriving any moment now, Alex thought. He drifted down to the cafeteria on the ground floor of the hospital where he told her that he'd be waiting. He bought a cup of coffee and chose a table near the main entrance but didn't have a chance to sit. Jennifer breezed in, stopped and scanned the dining area. He waved her over at the same time he approached her. "Jen, it's great to see you again." He wrapped her in a hug, lifted her off the floor, and growled.

"You too, Alex." She patted him on the back and kissed his cheek.

He looked her up and down. "Damn, woman. I swear you get more beautiful with age. I sure don't see gray in those long tresses of yours."

"Thanks. I guess. And, hey, watch how you use that word 'age'. We're only thirty-seven, ya know." She pulled her head back for a better look at him. "Has your hairline moved back a little?" She flicked his hair with the back of a finger and grinned.

He pressed his lips together and then licked them slowly. "Funny . . . real funny." He gestured to the chair across the table. "But, that does lead me right in to what I know about George's condition."

"Your hair? How so?"

Alex nodded. "When George saw me, he was shocked by my appearance. The first thing out of his mouth was, 'You have a full head of hair.'"

"Why would he say that?"

"Jen, until he remembered Marie and Louisa, he thought that you two were fifty-one years old with a fifteen-year-old daughter, Rachael Irissa, and had been married for over sixteen years. He was going nuts wondering where you were and why you weren't there in the room with him—that is, until the memory of what happened to his wife and daughter came crashing in on him."

Jennifer's jaw fell slack. "Rachael Irissa?"

"Yeah, y'all's supposed daughter. Why the shocked expression? Does the name mean something to you?"

She became emotional. She shuddered and began rubbing her arms as if chilled. Her eyes moistened. "A few days before we were supposed to have been married all those years ago, we were lying on a blanket in the grass behind his mother's house late one evening. We had a lengthy conversation about what our future together might look like. We toyed with names for children, finally deciding that we really wanted a girl. The name we settled on was Rachael Irissa. Rachael was a name I used for an imaginary friend when I was very young, and George would make fun of me for it." She looked down and stared at her feet for a moment, clearly envisioning the memory. "He was such a little shit." She smiled and thought about it for a second longer, finally reconnecting with Alex. "After we settled on that name, he pointed back at his mother's house and said, 'One day, Sweet Jen, we'll live right here and raise that child'."

"And that was the summer he came back from Houston, right?"

"Yeah. We were nineteen. I remember that when he called me 'Sweet Jen', I was so enamored with the pet name that I pounced on him and smothered him with kisses."

"He thinks he married you at thirty-seven, our present ages. That means in his subconscious he was aware of the death of his family and, I suppose as a defense mechanism, he married you while in that coma. Even if my imagination was good enough to wrap my head around such a story, I don't know how he crammed sixteen years of highly detailed life into a seven-day coma. But he did."

"You mean to tell me that George imagined a sixteen-year marriage—to me—all within seven days, with details?"

"Oh yeah, lots of details. I'm tellin' ya, Jen, he lived it. To him, you *were* his Sweet Jen. I've been in on some of the conversations between him, the neurologist, and a psychiatrist. Now that he has his memories back of Marie and Louisa, he's having a helluva tough time separating real from fantasy. Life events are all jumbled together in his head. I thought it might be helpful if you spent time talking to him. The psychiatrist agreed that it was worth a try. The doctor thought your presence might provide clarity so he could learn to set his feet solidly in reality, a place he doesn't at all want to be right now. He's literally torn between two worlds."

Alex allowed the suggestion to hang without pressing Jennifer for an answer. He saw hesitance in her eyes and pain because of George's abandonment of her all those years ago. Plus, she still harbored the additional ache of losing her husband, Sean. Alex became nervous that her answer might be negative, not wanting to reopen old wounds, and he would certainly understand it if she refused to stay. He had already committed to not appearing insensitive or insistent by asking her twice.

After quiet seconds, tapping the tabletop with a long fingernail, she nodded. "Okay. I'll do it."

Chapter 14 ~ Jennifer's Nervous Encounter

Jennifer Andrews leaned against the wall next to George Waller's hospital room fidgeting—hands shaking, feet seemingly frozen in place—scarcely able to function. She just couldn't allow herself to be seen until courage equaled commitment. The last time she had been face to face with him was sixteen years ago, the day before their wedding that never happened. She wished that her friend, Alex, hadn't gone home. At this moment, she needed a hand to hold to get a conversation started with George, but she also knew George needed family. Since he had none, a friend was the next best thing. Regardless how he had treated her, she couldn't easily dismiss a friendship carefully forged before that fateful incident that changed the courses of both their lives. Nor could she blame Alex or feel annoyed over his decision to go home. He had been away from his family for almost two weeks. If she and Lenny Poe were removed from the mix, Alex was the closest thing to family that George had now that Marie and Louisa were gone. She had never met his wife and daughter but, admittedly, wondered often over the years what they looked like—more to the point, what kind of person Marie was. She must have been quite a woman to have swept George so totally off his feet while, at the same time, pulling the rug from under her own feet. Jennifer couldn't see this initial meeting with George to be anything other than awkward. She had to do whatever it might take to get past hesitance as quickly as possible, to take the plunge, and breach the threshold into his room. Adding to this off-balance fear-induced paralysis were a stew of old emotions buried for over a decade—the hurt of an abrupt and brutal severing of a relationship left open and bleeding for years. But there was another sentiment working its way to the surface—affection—an honest desire to see him again and the result of her own lingering heartache over the loss of a spouse. She was adrift herself and in need of a tether, or her life might soon reel off into a dark place. She needed this as much as she needed to help George. She closed her eyes and clenched her teeth tightly. Time to take the plunge.

She forced her diaphragm into deep even breathing as if about to leap into cold water. Then, before she had a chance to think otherwise, stepped around the door jamb into George's hospital room. Standing between them was a stocky male nurse blocking her view of George and his view of the door. She walked in and used the moment to continue mustering courage while still unseen.

"That ought to do it for now, George," the nurse told him. "If you need anything before I come back to check on you, press the button."

George nodded confirmation, but never looked up at the man. "Thanks, Antonio. I will."

The weakness of his voice shocked her—a mere whispery rasp. Still, there was a wealth of good memories in the sound of it. The nurse spun around and smiled at her on his way out of the room. She detected a sincere warmth in his smile that told volumes of the man's humanity and integrity to his job. She returned the nurse's smile, hoping it contained at least a fraction of the friendliness she had seen in his. It crossed her mind that he resembled a childhood friend of hers—of theirs, the Smithtown Crew—who died a long time ago. As the nurse passed, he left a totally unobstructed view of a pale and drawn George Waller. Dark green circles beneath his eyes made them appear sunken in a colorless face.

He stared at her, as if awed. "My Sweet Jen," he cooed. "You're so young and your hair is so long, and you are just as beautiful as you were yesterday."

Yesterday? She thought.

George was speaking in such a way, with a dreamy lilt, that Jennifer wondered if he might not be totally conscious or aware. And since he so casually tossed out that word 'yesterday', it added considerable weight to that possibility.

A smile creased his face. "You're as beautiful as you were on our wedding day. As soon as I get out of here, I'll get back on that list of things you wanted done around the house." He flopped an open palm in her direction, clearly intending for her to take his hand. It was odd. He spoke as if it had only been a short time since they were last in the same room together, and it was clear that he imagined making promises to her.

She stepped in, lifted his hand, and kissed the back of it, but remained hesitant to say hello since he believed her to be something she was not. Still, there existed a growing urge to speak, brought on by the widening gulf of silence between them. Finally, "You are aware that that wedding never happened, right?" she asked in a low even tone.

The dreamy look in his eyes widened into shock. His lip quivered and then he closed his eyes. He squeezed out tears, finally nodding affirmation.

"When Alex told me what happened, there was no way I was going to stay in Abilene and make you endure this alone."

George sniffed. "Did he tell you everything?"

"Everything he was aware of, yes. I-I'm sorry about your wife and daughter."

"Oh, Jen, my head is so screwed up."

"If you like, I'll hang around a few days. Maybe I can be of help sorting it all out, but I'll only do it if you want me to. I can see where my presence might complicate and add to your confusion."

"You would do that for me ... after what I did to you?"

"Water under the bridge," she blurted abruptly. She paused and drew a deep slow breath. "Besides, there are a lot of really cool memories caught in eddies beyond that bridge." Her smile returned. "Friends don't let friends hurt like this. Of course I'll stay awhile. I'm surprised you felt compelled to ask. I don't know if you've heard but other than my job in Abilene, I have no reason to hurry home—not anymore." Her head lolled forward. "I lost my spouse to cancer a couple of years ago."

"I'm so sorry for your loss, Marie."

"Jennifer."

"What?"

"You called me Marie," she said with a smile, and then quickly added, "But it's okay. The blush of embarrassment brought a healthier look to his face. "Don't dwell on it, George. I understand what you're dealing with."

"Oh, Jennifer. I have lived two married lives that are equally clear in my mind and both are so tangled up in there that I'm having trouble separating fact from fantasy. Marie and my beautiful Louisa, I loved them so much. Now they're gone. Dead!"

"Shh." She patted his hand not trying to talk him down. All she could do was be there.

He cried. "I was stupid and reckless. Louisa pushed me to go faster because she was hungry and wanted me to get down the mountain into Taos quicker. I did as she wished and sped up just to see her smile." His voice choked off. "And that gorgeous smile was the last thing I saw." He couldn't stanch tears and didn't try. His chest heaved and shuddered with sobs.

As Jennifer squeezed his hand and stroked his shoulder with the other hand, she kept her expression neutral, but she couldn't prevent her own eyes from reddening and glossing with sympathy. The growing lump in her throat threatened to choke her. She attempted swallowing it away, to no avail. Jennifer struggled to maintain an even and calm demeanor, wanting George to have the moment to get it out without making it about herself. In his sad eyes, she saw the little boy she met on the first day of first grade in Smithtown thirty-one years ago—nervous about the new world he had just entered. Then, too, he needed a friend. Even at age six, she knew right away that George Waller was destined to be her friend. She had no idea that he would become her best friend, confidant, and eventually her fiancé.

After several minutes with no words exchanged, George settled. She thought it best to change the subject. "I hear they're going to transfer you to TrustPoint Hospital for rehabilitative therapy." She handed him a tissue.

He took it and wiped away the tears, taking a shuddering breath. He sniffed and nodded. "They've had me walking the halls here at Covenant. I'm shaky, but my strength is coming back. The drugs help the headaches, so I guess I'm ready to re-learn how to live." Again, he went silent. His eyes darted all over her face. "I-I can't get over how young you are. I just saw you two days ago, and you were fifty-one with very short hair."

She smiled. "Did I age well?"

"Oh God, Jen, you were beautiful. You are beautiful."

"Alex told me that you thought we had a teenage daughter. Was she pretty?"

He smiled. "Oh yes. Rachael is . . . was . . . a jewel." His still developing smile wilted away as he realized the girl never existed.

"Did she look like Louisa?"

On that question, he swallowed hard. Renewed grief drew his brows to a sad slant.

"I'm sorry," she said, "I let curiosity overtake good sense. Forget I asked that."

"It's okay." He drew a breath and let it out slowly. "I have to start compartmentalizing what was real against an overly vivid imaginary concoction." She saw the wheels of his mind turning. "Rachael was not born looking like you, but she grew to resemble you. My imagination may have made that happen, I suppose." He stared at the ceiling above his bed. His eyes darted as memories brightened his face. "But Rachael had her own unique look and style. I'm having a hard time believing that she was a fabrication of my mind and never existed. There has got to be more to it than that."

"Scientists are continually unlocking tidbits of information about the human mind: its capabilities and even what we as humans might be capable of doing with our minds after another evolutionary cycle. Of course, I believe there is *Someone* very important that will have a final say in that," she added, whispering and shielding her mouth with the back of her hand while pointing to heaven. "Who knows? Maybe you were blessed with a divine gift. Maybe while you were under, a portal opened and you saw an alternate universe or, perhaps, a glimpse into the future. Who am I to say it was not, or will not be, real?"

"A fan of science fiction, huh?"

"Not at all. You lived it. I didn't." She kissed him on the forehead. "Rest easy. I'll come over to TrustPoint Hospital tomorrow once you're transferred and settled. Exploring what you've been through might be tense, but it will also be a fascinating journey. Mind if I join you for the trip?"

"I think I would have begged you to if you had not asked." He rolled his head away. "I-I have no one else to ask." He jerked back to face her. "That doesn't matter. You would've been the perfect choice under any circumstance."

Jennifer backed away, allowing George's hand to slip from her hold before turning and walking toward the door, but was compelled to look back a final time. He was smiling and staring. She blew him a quick kiss and then continued out of the room. As she ambled down the wide corridor toward the elevator, the hard heels of her sandals clapped the floor with a rhythmic echo. She was unhurried by a need to be anywhere in particular and she thought about how aimless her life had become since Sean's passing. All her plans and dreams were shared with her husband and never were hers alone. When he died, so did her future. Now, purpose had been infused into her near-future. She had no plan to put an end date on it either. *I wonder if any of the law firms in Lubbock are looking for a good paralegal.*

Chapter 15 ~ A Future Seen?

Marie and Louisa float high in the sky clutching one another inside a large flexing, twisting, and rolling bubble—beyond the grasp of George's desperately seeking hands. A whine catches in his throat— impotent to intervene. The two loves of his life struggle to free themselves, clutching one another, slinging their combined weight into the pulsating film that entraps them. The bubble stretches and distorts but doesn't break—faces of mother and daughter scream anguish, but nothing of their torment is heard. There's no sound penetrating the seemingly flimsy prison. George doesn't want to hear what must be the result of pain-filled agony, although, he longs to hear their voices just one more time.

Another bubble comes into view and moves quickly to overtake Marie and Louisa. It's Jennifer and Rachael trapped in identical fashion. The bubbles collide but don't part, forming a single pliable, sparkling prison with only a soapy rainbow-laced membrane separating them. The two joined bubbles stretch to ridiculous shapes by its occupants, but it has no breaking point despite manic efforts by the four to free themselves. And then, in the span of time for a heart to beat once, Marie's and Louisa's bubble loses its rainbow luster. It goes colorless, reflecting no light, while Jennifer's and Rachael's shimmer in many different colors. In that flash of time, George's heart seizes, realizing that the bubble has popped, propelling Jennifer's and Rachael's floating prison beyond a cloud and out of sight.

The screams are abruptly shrill. George doesn't want to hear them. He attempts to block them, but cannot. The two plummet toward the top of a cloud. The whine that had been trapped in George's throat explodes into a loud tortured plea for God to intervene and save them at the precise moment he realizes the bubble has burst. He shouts their names over and over as they disappear into a roiling white cloud top, tumbling in free fall toward an unseen inevitability. Yet, deep in his heavy heart, he knows what that end will be.

He woke, covered in sweat, mumbling their names. As his clenched eyelids parted, he studied his surroundings, realizing he lay in bed at TrustPoint Hospital and it was just another bad dream. As a psychiatrist delved deeper into George's troubled and confused mind, the nightmares increased over the past few days. His brain worked overtime, attempting to sort what is, from what never was. Unlike his painfully vivid, but imaginary marriage to Jen while comatose, these were instantly recognizable as terrifying nightmares, nothing more. He had taken to praying nightly for the dreams to stop. He hoped therapy could help put them behind him eventually, but that day was sometime in the future, and the horrible dreams were an inevitable part of the journey.

Hearing George shout the names of his dead wife and daughter, Jennifer hurried through the door. "Are you okay?"

He ran a forearm over his sweaty brow. "Just another damn dream," he mumbled. He lay quietly for a few seconds and drew several controlled and deep breaths. He faced Jennifer. Amid his disturbance, a pleasant thought crossed his mind. "Twice in two days," he said, "you have appeared at my side like an angel." He felt a smile attempt to sprout, but was not ready to follow through and make it happen.

"An angel I'm not, but thanks." She pulled a chair in close to his bed. "How was your physical therapy and psyche session this morning?"

"Exhausting. That's why I came back here and drifted off to sleep."

"It'll be a while before all your strength returns." Jennifer looked at him, but only in nervous glances, never making hard eye contact. Her gaze flitted from one thing to the next around the room. Her body language indicated deep reserve and a touch of fear. She also seemed embarrassed, picking at a thumb cuticle and chewing the inside of her lip. George was so appreciative of her presence that he searched his thoughts for something to talk about, something soothing—at least therapeutic. He didn't want her to suddenly leave because of awkward silence. "The doctors here are good, but you're the therapy I need," he blurted. He raised his upper torso and scooted back against the pillows. "If you don't mind talking about it, tell me about Sean. I'd love to know what kind of guy he was."

George's calm request settled her. She relaxed her hands onto her thighs. "I don't mind." She began gently as she thought about her deceased husband. "Sean was a good man taken from me long before his time on this earth should've been up. I miss him terribly, but time is softening the pain of his abrupt departure. He was a CPA with a good clientele." She grinned and shrugged her shoulders. "I bet you can tell by his profession that he wasn't the wild or adventurous type. Sean was a good man with a huge heart and tremendous capacity for compassion." She fell silent, clearly drawing a mental image. "Anyhow, I worked as a paralegal for a small law firm right next door to his office, still do. For over a year now, I've looked at that damn 'For Lease' sign every day posted on what had been his office—a stark reminder of his absence and very difficult to overlook." She stopped talking. Her slowly drooping posture indicated a darkening mood.

"Do you have any children?" he hurriedly asked.

She sighed and straightened. "It was the plan, but never seemed like the right time to try. So, no. We kept putting it off until it was too late." Her eyes drifted down to the floor. "You talk awhile."

"It would seem we both have issues to work through."

She smiled nervously. "I thought that I'd be able to talk about it objectively by now but, maybe not."

"You don't have to explain," he said.

"How about you, George? What have you been up to since . . . well, since we were nineteen?"

"I own a small, but very successful, used car dealership here in Lubbock. I haven't thought about it much since I returned to the land of the conscious. I've been busy separating fact from fiction. I'm sure it's operating fine without me. I have good people running it that I trust. I've talked to them but, believe it or not, business is not always part of those conversations. I consider all of them friends and trust them all as much as anyone I've ever known to take over the business. They really don't need me or my opinions. The dealership is doing fine without me." He paused, shook his head and let it wilt forward. "Humph."

"What just crossed your mind?"

"I sold John Deere tractors and equipment in Smithtown in my so-called other life with you."

"You do realize that's what Alex does, right?"

"Yeah. I was always jealous of Alex finding employment in Smithtown—able to stay and raise a family right there in our hometown. Interestingly, while comatose, I never gave any thought to what he did for a living. I suppose it was a detail that never mattered in that life, so I assumed his career as my own. Weird, huh?"

"No stranger than anything else that happened to you during that week."

He sighed. "Back to this life. Marie was a housewife and Louisa had just finished her freshman year of high school as an A-student."

"Tell me about Marie."

George pushed around to the edge of the bed. Jennifer stood and gave him a helping hand. "Thanks. All it takes is a week of no muscle use to transform a grown man back into a baby. Muscle atrophy happens so fast. I'm still unsteady."

Jennifer returned to her chair. "If you don't want to talk about Marie, I'll understand."

"It's not that. I want to tell you something that you may not be aware of about Marie. Although, I'm not certain I should."

She shrugged her shoulders. "It's up to you. Tell me as much, or as little, about her as you're comfortable sharing."

"It's not so much that. It's as much about you as it is her."

"Oh? Now, you have stuck your foot in it. I must know."

"The day after our sojourn into a possible future while lying on a blanket in Mom's backyard which, of course, was only two days before our planned wedding, Marie called me from Houston. She was still on campus taking summer courses. She revealed to me that she was pregnant with Louisa."

As he spoke, Jennifer's jaw slackened as she obviously began getting a sense of where he was going with the explanation. "You're right. I was not aware of it 'til this very moment. Is that the reason you tried talking to me about her the day after that?"

"Yeah. It was."

"I guess I shouldn't have lost my temper and yelled at you. Of course, I still wouldn't have understood."

"Jen, it was never about loving her more than you. I didn't. I was torn, ripped right down the middle between desire and responsibility. I suppose Mama, God rest her soul, instilled a deep enough sense of accountability in me. It was a summer infatuation that happened to change the course of my future. I was too young and stupid to realize that that sense of accountability should have applied to you equally. The pregnancy screwed up my head. It took time, but I learned to love Marie. One day I realized that she was a good woman and deserved to be loved. She was a beautiful Latina with black hair and she was short, only about five-three. I often joked that if she ever got tired of walking I'd carry her in my hip pocket." He chuckled. "Let me tell ya, though, she may have been small, but she was tough." The image of her in various situations over the course of their marriage flooded his mind and made him smile, but then he remembered the down-side and that pleasant expression melted away. "All that aside, I was so ashamed of what I did to you. I still am, sixteen years later. It was a gutless thing I did to you."

Jennifer's eyebrows lifted slightly, and she nodded agreement but, otherwise, didn't respond.

Come on, Jen, yell at me or something. "I hate it that all I can do now is apologize. Saying I'm sorry is in no way strong enough to express my regret, but I *am* sorry, and I *do* regret it."

Jennifer sat next to him on the side of the bed and stared straight ahead, suddenly void of readable expression or body language.

Maybe regret and sorrow aren't the only things I can offer. I can redeem myself. I don't know how yet, but I will . . . as God is my witness.

* * *

Jennifer continued staring straight ahead—eyes following all movement beyond the hospital room door out in the corridor. *How do I respond to that? Of course, I think it was gutless to walk out on our wedding one freakin' day before it was supposed to have taken place, but that was sixteen years ago. I don't want to burden him with additional pain while he mourns the loss of Marie and Louisa. Re-opening that wound all these years later would be as cruel as he was to me then. It's not worth it.* She turned and made eye contact with him. *He's still my friend and, at one time, my best friend. I want it to be that way again. And, now, there's no reason that that can't happen. There is nothing standing in the way for either one of us any longer.* As she stared into George's apologetic eyes and thought about that, she smiled. "Like I've already said, it's water under the bridge. How about we not talk about it and keep our eyes forward to the day you're out of here. Looking back at failures and sad things doesn't do either one of us any good."

George was obviously touched. She saw it in his eyes.

Changing the subject seemed the best way to pull them both from the muck of unpleasant histories. "Say, do you still own your mother's house?" She asked.

"Yeah, I do. After she passed last year, I rented it out. I didn't want to sell it because Marie and I had discussed putting in a satellite used car lot right there in Smithtown and moving back home, making a life in the house I grew up in. It would be the only car dealership of any kind within a fifty-mile radius. I think it would do well—at least well enough to make a nice living for a couple of employees and myself."

"Interesting." She immediately thought of the only attorney in Smithtown. "Does Dwayne Brewster still have a law office there?"

"I think so. Why?"

"You think in terms of used cars. I think in terms of law practices. That's where my thoughts happened to go when you started talking about our hometown."

"That makes sense."

George picked up where he left off and spoke freely about the ins and outs of the used car business, what it might take to open a lot in Smithtown and keep the one here in Lubbock open and let his trusted employees operate it. She responded by saying only enough to keep him talking. He brightened when he spoke of the possibilities. She didn't want to spoil it, liking what she saw—a man looking forward to happier times and hunting for reasons to compartmentalize tragedy and not dwell on it.

As he spoke, she listened for key words and phrases that might indicate a future with her in it and not simply apologizing and begging for forgiveness for his actions all those years ago. *I wonder if Dwayne Brewster needs a crack paralegal.*

Chapter 16 ~ Another Revelation

George regained most of the strength, which was never very much, he had prior to the accident. Alex Burton was the strong athlete in his Crew. George didn't even finish attaining his full six-feet until after he graduated from high school and never did put on much muscle. The last time the hospital had him step on a scale his weight remained below what it had been. Before the accident, he had developed a paunch above his waist. That flab was totally gone now. The weight loss was probably for the best.

Headaches subsided and nightmares became less frequent. It seemed the psychological retraining was having the desired effect, but it was taking place in a clinically controlled environment and measured, keeping him grounded. After three weeks, he strengthened and was mentally stable enough that boredom had become the latest problem he struggled against. He wanted to go home.

Jennifer spent five days in Lubbock to be near him—a full work week, but had gone back to Abilene, having burned through her personal time off. He appreciated that she was hesitant to leave, and he disliked feeling obligated to encourage her to go home. He wanted her to stay, almost desperately. She had no choice if she wanted to remain employed. She had to go back. But the way she referred to that paralegal job in Abilene, the sour expression that came over her when she spoke of her boss, and how her face went dreamy when she spoke of Smithtown, George got the impression she'd get out of Abilene if the opportunity presented itself. He sensed in Jennifer a strong nostalgia for their hometown. He hoped that he had provided her with a reason to make that move back to Smithtown. Without spelling it out, she made it plain that she would hang around Lubbock longer if he wanted her to. All she waited for was his request which didn't come. George thought often and fondly of Jennifer's insistence that their friendship had survived the sixteen-year old turmoil. The incident that drove a wedge between them was now on course to developing feelings as strong as it was in times prior to those dark days. That was great, a foundation from which to build because he wanted more than friendship. He wanted to return to what they had—what he imagined they had. Still, he couldn't be selfish, no matter how much he wanted her to stay. She called him every evening. He quickly became dependent upon those lengthy conversations. He had no living family and simply chatting about everything, or nothing, was a treat. Calls from his employees at the car dealership about business and sundry small talk was welcomed, but certainly not the same—not at all. He had not yet considered that Jennifer had no one either, other than a few casual friends in Abilene that were likely married friends of hers and Sean's. George surmised that her situation was not that much different than his own.

He took to walking the halls of TrustPoint Hospital, spending as much time in the cafeteria as in his room. It was the beginning of another week. He hoped it would be his last under the hospital's roof. An evaluation was scheduled for tomorrow to determine if he was again ready to meet the world. As he sat at a small table eating a cup of frozen yogurt, he looked up to see a familiar face. "Hey, Doctor Levine . . ." He grimaced. "Sorry. I mean Levenson. Good to see you again."

The doctor abruptly stopped a purpose-driven march and came to stand next to George's table. "George Waller, right?"

"That's right." George thrust out his hand and shook the doctor's. "Got a minute? I'll buy you a frozen yogurt."

"Levenson checked his watch. "I'll forego the yogurt, but I'll sit and drink my coffee with you. I love frozen yogurt, but it leaves me lethargic. Nobody wants to see a doctor with sleepy eyes, especially if I'm coming at them with a hypodermic needle in hand." He snickered, and then added, "I'd better stick to coffee until late this afternoon sometime. Do you have something specific on your mind?"

"I've had a few questions about your insertion into my comatose fantasy. You mind helping me try to understand?"

"I came in to check on another patient brought in yesterday, but it's nice running into you. I heard you may be going home soon."

"Maybe. I'll know after the latest psych eval in the morning."

Doctor Levenson nodded. "You'll do fine. Now, about those questions." He sipped his coffee, set it on the table, and tented his fingertips in a receptive pose.

"Remember when I told you about the faces I saw during spells while in the coma, and that yours was the only one that ever appeared to me in full color, vivid detail and disturbingly close to me once?"

"Sure."

"Do you have any theories on why that was?"

Levenson tapped his fingers together and stared over the top of George's head for a moment. "Your coma, although not totally unprecedented, was odd because it seemed that you were never far from consciousness for the entire seven-day period. That said, early on—the second day I believe—your eyes popped open and I happened to be looking in on you at the time. Antonio handed me a penlight and I moved in quite close to check your pupils. It would be my theory that that was when my counterpart, Doctor Levine, took on my face in your subconscious world. I also believe that each one of those spells you were having within the comatose state were times that you would almost come out of it. That's why when you sunk back deeper, withdrawing farther from reality, you'd reawaken in *that* world with a bad headache. You really had a painful head injury that would come back to you briefly. It's becoming clear to me that your subconscious totally replaced your conscious mind and, I believe, you *always* had control over which one would dominate from day one of the coma. But, that's just a theory."

George pushed out his lower lip and nodded, slowly at first, then enthusiastically. "It makes sense. Using that reasoning, it's why I was so scared of your counterpart, Levine, hypnotizing me. I, somehow, knew what would happen. About Antonio, he was the nurse, right?"

"Yeah, Antonio Mendoza. Good man. Great nurse."

"How come I never saw his face like I did yours? He was in my room many more times than you."

"It could be because he never got down in your face while your eyes were open like I did. He was always on the sidelines assisting. I'd be surprised if he didn't register in your subconscious somehow."

"I keep thinking he did but—" As if his body had suddenly been electrified, George stiffened, slamming his body into the chair back, sitting bolt upright. His eyes popped large. "Oh my God!"

"George, what is it? What's wrong?"

"Bubba—Bubba Leal!"

"Stay calm, George." He frowned quizzically. "I don't know who Bubba Leal is."

"A friend." George couldn't control his shuddering body. Tears filled his eyes and spilled out, zigzagging down his cheeks. His hands shook so badly that he was compelled to clasp them together. "I-I created Bubba from Antonio."

"So, not everyone was real. Why would an imaginary friend cause you to become emotional like this?"

"Bubba was *not* a product of my imagination. He was real."

"I don't understand."

"Bubba Leal was my friend when we were in elementary school. He was clowning around and climbed about twenty feet up the ladder on the water tower in Smithtown. He fell and broke his neck. He was dead at nine years old. I created an adult version of him using Antonio as the pattern."

George couldn't prevent the free flow of tears, having lost the same dear friend twice.

* * *

"Stay calm, George. Your emotions are reeling," Jennifer said, as she paced the floor in her Abilene home with the phone to her ear. Revelations like realizing Bubba had been dead for many years threatened George's progress. *How much more must I endure? What else remained trapped inside my head that never happened or, conversely, did happen and I erased it from memory because it may be too painful to recall? Lord knows, I had forgotten a very real wife and daughter from my comatose mind for a week, or sixteen imagined years.*

She heard him take a wheezing breath. "Sorry, Jen, I didn't mean to go off on you like that. You've been a blessing to me."

"I can only imagine how difficult it is for you, dealing with two worlds and trying to figure out which is real and which is not. But . . ." She allowed a thought to dangle, unspoken.

"What?"

"You keep calling me Jen. Do you realize you never called me by that nickname when we were young, only *after* I came back into your life? I was Jenny to you, way back when."

"I guess that's right. But, it's only part of what I called you while we were, uh, married."

"Oh? What was that?"

"Sweet Jen. I called you Sweet Jen almost exclusively."

She let it roll off her tongue a couple of times. "I like it. Sounds kind of like a girlie cocktail."

"No double about it, you were the perfect blend of intoxicating ingredients. To me, it was not an adjective followed by your name, it *was* your name."

Jennifer's breath quickened as his voice descended to a dreamy lilt. Although she wondered where a rekindled friendship might lead, she realized it was too soon to be swept away by rebound romance that might well be fleeting. She understood her own weakness and must remain vigilant against falling back into an old but comfortably familiar rut too fast—or at all. He walked away from her once. Who could say that he wouldn't do it again once his life regained a semblance of normalcy? Still, she was compelled to know more. "You say we were married for sixteen years and even after all that time you still felt romantically drawn me?"

There was silence, only the hum of the open phone line for an awkward length of time.

Oh crap! I overstepped. Maybe he thinks he took it too far. Either way, I need to say something, and say it now. "George, don't answer that. I shouldn't have asked it."

"No, no. It's a fair question. It's just that it sent my mind shooting off on a fantastic aside, like a cue ball hitting the eight ball. It was a beautiful thought, but I wonder about the appropriateness of it now. I still have major sorting of events, dealing with this world versus that one. I fear that no matter how I answered that question, it would be the wrong thing. I don't want to say or do anything that might send you away, screaming in fear of me. You and I both know I'm a little crazy right now. I don't want you to have any reason whatsoever to think that I'm totally insane."

Her shoulders slumped forward on that comment. She pinched the bridge of her nose and closed her eyes. *I should be satisfied with that response, but I'm not.* She gathered herself and sat straight. "Look, I want to be your sounding board not an interrogator. Speak as freely as you wish about what you're dealing with. Anything I may ask that you don't want to answer, tell me so. I can handle it. I'm a big girl. And I promise that I won't run screaming into the night," she said, allowing a sardonic tone to slip in.

"It was not my intention to upset you. Really. I *am* sorry."

The conversation took a turn from romantic to sullen—not at all what she wanted. The only way out was to change the subject. "You know, since we've reconnected and talked so much about Smithtown, I started getting homesick for that simpler life."

"I know what you mean. I've been homesick since I woke up and it has nothing to do with Lubbock."

She knew exactly what he meant and chose not to comment, but then said, "I wonder if it's possible to go home again, as they say?" She clamped her jaws shut and cringed, realizing after it was already out that the question was ill-timed and highly suggestive. It was near overwhelming to keep conversation light and airy, considering their shared past. Everything about them both had been tainted by tragedy. George's mind remained trapped in the muck of two tragedies—losing two wives and two daughters within a week. And, the loss of Sean always remained near the surface for her. She pushed on. "I went so far as to call Dwayne Brewster. You were right, he does still have his law practice in Smithtown. He told me that having a paralegal would be nice, since he's getting a little older and slower."

"Are you going to move back there?" he asked.

"Don't know. Interesting thought, though. Nothing is keeping me tied to Abilene. That's for sure. In fact, I think that getting out of Abilene would be a healthy choice for my own sanity, far too many reminders of a life that has literally passed away there. And, a few things are going on that I would sure like to distance myself from."

"Believe me, I know what you mean."

"Brewster said he couldn't pay much but that doesn't matter. Cost of living is cheaper there. Besides, I know a guy that can sell me great cars very reasonably priced."

He chuckled. "You got that right."

"I told Brewster that I'd drive up this weekend and talk to him about the job. How about, afterwards, I keep driving north and spend Saturday afternoon and evening, plus Sunday morning with you. I'd hate to get that close to Lubbock only to turn around and come back to Abilene."

"That would be great." The excitement in his voice was encouraging.

"I bet no one would mind if I get you out on the town for an evening. Aren't you getting bored hanging around that hospital?"

"You cannot imagine how true that is."

"In that case, we have a plan."

George paced the halls of TrustPoint Hospital Saturday morning developing an almost desperate desire to be someplace other than this facility—anyplace else. It didn't matter that he was treated well. He had no complaints whatsoever about his care. It was the severe monotony of routine. He saw Jennifer as his approaching salvation from crushing boredom. Unfortunately, she couldn't give him a definite arrival time. He trusted her enough to know that no matter what problems she encountered in making her way here, she'd get to Lubbock as quickly as she could. Maybe her meeting with that old attorney in Smithtown, Dwayne Brewster, was turning out to be productive. Brewster was the only attorney that Smithtown had had in George's lifetime. *Who knows? Maybe Jen'll have a new job and a reason to leave Abilene for good.* Eager anticipation of seeing his Sweet Jen again and getting away from the hospital for a day accelerated mounting nervous energy. *Sweet Jen,* he thought, suddenly realizing that thinking of her by that name was wrong. She was simply Jennifer, a good friend, and nothing more, for now. Not only that, but in this light, on this day, in this existence, it simply didn't feel quite right, even to him. Still, he was hopeful that today might turn out to be the genesis of a new life, creating a path that someday Jennifer Andrews would again be his Sweet Jen. George remained grounded enough to realize that he might be placing too much faith in this brief outing with her. Escaping the prison of his own mind had to be the priority but that would be a weeks-long, maybe months-long, ordeal.

He was convinced that Jennifer was the key, moving forward into a brighter day and happier future, refusing to believe his fantasy world couldn't be made real, given time. Still, it remained a murky concept, a confusion of desires and a collision of different worlds. Now, it seemed virtually impossible to know what route to take to make that happen. Thinking of Jennifer in that way was always followed by guilt-induced images of Marie and Louisa for having romantic thoughts of another woman so soon after losing them both forever. Although, he didn't see Jennifer as the other woman. Even guilt feelings such as this remained a jumbled mess in his head that had to be sorted and dealt with.

A cute young nurse in floral patterned pink scrubs approached him in the hall—the same nurse he had passed half a dozen times during his morning meandering through TrustPoint. Her silken blond hair was pulled into a bouncy ponytail. She walked with a jaunty spring in her step. The girl could have passed herself off as a high school student. The young caretaker stopped in front of him, blocking his path. "Mister Waller, are you okay? Would you like me to page Doctor Lee? He may be in a therapy session but if you need to talk to a professional, I'd be happy to make that call for you. Every time our paths have crossed this morning, you've not appeared to be the calm man I've come to know. You look edgy, pacing like a caged cat."

Contemplations of the women in his life evaporated. As the young lady spoke, George smiled and gazed at her fondly. Her concern touched him. His smile widened, and he sandwiched her hand between his own. "There's nothing wrong—in fact, quite the opposite. I'm becoming happier by the moment. The best therapy I could hope for is on her way to see me today. I'm enthusiastic. No, not just enthusiastic, I'm excited and antsy to get out of here for a while. That's what you're seeing in me, a mountain of anxious anticipation, but in a good way."

"Why don't you go outside and walk off some of that nervous energy. It's a beautiful day. There's a touch of fall in the air that hints coolness. It feels really nice out there."

"That is an excellent idea. Thanks. I will." He gave her hand a final squeeze and pat, and then moved on, heading for the ground floor lobby. As the elevator doors parted, he didn't wait for them to entirely recede into the walls before sliding sideways between them. The young nurse was right. There was dry coolness in the northerly breeze under a brilliantly clear South Plains sky. Officially, autumn wouldn't begin for a couple more weeks, but its portent was in the wind. The obvious change of seasons held promise beyond the obvious. George breathed in the sweet fresh air and headed down the sidewalk at a brisk pace. High overhead, he heard the distinctive trills of a chevron of Sandhill cranes on their annual southward migration.

As he walked, he realized that even as his mind circled back to Marie and Louisa often, their treasured memories were indeed becoming just that, but slowly, one tiny bit at a time. After almost six weeks since that fateful accident and over a month since reawakening, he still mourned their absence from his life. But, he had struggled his way to the threshold of realizing that it would be possible to think of them fondly and with deep love but without tears, almost like a box of treasured items to be opened on occasion, thought of affectionately, while remembering the wonderful life they had shared. But then, place the lid back on the box for a time, resuming life, looking ahead to the future.

Even as that prospect grew, the final glimpse of Marie and Louisa alive stalked him. It would be years, maybe a lifetime, before that image of abject terror would fade—if ever. He frowned at the unwelcome intrusion on his good mood. His hurried pace on the sidewalk circling the hospital then slowed to a reflective stroll with his hands clasped at his back. His body softened and slumped as the uninvited image of his final view of his beloved Marie and Louisa repeated.

A car pulled up behind him on the street next to the sidewalk. "Hey, sailor, lookin' for a date?"

The smile that had cruelly been stripped from him returned as he recognized the voice. The car rolled into range of his peripheral vision. He straightened and lifted his nose to an indignant angle. He didn't turn his head. "I'll have you know, young lady, that I am of high moral standard."

"Too bad. It would have been fun. Maybe next time." Jennifer goosed the accelerator, lurching forward.

Suddenly, George became concerned she might be serious. "Hey, wait a minute! Come back here."

She came to a hard stop.

He jogged ahead and stopped next to her open window. He dusted the sidewalk with the toe of his shoe like a shy little boy. "All I meant was that I'm no sailor."

She laughed. "So, now you're trying to tell me that you think sailors are immoral?" She tilted her head, held a silly grin and waited for a reply.

His eyes narrowed to slits. He shook his head and waggled a finger at her. "Now, that's what I remember from way back when you were still Jenny. You were such a wise-ass. It appears things have not changed much."

"Of course not." A car pulled up behind her and honked for her to get out of the way. "Come on. Get in before I have to use some serious wise-assery on that dude behind me."

"'Wise-assery?' Is that a word?" The car behind her honked again.

"It is now. Shut up and get in."

As he sprinted around to the passenger side, George's heart lightened. In that brief exchange, he saw a kindling of the old rapport they had shared during the early years in Smithtown as they grew closer all those years ago, eventually falling in love. He longed to have that level of comfort with this angel for the rest of his life. He jerked open the door of the aging Toyota and dropped quickly into the seat. He studied the interior. "Except for the color of this car, it looks just like the one . . . never mind."

"Don't pull that stuff on me. Finish the statement."

"It looks like the only car you and I had during the early years of the imagined sixteen years together."

She grinned mischievously. "So, even in your dreams you weren't supporting me very well." The car behind her honked again. "All right, all right. I'm going." She over-accelerated, emphasizing displeasure at the trailing driver's impatience.

"It wasn't a dream, not to me. It was a very real life with lots of love, ups and downs and even tragedy. I lived it. I really, really lived it for sixteen solid years. It *was* life of sorts, at least a version of it. An odd feeling lingers of having left you behind without warning and wanting to get a message to you that I had no choice. Yet, here you sit right next to me and much younger." He shuddered. "Whenever this feeling comes over me, I have to consciously ask myself the question: just who do I expect to get a message to even if I could? It's too weird."

Jennifer's eyes darted around the parking lot, focusing on the traffic in tight quarters, but not her attention. That seemed obvious. George sensed that she avoided his gaze purposely for opening a conversation that might detract from a good time.

"Look, Jen, how about we set all that kind of talk aside for a while and just enjoy the afternoon?"

She finally glanced sideways. "That's my plan. I hoped it would be yours, too."

"It is. I promise."

George directed her to his used car lot and introduced her to his employees and his general sales manager, Bernie Moore. The visit was mainly for that purpose. He had been keeping up with business on the phone. Sales were up, going into the autumn season. So, there was no business to be discussed. Bernie and the team would keep things going smoothly until he returned to work full-time. He had no doubt. It was also the reason that prior to the accident he considered opening another car lot in Smithtown. This one was in great hands. He was more confident than ever that the Smithtown venture would happen. After an hour of light hearted banter with the crew at Waller's Pre-Owned Autos, George waved good-bye from the passenger side window as Jennifer pulled out onto the street.

"It's too early for dinner. How do we kill time 'til then?" she asked.

"How about I show you where I live? I need to check on things anyhow."

"Sure. Tell me where."

He pointed her toward an upper middle-class neighborhood in the newer section of south Lubbock and had her turn onto a circular cul-de-sac. He pointed to a specific house. "There. Pull in that driveway."

"Very nice," she muttered. When she killed the car, Jennifer's hands remained occupied with the steering wheel and the key, staring straight ahead at a closed garage door. It didn't take much to realize that she had suddenly become apprehensive and considered restarting the car and leaving.

He wondered if he was any more certain of what to do next than she appeared to be. *Can I hold it together once I get in there?* He had not thought about that until this moment. It was going to be emotional, in a big way. *Crap! I shouldn't have suggested this.*

* * *

Jennifer met George's gaze, but couldn't hold it. He turned his attention back to the house, eyes tracing its outline. She leaned toward him and craned her neck around, attempting to get a better read on his expression. "Be honest. Are you sure you're ready for this?" she asked.

"Look, maybe it wasn't such a good idea to come here, not today, not yet. I should do this when I'm alone. There's certainly no hurry to get it done. I wasn't thinking when I suggested coming here. It might drag me into a funk and take you with me."

She snaked her hand across and placed it on his knee. "I want whatever you want but please remember, I'm your friend — always have been, always will be. You don't *have* to do it alone if you don't want to."

He continued staring at the house. "I'm afraid I'll ruin your afternoon. I'm suddenly afraid that it's not just possible, but probable, that I won't handle this very well."

She squeezed his knee. "You would not be ruining anything, George. This is *your* afternoon. I'm along for the ride. Let me help — that is, if you want to follow through with this."

After a quiet moment of thought, he nodded. "Okay. Let's do a quick walk through. If I don't spend too much time in there, I might be all right."

As they walked abreast toward the front door, Jennifer flicked continual glances at him, attempting to gauge his mental strength to handle an assault by a house full of raw memories. She reached for his hand and squeezed it. "It'll be okay. Whatever happens I'm with you. Lean on me if you need to."

His shaky hand took several unsuccessful stabs with the key into the door lock. She wrapped her own hand around his to steady it. He offered a weak smile as he inserted the key, turning it and the knob simultaneously. The door swung open with a faint squeak of hinges that might as well have been a heralding trumpet for what lay in wait.

She couldn't claim to be calm, either. As the door opened, her nostrils filled with the strong smell of memories. As they tentatively stepped across the threshold and walked a short distance, she picked up a mixture of aromas — hints of perfumes, fabrics, foods, cleansers, waxes — all the things that make a house a home. A tingling chill coursed her spine, contracting the muscles in her neck. The emotion George felt was palpable, bleeding rapidly over into her.

He stopped at a tall narrow side table next to a staircase that led up to the second floor. On that table set his first test, a framed photograph. She assumed it was of a laughing Marie and smiling Louisa wearing elf hats with the comical attached pointy ears. They were standing next to a Christmas tree, presumably from the last holiday season. *Oh my God. I had no idea how beautiful she was. How beautiful they both were.* She shuddered, feeling what had to have been a mere fraction of what George felt. Standing loose-lipped and in awe, she gazed at and studied the picture. Until this very moment, she hadn't considered or tried to imagine what the loves of his life looked like. She suddenly felt ashamed and selfish. She threaded her arm through his. She felt his muscles twitching with emotion as he lightly caressed the surface of the framed photograph with fingertips.

He abruptly jerked his hand away from the picture. "I-I'm sorry, Jen. I thought I could handle this, but I can't."

Tears poured from his reddened eyes as he raised them to look up the stairs. His face practically screamed that he indeed saw the ghosts of two lives ended and of his own former life passing into the shifting sands of time. She pulled him around to face her, wrapped her arms around his waist, and pressed her cheek into his chest. They cried together.

Chapter 18 ~ Jennifer Decides

Following those tense moments inside the Waller residence, Jennifer found herself more affected by George's emotional breakdown than she thought possible. As George had predicted, the visit to his house cast a pall on the remainder of the afternoon into the evening. The air between them remained subdued and strained—dinner conversation virtually non-existent, perfunctory at best. Jennifer made half-hearted attempts at light banter only to wither and die into silence each time she tried. She struggled at not showing her discomfort, understanding George's fight to regain a measure of mental stability. Dinner ended in a most unmemorable fashion and she drove him back to the hospital.

They got out of the car and walked together to a bench near the entrance. She sat next to him, doubling her light jacket at the front and crossing her arms over it against the autumn chill. "You're being released soon, right?"

He nodded. "Monday, I think. I'll be back frequently on an outpatient basis for therapy and counseling." He glanced sideways and pulled an insincere smile. "You probably noticed that I still need it."

"Give it time. It'll get better." She pursed her lips and stared at her feet, legs crossed with the toe of the overlapping leg spiraled around the calf of the other, wanting to ask a question yet afraid to. It might breach a fragile state he had slipped into. But, she was compelled to know. "George, if you're released from the hospital Monday, are you going back to that house?" She uncrossed her arms and white-knuckled the edge of the bench on each side of her legs with both hands, fearing an emotional eruption that she didn't want to be responsible for, although the probing question might do just that.

"No." His reply was fast, decisive and surprisingly low-key.

She jerked her head around to connect with him, taken aback by the speed of his answer and the tone. "Then where will you go?"

George continued staring straight ahead. "I made up my mind at dinner that I'd never set foot in that house again. I can't. It would . . . I would . . ." He became frustrated. "Hell, I just can't do it again. I'll sell the house and hire an auction company to sell everything in it, down to the rag bag in the laundry room. I have to work, and work hard at moving on to the next stage of my life. I don't see it getting easier anytime soon and that house will only serve to keep me mired. The 'where' part I'll have to think about."

"I understand." On that comment, the wheels of her mind spun out several thoughts about the future. Every one of them had to do with simplifying her own existence. George's plan was not only a good one, but applicable to her life as well. She may be a couple of years farther down the road in her grief, but what he said spawned a notion. She could move away from Abilene to someplace neutral where everything hadn't been steeped with memories of Sean and end having to endure a suffocating boss at the law firm where she remained employed. Being near physical reminders of married life was holding her back from getting on with life, too. She sought happiness in whatever form it happened to take, and it would be nice to have reasons to smile and laugh more often.

George needed time, immeasurably complicated by sixteen years' worth of living while trapped within a one-week coma. Although, now their situations appeared similar on the surface, it was hard to make a heads-up comparison with what he had to be going through. His grief was two-fold—losing his beautiful family in this world and losing a wife and daughter he never had in another. By everything he had told her, the pain of loss had to be nearly equal, even though one had been the result of defensive imaginings, yet painfully real. Pulling up roots and leaving wouldn't work so well for him—not yet. Maybe in a few months it would be different. But even as these thoughts rolled through her mind, she might as well put an idea out there. "I know it's too soon to think about such things but, since you're already talking about moving, why not follow through on the plan to add that car lot in Smithtown and move back home? It sounds like you'd only be advancing the timetable on something you had planned on doing anyhow."

He was slumped over, elbows on knees. He began to nod, slowly at first. He looked over and up at her. "That makes sense. By my choice, I'm homeless as of today. So, why wouldn't I do that?"

She watched him begin to talk faster and toss out ideas that would bring the added business to fruition. It surprised her how quickly he latched onto the notion. George reanimated, sitting straight, returning to the level of enthusiasm he was at before that sorrowful visit to his house a few hours ago. As he went on and on about how to get it done, she realized that he didn't see her in the same way that she saw him. In his mind, she was still his spouse and that had to have been the reason he accepted her logic so quickly. She heard it in his voice and by the way he touched her. George had a strong connecting bond with her, beyond friendship, and still fresh in his mind. She sensed it. He trusted her implicitly. Her level of trust toward him had not yet returned in equal measure. There remained a small dark corner of her mind that harbored distrust, regardless how much she valued his friendship. It was hard to overlook that he had made a choice once before that broke her heart.

She had cried off and on for weeks afterwards. Could it happen again? she wondered. She watched him talk excitedly about opening another dealership, but her thoughts moved on to a wild roller coaster of ups and downs, trapped in a cycle of competing emotions.

* * *

En route home to Abilene Sunday afternoon, Jennifer had time to engage in objective thought without interruption.   She pondered George's accident, his loss, the coma, and the life he imagined within it—an existence that should have been reality, had life not taken a cruel turn for her sixteen years ago. All these things set her imagination into heated overdrive. The subjects of their many conversations since the day she swallowed her fear and walked into his hospital room in Lubbock's Covenant Hospital seemed to point in one direction. Possibilities billowed as the miles clicked off. Even from the first glimpse of his sickly face, she realized that affectionate feelings for the man were still inside her, simply strung with cobwebs and left untouched for years in dust-covered corners of her mind and heart. When their eyes met that day, it occurred to her that she and George Waller were in the same heart-breaking boat. There he lay, in bad shape mentally and physically, but single. In the days that followed she felt the magnetism of the situation—of him—drawing her ever closer to the precipice of a love she might not be able to recover from. She must keep her head in this reality and not be seduced into George's distorted version of it, even as appealing as that imagined life he described was. Jennifer knew too well that rebound relationships were dangerous and often short-lived under the best of circumstances. Although events might go a certain way, she committed to a slow, deliberate and thoughtful exploration of possibilities, rushing into nothing.

She gazed through the windshield heading south down the highway over the flat landscape of the Texas South Plains. The view of cotton fields had begun to yield to rocky pasture land dotted with rocking horse oil pump jacks and giant wind generators. The famous escarpment, the demarcation for the high plains of north Texas and the Rolling Plains to the south, was less than ten miles ahead. While driving atop the Caprock, a green highway sign appeared that read: Smithtown 4 miles.

She wondered if Dwayne Brewster had thought anymore about hiring a paralegal. The quasi-interview with him yesterday morning left it as an open possibility that fascinated him, but she left his house with no commitment from the aging attorney. Still, he seemed sincerely interested in having help in the office beyond secretarial functions. He'd had the same devoted secretary for years and wouldn't consider replacing her, even for someone with the depth of experience Jennifer could boast. She could, and would, be a true right hand for him. She could help him solicit new clients and then manage more billable hours. *That's it. That's the answer. I know how to close him on this deal.*

She glanced to Brewster's business card carelessly jammed into a crevice between the dashboard and the radio. She tucked her lower lip between her teeth, suddenly feeling devilish. *If I knock on his door and ask him directly if he's made up his mind. I wonder if he'd give me a direct answer? If not, I think I know how to get one.* She pulled the card from its wedged resting place and split viewing time between it and the highway. *Or should I call him first?* "Nah," she mumbled. *I know where he lives. I'll drop by.* Now infused with purpose, she pushed the aging Toyota faster. She was on a mission.

As she pulled into the sparsely populated northern outskirts of Smithtown, she noticed an old house set off by itself and off the highway about a hundred feet. It was small and the paint on the white shiplap siding was peeling. The composition roof shingles were blistered and curled at the corners, clearly in poor shape. The tabs on a few of the shingles were missing altogether. A black framed screen door stood open, resting partially atop a buckled and cupped wooden plank porch. Screen had rolled up from the bottom of the door, rendering it useless for its original purpose. It needed to be trashed. Nailed to the door frame, hanging slightly askew, was a large rust-streaked thermometer. It was a common style as an advertising novelty by cotton gins and feed stores handed out freely to customers in the fifties and sixties, but the practice had all but vanished as an advertising vehicle. The thermometers were intended for mounting outdoors on things like barn doors, not the front door of a residence. She thought it quaint—a visible piece of history. She smiled. There was a small and faded "For Rent or Sale" sign stapled to a stick and driven into the ground next to the highway. It was nearly hidden by tall dead grass around the base of the mailbox post. The little sign had a phone number on it. She braked to a screeching stop, snatched a ballpoint pen from the open ashtray and scribbled the phone number on her palm. She looked again at the house with a fresh state of purpose in mind, now disregarding all its noted faults. *It's cute. It wouldn't take much to fix it up. I wonder what the inside looks like.*

She accelerated out of the gravel at the side of the highway, the tires tossing small pebbles clattering up into the wheel wells. The thought of moving back to the town she grew up in appealed to her and added weight to her foot, pushing the little car up to speed. Seconds later, she drove into town and saw it through different eyes than she did just yesterday. She remembered how every landmark from her formative years held special significance, like the A & W Root Beer Drive-In that had gone through many incarnations over the years, still open with carhops scurrying about delivering cold drinks and hamburgers but no longer an A&W. As she slowed and drove by the drive-in, the aroma of burgers and fries wafted through her open window. She breathed in its perfume. Her smile grew even wider as the feeling of home washed over her.

Before going to see Mister Brewster, Jennifer felt as though she must first drive to the opposite side of town. It was an impulse followed by an urge to see the house she had lived in until graduating from high school. It was in a poor neighborhood, but not that much worse than it had been when she was growing up. For many years, the house had remained unoccupied and now uninhabitable, on the verge of collapse. It needed to be bulldozed and removed, but she was glad it hadn't been destroyed yet—too many memories that she held dear and it was the last physical commonality with her mom and dad. They had been killed in a motorcycle accident when she was only eight years old. The memories of them were few—only snippets, but each was a precious snapshot into her past. Her mother's younger sister, Connie, barely out of her teens at the time, moved into the house shortly afterwards and raised her to college age before finally marrying and moving away. Jennifer loved her Aunt Connie dearly and stayed in close contact. She now resided in San Antonio with two children of her own.

Jennifer remained parked at the curb staring at the decrepit old house. A sudden rush of sentimentality chilled her. Tears born of nostalgia brightened her eyes. She drew a breath and huffed it away through rounded lips. *Okay, I can't be crying while I'm talking to Brewster.* She started the car and hurried back to the main highway. Her detour to the poor side of town accomplished something very important. It cemented her love of Smithtown and strengthened her commitment to move back.

She turned off the thoroughfare that split the small town and drove a few blocks to the nicest residential area which was only two blocks long on the eastern fringe. Brewster's house was the last one on the left. Nothing beyond or behind it except for a cotton field. His late model Buick sedan was in the driveway. *Good. It looks like I'll catch him at home.* It was a long ranch style structure and about forty years old. She knew the house well from her childhood as having always been there. So, it had to have been at least older than her thirty-seven years. The yard was immaculately landscaped. She wheeled into the driveway behind Brewster's car and parked in the shade of a large live oak tree. With a strong desire and ample confidence, she bounded out of the vehicle and marched to the front door. But, as she raised a finger to the doorbell button, she hesitated. From somewhere in the depths of her consciousness a voice murmured, *You can't go home again.* Courage wavered. She clenched her jaws, angered by her sudden and surprising indecision. "Bullshit!" She whispered. "I damn well think I can." She rang the bell.

Moments later, the door whooshed open and there stood an attractive woman with silver hair, slender and tall. "May I help you?"

"You must be Missus Brewster."

"That's right." She was wiping her hands on a dish towel.

"I dropped by yesterday morning and talked to Dwayne about the possibility of going to work for him in his law practice."

The lines on the woman's face smoothed as her expression brightened. "Oh yes. You must be Jennifer—Jennifer Andrews. Is that right?"

"That's right."

"I remember your parents so well. They were fine people. I also remember your Aunt Connie. How is she?"

"Very well. Thank you. She moved to San Antonio a number of years ago. She seems happy. She has a wonderful husband and two beautiful children."

Missus Brewster held out an inviting hand. "I'm Anna Lee, but folks around here just call me Anna." She stepped aside and gestured toward the inside. "Please come in. I was preparing an early dinner. Dwayne and I usually eat early on Sundays and then take in the evening service at the church. We'd love to have you join us."

As Anna made the offer, Dwayne, holding the front section of the Sunday edition of the Lubbock Avalanche Journal, came into the room. "Come in, come in. This is a pleasant surprise. I didn't expect to see you again so soon."

Jennifer blushed. She stepped inside and noticed the living room. It was somewhat dated but lovely—a cathedral ceiling with dark stained rough-sawn beams rising to meet a larger, but equally rugged, central beam. A rock fireplace made the room appear majestic with a woodsy feel, like a log cabin. Smoky stains streaked the rock above the firebox. It obviously was used often during the cold months. "Honestly, I didn't expect to be here. But, since I had to pass right through Smithtown on my way back to Abilene and, since I was alone and had plenty of time to think between Lubbock and here, I came up with a plan that I wanted to propose. It would be much better if I ran it by you in person."

Anna turned and walked back toward the kitchen. "Go ahead, Dwayne, you two visit. I'll finish with dinner."

Dwayne gestured Jennifer toward a chair. "Make yourself comfortable." He sat across from her. "Okay, what is this proposal you have for me?"

"Mister Brewster—"

"Call me Dwayne."

"Okay . . . Dwayne. I know you're hesitant about hiring me because of salary concerns but what if we do it on a graduated scale that would be gentle on your payroll. For example, I'll rent the cheapest house I can find here in town and if you'll cover monthly rent and utilities with a small stipend for groceries and gasoline, that's all I'll require to begin with. And then, once I prove my worth at client solicitation and increasing the company's billable hours, then it would become possible to incrementally push my salary upward in direct proportion to those billable hours. That way your initial outlay and future financial risk would be minimal. How does that sound?"

Dwayne, flabbergasted by the generous offer, slid backward into his chair as a smile grew to such proportion that it disappeared into deep pale dimples. "Jennifer, I like your style and I love your confidence. I can work with that. Give me a couple of days to hammer out specifics and get them in writing." He rose and came around the coffee table and shook her hand. "I believe we definitely have a deal in the making here. I'll be calling. Now, how about joining us for roast beef and mashed potatoes followed by a church service?"

"Uh, the roast and potatoes sound good."

He laughed.

Chapter 19 ~ Back into the World

"I've grown fond of everyone here at TrustPoint. So, please forgive me when I say that I hope I never see any of you again." George flashed a toothy grin.

The plump lady with a too-perfect hairdo chuckled. She sat at a desk behind a waist-high counter that George was leaning against and continued inputting information into a computer. "I understand completely, Mister Waller." She filled out a form, the final step before releasing George back into the world. She hit print and offered him full attention. "The only thing I would add is that as long as you're careful out there, you won't have to see us again. How about that, handsome?"

"Touché." George felt a hand on his shoulder and turned to see Doctor Levenson. Hey, Doctor Levine." He cringed. "I'm sorry. I can't seem to stop making that mistake."

Levenson extended a friendly hand and shook George's. "Don't let it trouble you. After all, by your accounting, you've known Levine for years and me for a few weeks. Levenson smiled. And, if I said that in the company of anyone else on this planet, they would think I was out of my mind." He chuckled. "I'd be in therapy myself soon after making the comment."

George nodded and smiled at the doctor's stab at humor. "Do you have business here today?"

"Just you. I thought I'd drop by before going on to work over at Covenant to wish you well in your challenging trek back out into the world."

"It's lucky you caught me at all. I'm *so* ready to get out of here that in another couple of minutes I'd have been out of here like a shotgun blast."

Levenson's pleasant demeanor slid from his face. "I know that Doctor Lee, your psychiatrist, has already spoken to you about it, but I wanted to add the weight of my words before you take this leap. And the fact that you still see me as a trusted friend and advisor by the name of Levine is the reason."

"Oh?"

"I feel like you had bonded with me before ever coming out of the coma. Therefore, I hope you trust this advice. I want you to know that challenges are coming your way. You'll be blindsided and tested, sometimes severely, by many of them. Here's the heart of the advice: whatever shocks come out of the gates at you, deal with them one at a time. Don't allow a single one to fester unresolved, waiting for the next one. Don't become frustrated. You're juggling two lives, both equally real *to you*. Once you get out and start piecing together a life again there'll be things you assume to be real that will turn out to be false and the opposite of that will occur as well. These things, and many others I can't fathom now, will threaten your confidence and might send you over the edge emotionally. You must galvanize yourself against inevitable contradictions yet to come."

"Is there any way to prepare for it?"

"Be vigilant and aware that it *will* happen—likely many times in the months ahead. That's about all you can do. Remember, don't allow any of these things to drag you down, simply process each occurrence and then move on." Levenson's smile returned as he handed George a business card. "Of course, I'm speaking to you as, I'm guessing, your friend and neighbor Doctor Levine would have."

"Thanks, Doc. You've gone far out of your way for me. I'll not forget it."

The doctor shook his hand again. "Call me if you ever need to talk," Levenson said. He turned and hurried toward the front door on his way to begin his day at Covenant Hospital.

George watched him walk away, feeling awed by the man's beyond-the-call-of-duty sense of compassion. He was a neurologist and his responsibility to this case ended weeks ago. He took a moment to read over the business card in his hand.

The cute but squat clerk just past her prime stood from her chair and handed him a piece of paper and a pen. "Sign next to the "x", doll face, and you'll be on your way."

He scribbled his name and slapped the pen onto the paper with a decided show of finality.

"I would say don't be a stranger. Come back to see us," she offered, "but I know how you'd respond. So, let me just say, go have a good life."

He laughed while waving over his shoulder on his way to the front door. He waited for the automatic sliding doors to fully open, savoring the moment of stepping into freedom. It was a cool sunny morning, as most mornings were this time of year in this semi-arid climate. He crossed the threshold into a new day and a new life, but then abruptly stopped walking. It occurred to him that the last time he'd been out here, he did so with purpose—to take a brisk walk while waiting for Jennifer to arrive. Today, he had no one waiting for him. His only purpose was to get out of the hospital—no plan beyond that. He didn't even have a car here. *For Christ's sake. What the hell am I thinking? I need to call a cab.* He slapped his pocket for a cell phone. It was an automatic response because he hadn't had access to a cell phone since before the accident. Feeling silly for lack of preparedness, he stared off into the sky.

It struck him that even if he did call a cab, where would he tell the driver to take him? The cocky spring in his step vanished. He shuffled to one of the benches lining the broad walk in front of the hospital and lowered himself onto it. He had no place to go, no family, and very few friends here in Lubbock, other than his employees at the car lot. Gloom dropped a veil over his mood. Levenson's words of only a few minutes ago came back to him with stinging clarity, 'Many challenges are coming your way. You will be blindsided by many of them.'

George was in a downward spiral. *Levenson knew — he damn well knew this would happen.* He looked back to the front door of the hospital. *Hell, I couldn't even make it a few feet before it began.* He rolled his fingers into tight fists and slammed one of them into his thigh and said aloud, "I need a plan and I need it now."

An old man shuffling by in a walker stopped. "Excuse me?"

"Sorry, sir. Just thinking out loud. Didn't mean to startle you."

The old man smiled, showing a couple of gaps in his worn teeth. It was clear that the old guy had grown up in a rural area and raised on well water right out of the Ogallala Aquifer — notorious for leaving brown stains on the teeth. "Well, young man, I hope your plan turns out well. Have yourself a great day, ya hear?" He shuffled on.

"Thanks. I will." He thought about that simple statement. *A great day? Is that even possible? How about I just make it through the day.* He mulled several potential plans of action and finally settled on one. *I need to get over to the car lot and talk to Bernie.* With a first step decided upon, he sprang to his feet and headed back inside to a phone. He now knew what he needed to say to a taxi driver. He'd make a quick stop at a cell phone store and then on to his car lot.

* * *

As the cab approached the car lot, George noticed how impressive the business looked. Long banners were suspended beneath a string of lights fronting the vehicles that would light it all up like a carnival when the sun sets. The business had grown to an imposing size since he founded it. Over the years he had purchased adjoining lots to increase frontage and vehicle display area. The cab driver slowed and pulled onto the fully paved lot lined with pre-owned cars and trucks. The cab driver stopped broadside to the small office at the rear of the third row of vehicles. George's general sales manager, Bernie Moore, hurried out to greet him with a huge smile. "George, are you home for good now?"

"Yep, for good *or* bad." He accepted Bernie's enthusiastic hand as they came together. "Bern, I hate to do this to you, but do you have enough cash on you to pay this man? All I have is a credit card."

"Heck yeah," Bernie said, pulling out his wallet. "Look around. The inventory looks kind of sparse doesn't it?"

"It does for a fact."

"We've sold eight cars and three pickup trucks since you and your friend were here Saturday. Business is good."

While Bernie paid and tipped the man, George scanned the lot. His eyes settled on a vintage gold '69 Dodge Charger that appeared to have been totally refurbished. "That one looks interesting."

Bernie winked at him. "Got a great deal on it this very morning. A young man going through a divorce had to sell it. It has been totally renewed with one of the hottest 440 magnum engines under the hood that I've ever driven."

George sauntered to it, thinking that a car like this was exactly what he needed because it, in no way, reminded him of his previous life. "In good shape, you say?"

"I don't think there is a used vehicle on any lot in town in better shape—many new ones either for that matter," Bernie said.

George walked along beside the car, running his hand over the high gloss metal flake gold finish. "Good, unless one of you guys have a claim on it, I want it."

Bernie grinned. "Decided to have a second childhood, have ya?"

"Yep. Starting today."

"It's yours. Take it away."

George opened the door and slid in under the steering wheel. While he scanned and admired the interior he said, "Remember that conversation we had before the accident about putting in another lot in Smithtown?"

"Sure do. You still thinking about it?"

"Yeah," he continued admiring the craftsmanship of the restored vintage Dodge Charger. "I want you to help me make it happen. I'll operate it and live there. You can continue running this lot. I'll begin calling you general manager, not general sales manager, and up your percentage on each vehicle sold. You've already proven you don't need me around to keep it successful. How does that sound?"

The short paunchy man offered George a knowing nod and a warm fatherly smile. "It sounds like a damn good plan to me and, maybe, something you need and should do." Clearly, Bernie knew exactly why George felt the need to move away from Lubbock.

George cranked the power plant in his brand new forty-five-year-old muscle car. It roared to life and then idled with a healthy rumble. He patted the top of Bernie's hand that rested on the door in the window opening. "You're a good man, Bernie Moore. I'll be talking more about the plan soon." He pulled the floor shifter into reverse and inadvertently over accelerated backing out. "I'll have to get used to the power of this thing," he called out as he wheeled out of the lot onto the street while waving out the window.

His only desire was to be alone out on the open highway and enjoy the freedom. Heading south out of Lubbock toward Slaton, he grinned at the fact that he'd have to remain vigilant about his speed. This stallion with a steering wheel had a speed it wanted to go and it wasn't slow.

After a few miles it occurred to him that he needed cash. He hadn't used his debit card in months and needed to make sure that he still had it. He yanked his wallet from his hip pocket and fumbled it open onto the passenger seat across the console, spilling cards that included the debit card and a small photograph. It was an old creased picture of Marie in a hospital bed holding the newly born Louisa. She was young with a beaming smile and so happy. The sight of it held his gaze too long.

The air horn of a truck blared.

George looked up to see that he had drifted across the center line of the highway and quickly jerked it back before running head-on into a sixteen-wheeler. The near-miss left him shaken. After another mile, he approached a convenience store and pulled off the highway onto its graveled and pitted parking lot. He sat still, allowing time for his racing heart to settle and get his breathing back under control. He noticed a lighted red neon sign in the window of the store that read: ATM Inside. He looked again to the open wallet and spilled items in the seat next to him. This time there was no hesitation. He retrieved the picture and shoved it back inside the wallet and closed it while palming the debit card in his other hand.

With five crisp twenty-dollar bills in hand, he was quickly back on the highway. He forced his mind onto a plan to open another dealership in Smithtown. The car rumbled gently—no strain even at seventy-five miles per hour.

As he mulled the mundane ins and outs of setting up a satellite dealership, he began to think about his childhood and the friends he grew up with. Alex sure proved the value of their lifelong friendship by dropping everything and coming to Lubbock to be at his side after the accident. He wondered about his old buddy, Lenny Poe. He hadn't seen him in nearly a year, or about a month, depending on which version of life he happened to be thinking about. For the first time, the absurdity of it all brought on a grin. It suddenly occurred to him that he was having trouble separating fact from coma. Did Lenny still live with his dad or was he married?

An abrupt shuddering chill washed over George with such ferocity that he violently jerked the steering wheel, coming dangerously close to disaster number two within the span of about fifteen minutes. He pulled off the highway and stopped—hands still clutching the steering wheel with a vice-like grip. "No! No! It can't be!"

George remembered back to the day, while in the coma, that the deranged drug addict came into the John Deere Dealership and shot Buck Poe, before turning the pistol on him, poking it into his gut, and then squeezing off a round. Yet, somehow, the would-be robber missed the pointblank shot into his stomach. Disbelieving that his memory had again lied to him on such a grand scale, it threw him into a quandary. He rolled it over and over in his mind before coming to terms with the truth. Buck Poe was the one who had been shot pointblank in the stomach and didn't survive. George had been nowhere around when it happened nearly five years ago. He had only seen the hole in the calendar and wall from the bullet that passed entirely through Buck's midsection. He thought, after awakening, how could I have accepted so readily that the job at the John Deere Dealership was Alex's job and never mine, yet, totally accept something like this? He had even attended Buck's funeral and still had trouble believing Lenny's father was, in fact, dead.

The stone-cold realization left him numb. He now didn't know where to go or what to do. This fantasized ideal of being alone out on the open highway wasn't working out so well. He looked up the road and noticed a small cluster of businesses standing alone in a cotton field at the side of the highway. *I wonder if I can make it the few hundred yards to those businesses without killing myself.* After two near deadly missteps, he wasn't so sure. Still, he put the car in gear and eased back onto the highway. The sun was high in the sky now. He wore no watch but assumed it had to be about noon. As he again pulled off the highway, he noticed one of the signs. It read: Donovan's Tack Shop and Bar. *What an odd combination of businesses.* He didn't need a saddle, but he sure could use a drink. There were no cars in front of the building, only an old dinged and dirty pickup truck off to the side. He assumed it belonged to the owner.

George parked and walked up to the door, expecting it to be locked. It wasn't. It opened easily as a small bell tinkled above it. He went on in. The front of the interior was an assortment of displays for the horse enthusiast—the smell of tanned leather strong but pleasant. There was even the musty smell of dust, but that was common to this area of Texas in poorly insulated buildings not aired out frequently. He looked around but saw no one.

"Be with you in minute," a voice shouted from the restroom next to the bar in the rear of the large open room.

George examined the bar area. Two ceiling fans hung down from the ornately stamped tin tiles in the ceiling. The speed of the fans above the bar mimicked what George thought this place would be like—slow paced and laid-back. "No hurry," George replied in raised voice and ambled on back toward the bar over the bare and badly cracked concrete floor. As he moved toward the back, the fluorescent lights up front gave way to a dimmer setting. He figured that was by design. A blue neon light outlined a beer sign. It flickered and buzzed over a mirror behind the bar.

He heard a toilet flush. An elderly man came out while still zipping his fly. "What can I do for you, son?"

George eyed the old man. If not a cowboy now, the old guy had to have been at one time—bowed legs, big gut, no butt, wearing Wrangler jeans stuffed inside tall boots almost to his knees. "Well, I have no need for your merchandise, but I sure would like a Crown and water, neat." He mounted one of the five stools fronting the bar. The bar top had clearly seen many decades of use—gouged, scuffed and pitted across its surface. The stools were in no better shape. The one he chose to sit on had a rickety squeak. The mirror centered above the back bar had begun to lose some of its silver and was cracked and stained across its bottom, although, two rows of glass shelves holding a variety of liquor bottles did a satisfactory job of hiding the worst imperfections.

The old man shuffled over behind the bar and retrieved the bottle of Crown bourbon whiskey from one of those narrow glass shelves over the back bar. "Gettin' an early start, are ya?"

"I almost ran head-on into a sixteen-wheeler. I need it and, maybe, the one after that, and even the one after that. Anyhow, let's get 'em started."

The old man grinned. "You got it. Where're ya from?" he asked as he set the short square glass in front of George.

"Lubbock. For the past sixteen years anyhow. I grew up in Smithtown."

"You're not too far from home in either direction."

The comment made George realize that he was only about twenty miles north of Smithtown. "I guess that's right." He looked around. "You have an interesting place here."

"Got too old to rodeo a few years back and opened the tack store. A few years later, I got damn tired of listening to local farmers and ranchers complain about no waterin' holes close by. You know, a place to gather, grin, and drink. So I added the bar." He leaned over the bar and shielded his mouth with the back of his hand as if sharing a secret. "The bar makes me a living. I'd starve to death if I had to depend on selling all that crap up front in the tack store." He thrust out a friendly hand. "My name's Bradley Donovan."

George took his hand. "George Waller. Nice to meet you." He turned up his glass and downed the final swallow.

The old man didn't wait to be asked. He refilled it. "I had a good buddy, once upon a time, that lived in Smithtown. His name was Buck Poe."

Although inebriation had begun to set in, the name made George sit straight. "You knew Buck?"

"Sure as hell did. Aw yeah, we used to travel all over the country ridin' bulls at rodeos where we could afford the entry fees." He laughed, but it was more of a wheezing chortle. "Maybe I should say that we competed at rodeos we hadn't yet been banned from for fightin', cussin' at the crowd, or some other such crap. We had a lot more piss and vinegar than good sense back then. Life was a hoot." He thought for a second and then laughed that raspy laugh while shaking his downturned head. "Yep, good times for sure. Then we got older, broke some bones and had to stop ridin' those damn bulls before we crippled our fool selves for life. I opened this place and Buck started fixin' tractors." The old man's ready smile faded. "Buck died a few years back . . . gunned down by some asshole drug addict." He paused. "Enough about me. Tell me, son, what has you out on the highway in the middle of a weekday?"

"Let me start by saying that the reason I pulled off the highway here was, coincidentally, because of Buck Poe. But the story doesn't start there. It began over a month ago by your calendar, but over sixteen years ago according to the calendar in my head."

The old man poured George a fresh bourbon and water and then pulled a stool in close to the back side of the bar, centered his butt, and dropped onto the seat with a wheezing grunt. "I don't know what the hell you're talkin' about, but it sounds interesting." He twirled his hand at George. "Don't leave me hangin' with that tidbit. Tell me the story."

George pulled a half grin. He took a sip. "I know where the story begins, but don't know how to end it. I'm not sure you have that much time."

"Look around, son. You'll see that I'm not overrun with customers. All I have is time. If you want to tell it, I'll listen to it."

Over the next hour and three more bourbon and waters later, he had told the old guy the rudiments of what he had been through. The old cowboy offered occasional encouragement for George to keep talking. It clearly captured Donovan's fascination, leaving his chin propped on an open palm for long periods without moving. George did omit a few details so he'd have a chance to finish it before sundown. "And that brings me to this moment," George said.

The old man let out a breathy whistle. "I'll be damn, son. I don't think I've ever heard a tale as odd as that one."

"Yeah, well, if you think the story is odd, ya ought to try living it." George smiled and turned up the last swallow of his latest drink.

"Can you handle another Crown and water? Or, would you even want to? I'm a little concerned about your ability to drive. You've put away a goodly number of those things."

George held up an unsteady finger. "Hold that thought." He fumbled through his pockets and found the scrap of paper that he searched for. He pulled out his new cell phone and dialed the number scrawled on it.

"Hello," came the reply.

"Jen, its George."

"Sorry I haven't called," she quickly replied. "The last couple of days have really been hectic. Did they release you from the hospital?"

"Oh yeah, I've been cruising the highway in my new, very old car."

"Your what?"

"Never mind. Are you in Abilene?"

"No. Smithtown."

"Aha, I thought so."

"And, just how would you know that?"

"'Cuz I feel ya, baby," he said then blew a slobbery snicker, followed by a long unanswered silence. "Still there?" he asked.

"Are you drunk, George Waller?"

"How should I answer that?" He took a sharp breath, pulling air between clenched teeth. "I know. I haven't fallen off this bar stool yet. How's that for an answer?"

"Oh jeez, where are you?"

"Ever hear of Donovan's Tack Store and Bar?"

"Are you talking about that little place on the highway about twenty miles north of here?"

"That's the one."

"I always figured it was some kind of joke. So, it's really a bar?"

"And a tack store—for real! Want to join me for an afternoon cocktail?"

"I'm feeling an obligation to come whether I want a drink or not. It sounds like you don't need to be behind the wheel."

"Don'tcha just love it when a plan comes together?" he slurred.

She let out an exaggerated sigh. "This is not a good way to start a new job."

"You have a job in Smithtown?"

"I'll let you know tomorrow after I ask my new boss for the afternoon off from my first day of employment."

"It seems we have things to discuss," he said, his tongue thickening.

"I'll be there in about half an hour."

* * *

Shadows lengthened as Jennifer pulled into the small graveled parking lot of Donovan's Tack Store and Bar. There was only one car parked in front, a shiny gold vintage muscle car worth a lingering admiring look as she walked toward the front door of the place. When she opened the door, the late afternoon sun shot a beam of light all the way to the rear. It was an odd sight because it was like a spotlight had been switched on and isolated George and an old man at a bar along the back wall. George swiveled around on the stool and had to steady himself on the seat next to him. "Hey, you made it. That was fast."

"Not really," she said. "You're just thinking very slowly."

"Touché."

The old man pushed himself backward off the stool and leaned against the bar. He flipped a finger in her direction. "Well, son, is this the mother of your child—until you woke up, that is?"

"Sounds to me like the two of you have been talking," she said.

"Yep, for several hours as a matter of fact," George said and then faced the old man. "And, yes, this is Jennifer Wal, er, Harv, uh, I mean Andrews—Jennifer Andrews.

She patted him on the back. "Oops. Faux pas. It would seem you and I have work to do."

He sheepishly looked up at her. "Sorry about that."

She sat on the stool next to him. "Talking to someone, anyone, is probably a good thing, I suppose. You need to talk about it openly and honestly so that someday you might get your head right again."

Jennifer told him about her new job with Dwayne Brewster and how it came about. He shared with her his drive south that turned more careless than carefree and the reasons for the episodes. She then began telling him about the small house she rented as a temporary residence until her income hit a point she could afford something better.

"Are you talking about that rundown little one-bedroom place north of town?" he asked.

"Yeah, that one. So, you remember it."

George seemed to lose his lackadaisical alcohol enhanced good mood. "Yeah, I know it very well." He turned away from her and stared past Bradley Donovan to the aged mirror on the back bar.

"Let me guess," she said, "would it have played a part in the sixteen years you lived during the coma?"

"It was the first house you and I lived in after we were married."

"You've been inside it before?"

He thought about that and cocked his head quizzically. "Actually, no. I never have been. I guess I concocted the way it should have looked."

"Damn, son, this story just keeps getting better and better," the old man said. "Care for sumthin' to drink, ma'am?"

"A glass of Chardonnay would be nice."

"Sorry, ma'am, I don't keep any of that frou-frou stuff. Not many of the cowboys and farmers around here drink it. But, I can sure pop the top on a cold beer for ya, if ya like."

"Sure."

The old cowboy lifted the lid on a refrigerated box beneath the bar and retrieved a bottle and twisted the cap off. He set it on the bar and slid it toward her. He again took his seat on the stool across from them and dropped his chin onto his open palm. "I don't want to miss a word of this conversation."

The old man sat near enough that Jennifer could smell his breath. It was not pleasant. She wanted to talk to George but not at all sure she wanted this guy to hear every word. She stared at the old man and frowned. It was obvious that George saw what was going on and smiled at Donovan while shrugging his shoulders. "Sorry, buddy."

The old man's eyes darted between them until the light of realization switched on. He sat up straight and pushed away from the bar. "Uh, but I really should go out back and feed my goats and that old mother cow penned up out there."

Jennifer and George watched the old cowboy disappear through a door next to the back bar. "Did you have something sensitive that you wanted to discuss?" he asked.

"Nah." She took a drink of her beer. "I just wanted you to myself. I'm selfish that way. Besides, the old guy may have been nice but his breath sure wasn't."

He stared at her for a moment with a loopy drunken look until he finally realized it was a joke. A grin slowly stretched his face. He wagged a finger at her. "Funny. I like your style."

"Now, for the part I didn't care to talk about in front of your new friend. I rented a motel room in Smithtown for a week until I get some furniture to furnish that little house and move in. The motel room has two beds. Why don't you leave your car here and come with me."

"Sure," he replied quickly but then paused. "But . . . what if I can't trust myself with you?"

She backhanded him on the arm. "Then I'll cut a switch and make you mind."

They traded small talk and shared childhood memories until his glass and her bottle were drained. The front door swung open and the bell above it tinkled. Standing there was the first regular customer of the evening, a cowboy wearing a light gray high-crowned western hat with a grimy sweat ring around its base. It was slightly askew and tilted to an odd angle as if he was tired and simply looking for a place to throw it down. The man had clearly been working outside all day. Before he could walk all the way to the bar in the rear, Bradley Donovan reappeared from the back.

Jennifer leaned sideways and whispered, "It's getting crowded in here. Let's go home."

"Home?"

"You know what I mean." Jennifer slid off the back of the stool, cringing at her choice of words that were meant to be humorous. She saw in George's face that the word "home" meant something entirely different and much deeper.

Chapter 20 ~ Getting to Know You

"Bradley Donovan," George murmured in a slow drawl. He sat slumped down in the passenger side of Jennifer's older model Toyota.

She looked sideways at him as she headed south down the highway toward Smithtown. "What about him?"

Bradley Donovan is a cool name." It was clear that George was inebriated beyond the point of clear speech—capacity to make his mouth form words had suddenly become a nearly unattainable art form, exaggerating every word with overly precise lip movement. "When Donovan said that he and Buck had been friends, it occurred to me that both those names are cool." He snickered and sprayed a little slobber. "While I'm stuck with a name like George Waller. How cruel is that?"

"Don't talk that way. I like your name."

He pulled his knees up, rolled sideways in the seat to face her, and then folded his arms tightly across his chest as if he would have preferred being asleep. "Really? What image pops into your head when you say my name?"

A playful grin pulled at her lips. "Well, let me think. Oh, I know. How about a sexy, sexy CPA?" She laughed.

"Sweet Jen," he slurred, "you are such a wiseass." He closed his eyes and dozed.

Sweet Jen. Sweet Jen. Jennifer rolled the pet name over in her mind—the name he had for her during their imaginary marriage. It sounded amazingly warm and sincere, even uttered in his drunken state. She liked it. She liked it a lot—maybe too much. She glanced repeatedly at him. It was difficult to determine if he had dozed or passed out. Selfishly, she didn't care much which it was. She took the opportunity to split viewing time between his face and the highway. He looked peaceful, even happy. As afraid as she was about abandonment a second time, it was increasingly difficult not to imagine this man at her side at some point in the future—the way it should have been—the way comatose George believed it had been. His conviction in that regard was rubbing off. Thoughts spawned were good and comfortable. She wanted to recreate that life he experienced, but she had to get past personal issues if it were to become reality. She wondered about George's ability to differentiate her from Marie and his idealized version of her as Sweet Jen. None of it would be real or durable if not.

As Jennifer slowed and drove through Smithtown toward the south side, she attempted rousing him. "Wake up, George. We're almost there and you're nuts if you think I'm going to carry you in and put you to bed. That's all on you, buddy."

He mumbled incoherently and stretched his legs but was abruptly stopped in the attempt by the confines of the floorboard. It was obvious that he, even drunk, became aware he was somewhere other than in a bed. He opened his eyes.

She studied his face and saw that although his eyes opened, there didn't appear to be recognition in them. The red-rimmed bloodshot orbs searched for clues around the car. He didn't know where he was. "Yoo-hoo, George, it's me, Jennifer. Sit up and get your bearings."

"Oh yeah," he mumbled as he pushed himself upright.

Indignantly she replied, "You could at least act a little more excited that your Sweet Jen is helping you out."

He'd been rubbing his eyes but suddenly stopped and looked at her when she used the pet name. He glanced through the windshield and then the side window. "Smithtown?"

"Sure is."

"Are you . . . I mean . . . are we married?" George truly wondered.

A knot of shock drew tight in Jennifer's abdomen, realizing that fatigue and alcohol had taken a toll on him in another way. She offered the name as a joke. It was no joke to him. The sight of Smithtown, her use of the name Sweet Jen, and her car that by his own admission appeared like the one she drove during the coma had thrown him back into that fantasy world. He had broken with reality. Suddenly, she was fearful of telling him the truth. In his present state of inebriation and confusion over what was real and what was fantasy, it might go either way—send him over the edge or he might simply shrug it off. She was scared to test it.

Not getting the answer he sought, George asked, "What are we doing on the south side of town? Why don't we go home? I'm tired, Sweet Jen, and more than a little drunk."

Not wanting to tip him one way or the other, she thought it best to probe deeper. She remembered the story he shared of falling from the roof while patching it in that alternate life. "We will. Are you going to get started patching that roof tomorrow?" It was a strategic question meant to determine how deeply he had slipped back into his imaginary life.

"I do need to get that done before the baby comes. I'll get it done tomorrow. Promise."

A chill raised the tiny hairs on the back of her neck when he answered so quickly and positively—proof that George, in his mind, was back in that world. They were married, they lived in his mother's old house and she was presumably pregnant. She attempted lightening the conversation while staying in character. "You really have had too much to drink. You've forgotten that I've been painting and have the furniture all out of place and drop cloths everywhere. I rented a motel room so I wouldn't have to straighten up just to go to bed."

He tilted his head and blinked his eyes in a sleepy way. "You did?" He paused but didn't wait for her to answer. "I guess I did drink too much. I don't remember that at all." His speech was slow and labored as if his tongue refused to cooperate. He rubbed his face but abruptly stopped. "Why did I get drunk? Why was I drinking at all?"

"I'll explain it in the morning. Okay?" She eased off the accelerator as she neared a small motel off to the left beneath an outdated neon sign. A couple of the lighted letters were non-operational. Another flickered and appeared to be about to go out as well. The remaining lights outlined rusting and faded letters in a soft amber glow that read: Sundowner Motel. Beneath it blinked a red neon vacancy addendum. "Here we are," she said, steering into the parking lot. She drove directly to a particular door and parked. As she turned off the ignition switch, Jennifer held on to the key and stared at George for a moment. *I think it's best that I don't rock this boat, not tonight.* "Come on, George, let's get you into bed. Things will be much clearer in the morning." She opened her door and turned away from him as she got out of the car. "At least I hope so," she added, whispering."

Getting him inside was more exercise than Jennifer bargained for, but finally spun him around on rubbery legs and let him fall backwards onto the bed. She pushed him around to lie correctly and then pulled his shoes and socks off, tossing them to the floor off the foot of the bed. Without thinking, Jennifer reached for his belt buckle, but her hands stopped abruptly as she thought about that. *It has been over a year since I've slept with a man and if I know he's lying in a bed next to me without pants, I might not be able to control myself. Besides, if I ever follow-through on such a thing, I want him sober and realizing which Jennifer he's making love to.* She remembered the last, and only guy, she had slept with since Sean died. It had been a matter of loneliness—a desire for warmth and closeness of another human being and, as it turned out, a huge mistake. Michael Lassiter was the principal attorney and managing partner of the law firm she resigned from in Abilene. Dating him was a regret she'd have to live with. Even up to the day she walked out of that office for the last time, the guy still believed that a window of opportunity existed for a relationship with her, despite her non-stop and loudly vocal assertions that it wasn't possible. She told him repeatedly that she wasn't interested in him that way. Michael was not interested in her that way either. It was about sex and only sex. She was sure of that. The man was all about sexual conquests, regardless how he framed his propositions.

What she was doing at this very moment with George might be the same mistake in the making, only taking a different route in getting there. Having thought on her weakness, she re-inserted the belt end into the loop on his pants and patted it down. She removed his shirt and covered him with the bedspread.

As the cover drifted down over his body, he roused slightly and licked his lips and cleared his throat, but never opened his eyes. "I love you, Sweet Jen," he muttered. "I only wish I knew stronger words to let you know just how much, because it's deep . . . and . . ." His voice trailed into garbled mumblings.

Jennifer's exhaustion played upon her emotions. A sentimental lump rose in her throat that refused to be swallowed. She placed a hand on his chest and felt his heart beat. She wanted desperately for those words to be for her and not some imagined version of herself. His words came from his subconscious, a place she knew only spoke truth. She wondered, could it be possible that those words were indeed meant for her in the here and now although he had used the pet name? Did he, or could he, tell the difference between the imaginary Missus George Waller and the reality of Jennifer Andrews? Did it matter? For God's sake, they were both the same person, her.

Somehow, though, it did make a difference. She wasn't certain that she could live up to his sixteen-year imagined version of her that had been crammed into a week. All her childhood affection and teen fondness for this man tightened a grip on her. Tears filled her eyes. She was falling in love all over again, and that frightened hell out of her. Everything she had done since the day that they reconnected drew her closer to him.

For the first time, sitting in the dark with George lying in the bed next to her bed, Jennifer questioned the wisdom of moving back to Smithtown, knowing he'd begin working on opening a pre-owned auto dealership here. She wanted it. She wanted him. But, the question remained—a big one: could her heart stand another break like the one that he had dealt her sixteen years ago in this world, the real world, if things didn't go the way she assumed they would? It took years to heal and left scars on her ability to trust. She needed a guarantee it wouldn't happen again. Staring at George, a bourbon reeking lump under the bedspread, she was torn by this internal battle.

The urge to lie at his back and feel his warmth proved to be a strong beckoning call that reached out to her. The draw wouldn't stop. The desire for a moment of tender warmth with this man was fast becoming an irreversible need. If she gave in, it wouldn't—couldn't—stop at cuddling warmth. It would reel out of control and she'd give herself to him completely. She attempted justifying to herself that it might be okay to follow through on these feelings. He was drunk, after all, and probably wouldn't remember it. She might satisfy an itch without having to explain anything when the sun rose in the morning. Eventually, after a brief internal give-and-take, she rolled both hands into fists and hit herself on the thighs hard enough to cause pain for allowing the idiotic notion such latitude. She fell back and lay on her own bed, rolling away before the urge to feel his warmth overwhelmed her. She couldn't—she simply could not give in, not yet. There were miles to go in this relationship. She should take it slow to be sure that, this time, there was a future in it—a real future. There existed a dark corner of her mind tugging her away from him, albeit shrinking. Her conviction finally caught up to her better judgment to remain aloof romantically—just be friends with him and leave no door open for that kind of relationship this soon. Such conviction was not born of strength, but from weakness, afraid of being left alone to fend for herself yet again. Lying on her side, she pulled her knees up high into a protective fetal ball as a free flow of tears soaked a spot beneath her eyes on the pillow. Visions of Sean Andrews and George Waller whirled in a kaleidoscopic frenzy. Exhaustion took her down.

* * *

George snorted. The sudden sound from his own throat woke him. He smacked his chapping lips. He had been mouth breathing for quite some time. For how long, he had no idea. But long enough to dry it out. His tongue felt like a cottony foreign object. He swirled it around to work up the blessed feel of fresh saliva. As that happened, the foul stench of his own breath drifted out of his mouth and up his nose. It was as effective as smelling salts stuck under his nose. He was suddenly alert and sat up. It hit him that he had a hangover—a bad one. The throbbing pain in his head wasn't so different than the pain he experienced when he came out of the coma. His heart felt as though it had taken up residence inside his skull and pumped pain with every beat, nauseating him. Water. He needed a big drink of water. That might help.

George swung one leg, and then the other, off the bed. He rubbed his neck and rolled his head, attempting to alleviate the pounding headache. He abruptly stopped, realizing he didn't know where he was or, how he came to be here. The bed next to the one he sat on had been slept in, but empty. He searched his memory, wanting to piece together facts that brought him to this moment. The clearest memory was having a wonderful conversation with a colorful old cowboy by the name of Bradley Donovan at a country bar he stopped at. That's where his memory of the afternoon and evening before began to fail, turning into random snippets of events, some not seeming to relate to others. But, once he established that beginning point, memory scraps began falling into place and piecing together. It finally occurred to him that Jennifer was part of it. "Jennifer?" he asked aloud, but not expecting a reply.

"I'm in the bathroom," she called out. She opened the bathroom door and poked her head out, brushing her teeth.

He frowned. "Where are we, and how did we get here? Did you spend the night here, too?"

She pulled the toothbrush from between her teeth and pushed the diluted paste into a bubbled corner of one cheek and held it. "Give me a minute." She disappeared back into the bathroom and then came out to join him.

He eyed her up and down. "Did you just now get up?"

"Yeah."

"You sure look good for someone having just climbed out of bed," he said, watching her with one eye closed while massaging his temples.

"Thanks. Too bad I can't say the same about you." She smirked. "You look like shit."

"Oh yeah? I don't know what I look like, but I'm sure I feel worse." He tried to smile, but couldn't make it happen. "Meaning, I suppose, you have ample reason to use that language."

Jennifer snickered. "Sorry, I don't mean to make merry with your pain. Unfortunately for you, that's who I am and what I do." She smiled. "Tell ya what, wash your face, put your clothes on, and I'll buy your breakfast over at the Village Diner."

"Village Diner? Are we in Smithtown?"

"You really don't remember much about last night, do you?"

"Afraid not." He looked around the room. "Judging by all your stuff lying around, it looks like you're living here."

"I am, but it's only temporary. Less than a week, I hope." She stepped over and sat beside him on the edge of the bed and patted his knee. "We have a lot to discuss. But let's do it over breakfast. I'll start by filling in the gaps on your day yesterday." She handed him the toothbrush and a small tube of toothpaste. "Here. Now that I'm sitting close to you, I can tell that you need this more than me. Whew!" She fanned his breath away from her nose and gave his knee another reassuring pat. She then sprang off the bed.

When George stepped outside, a brisk autumn breeze met him when he faced north up the highway. It did wonders to settle gurgling queasiness. Not that he didn't believe Jennifer, but the view from where he stood in front of the motel room at the Sundowner proved that he was indeed in their hometown. Up the highway, he saw the A & W Drive-In. Although it no longer had that name, he would always know the burger joint as the A & W Root Beer Stand because it was his crew's favorite high school hangout.

"How ya feelin'?" Jennifer asked.

George breathed the morning air deeply. "Better. Let's go eat."

There was little conversation exchanged in the car during the short drive to the diner. George spent the time collecting his thoughts. As they stepped inside the popular eatery, the warmth of the place was inviting and in sharp contrast to the dry chill outside. Smells of sausage and bacon, syrups, pancakes and other morning standards made his mouth water. "I'm glad you had this idea. I'm suddenly hyper-aware of my hunger," he said while scanning the many faces enjoying breakfast. He thought he might see someone he would recognize, but not this time.

"Then let's get you fed." Jennifer guided him to a booth at the far end in a corner where large windows came together.

The waitress promptly came with mugs, a coffee carafe, and two menus tucked under her arm. "I assume you folks want coffee. Am I right?"

George offered the lady a sad desperate face. "Oh yes. God bless ya, girl."

The waitress chuckled. She poured two mugs full and dropped the menus on the end of the table. "I'll be back in a moment to take your order," she said. She hurried up the row of booths, topping off mugs at every table and booth along her retreat.

"Tell me truthfully," George asked, "was I a gentleman last night or, God forbid, an asshole?"

"It leaned heavily toward gentleman."

He sighed. "Good."

Jennifer's pleasant expression lost its sparkle. "Last night you had it fixed in your head that I was Sweet Jen, we were married and wondering why we didn't just go home. It made me nervous. I was afraid to burst that bubble—not sure what it might do to you if I forced the truth on you while you were in that condition. So, I played along."

"I'm sorry if I made you uncomfortable."

"Don't worry about it . . . seriously. I know first-hand how alcohol can distort reality in the best of circumstances. I was doubly aware of it in your case."

As Jennifer spoke, Marie and Louisa crossed his mind. Oddly, the thought and images didn't linger. Moments later, he thought back and took note of how his two dear ones floated into and then out of his consciousness so easily. His face expressed a twinge of guilt and observable sadness.

"Are you okay? Was it something I said?" Jennifer asked.

"No, no," he blurted, "My mind drifted." He grinned. "Must be a hangover thing."

"Anyhow," she continued, "you were a perfect gentleman last night—quite affectionate actually." She raised one eyebrow.

"Oh God, I didn't try to force myself on you, did I?"

Jennifer laughed. "No. You just said things—very nice things." Her smile smoothed away as her head tilted to a thoughtful slant. "But the situation, as it was . . . you know, both of us in the same motel room, made me think about the only man I've dated since Sean's passing. His name is Michael Lassiter. It was only three dates, and I let it go too far on that third one. It wasn't awful. But, it *was* a huge mistake. I felt compelled to tell him later there could never be anything between us and broke it off with him. I knew that I had to put the brakes on that situation before it spun out of control. The man never backed off. It was complicated by our work proximity and his position there. We both worked in the same office and he was a managing partner and part owner of the law firm. I had inadvertently created a tightrope that I had to walk every day if I wanted to remain employed. It got tiresome. Being courteous but not overly familiar and nice but not too nice. He even became belligerent when I broke the news to him that I was resigning and moving back to my hometown. He took it as a personal affront. He didn't believe me when I told him it was due to Sean's passing and nothing to do with him. I told him over and over how much I appreciated the opportunity of working with him and that I would always remember it as a positive experience. Nothing worked. His last words to me weren't goodbye, but 'get out and don't come back'."

"Sounds to me like you successfully left a problem behind."

Jennifer's smile bounced right back. "Yeah, I did." She paused. The smile drooped, and she frowned. "But, I know him well enough to realize he doesn't give up—ever. So . . ." She said nothing more about it, but the meaning was clear without further explanation.

George was so hungry that eating breakfast was taken care of in glutinous fashion. He washed down the last bite of pancakes with a gulp of cooling coffee. He sat back and rubbed his stomach. "Ah, that was great."

"Feeling better?"

"Much." He straightened and looked out the window next to their booth to the highway. "What's the plan now?"

"I suppose this is where I take you back to your car."

George hadn't thought about the car. "I don't have a car here. Do I? Is it still at Donovan's?"

"Yep. Hopefully, no one stole it."

"Oh Geez, don't say that. I'm already homeless. I don't need to be without wheels, too."

Jennifer slid out of the booth and stood. "Now that *would* be funny. The owner of a prosperous automobile dealership who has no car." She snickered. "Come on. Let's go get it."

As Jennifer drove them north out of town, George noticed the old and poorly cared for small white house off to the left with the black roof. As they sped by, his eyes stayed on the place for a moment.

"See something interesting?" Jennifer asked.

"It's, uh, the house you—I mean Sweet Jen and I rented for the first year of our marriage in that other life. Sorry, I didn't want my head slipping back into that mode, not this morning." He looked sideways at her and noticed an expression that he couldn't determine. "What?" he asked.

"Yesterday morning I rented that house."

"Seriously?" He glanced back at it one last time. You mean that little rundown white house back there?"

She nodded. "The job I accepted with Dwayne Brewster's law firm will pay very little for the first few months and that place was cheap. It only made sense."

For the remainder of the trip up the highway to Donovan's Tack Shop and Bar, there was little conversation. The words that were exchanged were trivial and without substance. It was clear that he and Jennifer swam in their own pools of thought. He also realized those pools were connected and would always be, whether they were conscious of it or not.

Jennifer pulled off the highway onto the graveled parking lot in front of the little red rough-sawn building that housed Donovan's place. George's car was not where he remembered parking it. "What the hell?" he muttered.

"Don't panic. I asked Mister Donovan to pull it around back to remove theft temptation by someone that might appreciate a slick vintage car as much as you apparently do. I take it you don't remember handing him the keys."

"Hmm. Not at all. If you hadn't been there, the old man could have stolen the car and I would never have known it."

Jennifer drove around to the side and eased forward until the slick gold '69 Dodge came into view. It caught the morning sun, exploding in a brilliant reflection off its hood once it was fully in view.

The old cowboy stepped out the back door sporting a big grin. He dangled George's car keys between his fingers. "Howdy," he called out as they got out of her car. "How ya doin' this fine mornin', Mister Waller?"

"Amazingly well," he replied. "Call me George. I have a feeling I'll be back to see you soon."

"That'd be mighty fine," Donovan said. He looked to Jennifer then back to George. "You two make it through the night without a hitch?" he asked in a slow calculating way, and then grinned lasciviously while fingering the gray stubble on his chin.

"Yes, without a hitch," Jennifer blurted. "And no—nothing happened last night between us, if that's what you're wondering."

Bradley Donovan offered a one finger wave. "Well, I'll leave you to it then. Y'all have a great day and come back to see me." He walked back inside and closed the door behind him.

"Can you believe that guy?" Jennifer asked.

George came around the car to face her. "Actually, I can. I do a very poor job of hiding my feelings." He reached for both her hands and held them, staring into her eyes in a much different way than any other time. "You're such a good friend. I don't deserve everything you've done for me."

Her eyes darted around, showing signs of embarrassment. "It's nothing. Really."

He continued with a locked stare on her beautiful nutty brown eyes. "Oh yes, it is. It is something—a big something." He leaned in toward her and slid his hands up her arms above the elbows when he felt her attempting to step back.

"Oh, George, I don't think it's a good idea to—"

He pressed his lips to hers.

She stiffened and tried once more to back away. The struggle was slight and brief. He felt her lips become receptive and soft as her body relaxed. He pulled her into full body contact and kissed her deeply. When he slowly broke the connection, he saw her eyes open in a dreamy way. In an instant, her eyes burst large. She reared her head back. "What the hell are we doing, George? What the hell am I doing?" She did not wait for a response, broke his grasp on her arms, and hurried away.

"Wait, Jen. Come back."

She glanced over her shoulder but kept moving toward her car.

He glimpsed her face twisting into anguish. She appeared on the verge of breaking into sobs. In a rushed and clumsy maneuver, she got into her car and over accelerated out of the parking lot, spraying gravel as she went.

There were many things that ran through his mind as he kissed her. That reaction was not one of them.

Chapter 21 ~ Regrets

Dwayne Brewster, Jennifer's new employer, graciously allowed her to meet the moving van at her recently acquired rental just beyond the city limits on the north side of Smithtown. As she drove toward the rundown little house just beyond the northern city limit sign to meet them, the image of George's surprised look yesterday circled her thoughts like vultures waiting for the moment of death to swoop in and pick clean the bones. *It was just a kiss! Why did I run?* Fist tightly clenched, she hammered the top of the steering wheel. Even as she thought it, she knew the answer. It was not that she didn't want George to kiss her. She did—very much. Fear of her own weakness and that dark voice inside her surfaced and seized control at the worst possible time, spiriting her mood to a negative place. Jennifer's abandonment issues were deep and wide. Tears lapped at her blinking eyelids threatening to spill.

She wheeled into the driveway of the old house. The moving truck was there, and two men were removing the larger items onto the unruly dead grass in the front yard. After a cordial but quick introduction she showed them where to set the largest of the appliances and furniture. Afterwards, all that remained were boxes and those were clearly marked with the rooms they belonged in. She handed one of the men a key. "Look fellas, all the rest of that stuff, just put it in the rooms that are written on the tops of each box and then lock the door when you leave." She pointed to a flower pot with the dried skeletal remains of some type of plant still in it. "You can leave the key under that red terracotta pot over there."

"Sure," one of the men said. His partner quickly added, "We'll get it done for you, ma'am."

"I started a new job and more than a little nervous about being away from it so soon for any reason, even a good one like this."

The older of the two men smiled. He was a big man with a rotund belly and not old, but a little past his prime, early fifties perhaps, but he had a kind and gentle way about him. "We understand. Believe me. Go on and don't worry. Timothy and I will take care of things here and button it all up when we're finished."

The man had an honest face and Jennifer trusted him. She got back in her car and left them to the task. *I wish I trusted myself as much as I trust strangers,* she thought. After driving a mile, she made up her mind to call and apologize to George for what she now believed to be her childish behavior yesterday. She pulled off the highway and retrieved her cell phone from her purse. As she dialed, she rehearsed ways to get it said quickly, while maintaining the truth of her sincerity. Sure, it had to be honest, but it had to strike the right note as well.

"Hello," came his flat reply.

"George?"

"Jennifer?"

"Yeah, it's me," she replied. "After my little stunt yesterday, I thought I should call and apologize." She paused. "Are you back in Lubbock?"

"You don't need to apologize. I succumbed to an urge and shouldn't have. Secondly, no I didn't go back to Lubbock. I spent the night with Alex and Patricia and, right now, I'm sitting in Alex's office at the John Deere Dealership telling him how to better sell tractors and implements. I have sixteen years of imaginary experience, you know." He chuckled as Alex guffawed in the background.

Jennifer's nervous tension left her. George's light-hearted comeback was perfectly timed.

"Look, Jen," George said, his tone sinking to a serious timbre, "what I did yesterday was not right. I spoke to you as a friend, but I was seeing you as my wife and acted in accordance with the latter. In that moment, yesterday, in my mind, we were a couple—husband and wife type of couple. I must do a better job of separating what is and what never was. Plus, if—"

"Stop talking before you make me cry."

"Jeez, did I say something wrong?"

"Quite the opposite. You said everything perfectly. It's just that . . . well, honestly, you're not the only one with a problem. I'm messed up in the head, too, where it concerns you and me." She paused. "You know what? We need to have a party, and soon, too—just our crew. It has been a long time since you, Alex, Lenny, and I have been in the same place at the same time for no other reason than to enjoy one another's company."

"That's a great idea!" he said, and then shared the idea with Alex while she listened on the phone. He came back on the line. "Alex said we could get together at his house and that he'd call Lenny. It's . . ." His voice trailed off.

"It's what?" she asked.

"I know you get tired of hearing my stories about my life that never was, but in my mind, it was only a couple of months ago that you and I were in our fifties and we had Lenny, Alex, and Bubba over for a backyard barbeque at our house, you know, my Mom's place."

"It's okay. I enjoy hearing your stories of that other life. Regardless what you think happened in that alternate world, in this life I *am* your friend. Don't ever forget that—always was, always will be. You can trust me with anything. That's the reason I want to be close to you, to help with this process." She paused, and then continued slowly, searching for the right words, "I'm still amazed though that Bubba Leal was an adult part of that world, since he's been gone since we were nine years old."

George remained silent. In that moment, the quiet was steeped in sadness. "Yeah. Amazing," he finally replied. "I guess that I missed him more than I knew. It must have been tucked away in my subconscious. Of course, he did have the face and body of Antonio Mendoza, my nurse, while I was in the hospital. "Even more amazing is that I'm holding onto a certain amount of grief for a person that never actually existed beyond childhood, yet Bubba was there—laughing, playing, and partying with the rest of us." George's voice fell to a whisper before he cut it off. It seemed as though he may have wanted to say more but couldn't. It was time to intervene.

"Look, she said, let's cut this conversation short. You guys get things arranged and then call me later with details. How's that?"

"Great idea. We'll talk later."

Jennifer ended the conversation and tossed the phone back into her purse. She determined the conversation did two things, one good—one not so good. She had apologized for breaking and running away from the kiss yesterday like a child scared of the dark. As it turned out, it was not the problem for her that she was fearful it might be. George graciously and quickly made it a non-issue. The other side of this coin was the downside. George slid back into that other life with alarming ease. His too real memories of Bubba Leal as an adult served to harden her conviction to be the best friend possible and help him any way she could. But, she had to remain at arm's length from any romantic moves he may attempt. She figured it was only a matter of time before George would again slip up and see her as his Sweet Jen. Keeping a respectful distance from him in mind and heart was the best way—for now the only way. But, that arm's length distance was as far as she wanted to push him because affection deepened by the day.

Jennifer checked her watch and felt a tiny streak of panic bolt through her when she noticed that it was a few minutes shy of noon. She had been gone over two hours to handle a chore that she promised Dwayne Brewster should take less than one. She over accelerated up onto the highway with a screech of tires, now in a rush to get back to the office.

She aggressively pulled into an angled parking space on the west side of the square surrounding the courthouse in front of a row of offices and storefronts. Her tires hit the curb and the car bounced back, causing the vehicle to rock and sway on worn shock absorbers. Brewster's law office was directly in front of where she parked. She hastily retrieved her purse and was about to bound out of the vehicle when she noticed that the car parked next to hers was sickeningly familiar. Instantly angered over the sheer possibility of who it might be, she clenched her jaws. She threw open the car door and marched up onto the curb, hoping she was mistaken.

As she opened and stepped through the front door, she saw Dwayne Brewster beyond the open door into his office sitting behind his desk talking to someone off to the side and out of sight. "Ah good, you're back," he called out to her, adding, "I've been having a nice chat with a friend of yours."

Those words were all it took for her heart to take a quick slide into her stomach. She felt a mixture of things as she slowed her approach, none of them good. She stepped inside Brewster's office. Sitting in the chair to her left was Michael Lassiter, her former boss, and one of the reasons she left Abilene, maybe the biggest reason. She wanted to get away from the guy. "Michael, what are you doing here?" she asked with no hint of a welcoming expression.

Michael smiled. It lacked pleasance. What Jennifer saw in that grin was connivance. "I'm here on business," he said.

Before Jennifer could respond, Brewster added, "Mister Lassiter has made this firm a very interesting offer, certainly worth consideration."

"Oh?" She redirected attention to Michael. "What might that be?" she asked with ample skepticism.

Michael's smile transformed into a smirk. "Here's the deal, Jenny, since—"

"I'd appreciate it if you addressed me as Jennifer or Miss Andrews."

Michael's mouth remained open from the interruption. "Okay, Miss Andrews," he replied slowly, over-enunciating, "Since you did most of the legwork on that Sweetwater lawsuit, and since the clients are, within reason, halfway between our two firms, I proposed to Mister Brewster that his firm and ours collaborate on the case. Although we took it on a contingency, it's a strong case and could be a big payday for both our firms."

"What do you think, Jennifer?" Brewster asked with tented fingertips and a hopeful sparkle in his eyes.

She drew a deep breath and forced her body to stand down from its defiant posture. She let out an exaggerated sigh. "Yes, it is a compelling case, and, yes, it could earn a sizable settlement. Here's the case, as I recall it to be: a company came in and offered farmers and ranchers a contract to place electrical wind generators, a wind farm, on their properties at a given price. Landowners were given a deposit, equally divided among them, but when it came time to pay the balance, the company decided some of those properties were more important than others and the payouts were all over the place, no two the same. It's a clear breach of contract case, but for some odd reason the company is choosing to deny that they are in breach and not living up to the terms of the agreement. It involves seven large land owners that have gone together and filed suit jointly, even the two land owners who received what they were promised have joined in support of the other farmers and ranchers. And that makes it a strong case in favor of the landowners." Her face showed contempt as she turned to Michael. "Michael's firm can, and does, boast a litany of successful lawsuits in these types of cases. So, now, his firm is the sole legal counsel of record for the seven owners."

Brewster nodded. His smiled widened. It appeared clear enough that the old guy was seeing dollar signs. "Then I'm of the opinion we should draw up some paperwork and make the deal with Mister Lassiter," Brewster said. "It comes at the right time, too—just when you're starting and in need of the income so that I might keep you on the job. I really want you to be happy here. I believe with your help, Jennifer, we can accomplish some good things."

Jennifer was really beginning to love old Mister Brewster, compelled to do everything she could to make him happy with his decision to take her into his firm even when he couldn't afford it. She smiled weakly and affirmed his opinion. "You're right. We do need this."

Brewster clapped his hands once. "Good! Mister Lassiter and I will hammer out the details and when Clarice returns, I'll have her type it up." Brewster looked to Michael. "Clarice Beatty is my secretary. She had a doctor's appointment. You'll meet her shortly. It won't take but a few minutes to get details down and then let's give Clarice about an hour to get her part done. That way we can have the deal done before you leave town. Is that plan all right with you, Mister Lassiter?"

"Absolutely," Michael said. "Maybe Miss Andrews and I can grab a bite to eat while it's being typed."

"Excellent idea," Brewster said. "Jennifer, why don't you take Mister Lassiter to lunch over at the Village Diner and charge it to the office? I have an open account with them for just such occasions. By the time you return it will be ready to sign?"

Jennifer nodded. "Okay." She wandered into the outer office and sat to wait for Brewster and Michael to finish their discussion. Her mind reeled with frustration and anger. She felt as though she had just caught a tidal wave, riding atop it on a rudderless surfboard and no control over the direction, caught between the man she wanted approval from and another she wanted nothing to do with. Suddenly, she found herself smack-dab in the middle. She'd be working closely with Michael again. Just the thought forced her to swallow an urge to explode into obscenity laced vitriol, knowing the real reason he cooked up this scheme. There was no way in hell this arrangement would have crossed Michael's mind had she not left Abilene to come to work here.

After ten minutes of stewing over the situation, Michael emerged from Brewster's office. She sprang to her feet and spun on her heels toward the front door. "Come on Michael," she said tersely, "let's go get something to eat and let Dwayne work."

"I'll drive," he called out to her as she walked out the door, not waiting for him to catch up.

As Lassiter drove toward the diner, Jennifer wanted to say nothing and get this luncheon behind her, but Lassiter's light-hearted banter grated her to the point she couldn't remain quiet. She interrupted his babble on the joys of small town living. "What are you really doing in Smithtown, Michael? Your last words to me as I left your office in Abilene were, 'Get out and don't come back', which I planned on honoring and, quite honestly, looked forward to. So, just what the hell are you doing here? And, don't insult me by offering up that 'business' bullshit."

As she spoke, Lassiter glanced repeatedly at her and smirked. "Maybe I felt bad about what I said. Have you thought of that?"

"Again, I call bullshit. I know you, Michael. You're a spoiled rich kid that never grew up, a tantrum thrower when things don't go the way you want. Unfortunately, you have the resources to back up those tantrums. Case in point: this proposed legal partnership on the Sweetwater lawsuit. I think you're here because you're ulterior motive is to continue your pursuit of me, not that lawsuit. You don't need a collaborative partner on it. That's just a crap reason. I believe your goal is to get me back in the sack or make my life miserable while you try. You don't like to lose."

"That's not true at all! I do like you, very much." Lassiter pulled into the lot of the Village Diner and parked. He turned sideways to face Jennifer. "Do you truly think that I'd be that crude and petty?"

"Yes."

"Whew! Boy, do I have my work cut out for me, proving to you that my intentions toward you are sincere."

"Sincere? Maybe. Honorable? I doubt it. In that one statement, you just told me everything I need to know about your reason to be here," Jennifer said as she was getting out of his car. "If this is *business*, as you say, let's keep it businesslike."

He came around the car and met up with her. "The first thing we need to establish is a meeting place in Sweetwater to collaborate on the case as needed."

She rolled her eyes and looked away from him. "And so it begins. Hell has followed me to Smithtown," she mumbled, as she turned her back to him and walked away toward the diner.

George spent the remainder of the week in Lubbock at his used car dealership, but his mind and heart were not in attendance. His essence was left behind in Smithtown. He had entered a stage of metamorphosis—his nights spent alone in a nearby motel brooding. Loss and loneliness peeled away allegiance one layer at a time to this place known as the Hub City—Lubbock, the place he had called home for his entire marriage to Marie. As loyalty to this town and his past sloughed away one fibrous strand at a time, reasons continued piling, one upon the other, to be in Smithtown permanently and get it done as soon as possible. No longer did anything hold him here except the dealership and that provided insufficient distraction to quell memories of Marie and Louisa. Reminders at every turn kept his heart heavy. Winter was only a frosty breath away. Dreary gray skies and chilled north winds amplified pangs of loss. Now, only thoughts of a future in Smithtown kept him warm, with Sweet Jen at his side. George believed it a reasonable and possible goal—a bright spot—a forward-looking plan with his hometown at its shiny center.

When a blue mood threatened, all he needed to do was consider the upcoming party in Smithtown Saturday night with Alex, Jennifer and Lenny. Visualizing the way they had been once upon a time—laughing, joking and as comfortable in one another's presence as family. That wonderful thought led to others—moving back into his childhood home and the beautiful nostalgic tug of his early life that had been filled with happiness, thanks in large measure to the same people he would see again this weekend. It excited him. Born as a novel idea, the coming life's change had become a hardened plan, like fast-setting concrete. He wouldn't return to Lubbock as a resident. Instead, he'd begin the process of securing property for a used car lot in his hometown. He had already notified the renters in his mother's house that he'd not renew their lease and explained to them why. They were upset. He had difficulty caring too much about that. Although, he did plan on refunding all their deposit money without quibbling. It would be vacant by December first. From that day forward, George could call it home. Every thought, every notion, every plan came to him with Jennifer in mind. There would come a day, and soon he hoped, that Jennifer Andrews would once again be Sweet Jen Waller.

Saturday morning every mile that clicked off on the odometer brought him one mile closer to his hometown—one mile farther from his past. He cranked up the radio and moved with the tunes, singing along on occasion. The countryside was rife with pickers stripping dead dried stalks of fluffy white cotton bolls and large compacted ricks of harvested cotton ready to be taken to the gin for processing. It was a pleasant sight and filled the air with an aroma that only a person that grew up in cotton country could appreciate. A visual representation of a good crop season and of a job well done.

As George drove past Donovan's Tack Store and Bar, he smiled and said aloud, "I'll be back to see you soon. You're a good man, Bradley Donovan." He drummed the top of the steering wheel with his thumbs as he continued singing along with the old Righteous Brothers tune "Soul and Inspiration". It seemed appropriate coming from the radio inside a car manufactured in 1968. As he neared Smithtown, his foot became heavier on the accelerator, eager to get there—his attitude devilish toward the climbing speedometer. He kept an eye out for familiar black and white cars, but he had no intention of backing off on speed. His timing was near perfect. He'd be at Alex's house at six o'clock—right on time.

He pulled into Alex Burton's driveway at six and parked behind Alex's aging blue Buick. *That boy needs a newer car. I should be in business here in time to make that happen for him.* Along the curb out front were Jennifer's old Toyota and Lenny Poe's dinged and dirty green Ford pickup. He laughed aloud, thinking, *I should have a pretty good customer base in this town if the condition of my friends' vehicles are any indication.* The sight of those vehicles fluttered his heart, knowing that inside the house were three excellent reasons to smile and it had very little to do with selling them cars. He couldn't think of anywhere in the world he would rather be right now.

George didn't slow down to knock. He flung open the front door with a whoosh and quipped in a loud sarcastic voice, "Honey, I'm home."

"Back here, Sweetheart," came Alex's equally absurd feminine impersonation.

George heard laughter as he sped toward the voice in the kitchen at the rear of the house. As he rounded the corner, Jennifer, Alex and Lenny sat on tall stools at the kitchen's center island. All three had beverages that he assumed were alcoholic, and all were in various stages of consumption. "Hey, I thought the party started at six. What are y'all doing with mostly emptied drinks in front of you?"

"My little house, that I will henceforth affectionately refer to as The Hovel, was closing in on me so I came on over," Jennifer said and then hoisted her glass. "Cheers."

George patted her gently on the back. "Cheers to you, too." He stepped behind Lenny and began massaging his shoulders. "Hey, Len, I haven't seen much of you lately. Ya doin' okay?"

"Aw yeah, fine, just working for a living. It takes up far too much of my free time. You think anyone would notice if I retired at thirty-seven?"

"Someone might," George said. "Do you think you can sell cars?"

Lenny twisted around and looked wide-eyed up at George. "Really?"

"Really."

"We'll talk about that some time," Lenny said.

"You got it." George's smile wilted somewhat when he looked at the empty stool next to Lenny. He suddenly had a strong sense of something not right—something missing. A chill prickled the hair on his neck when it occurred to him that he was thinking of Bubba Leal, the fifth member of their crew that died when they were nine, but was a vibrant living adult with a wife and children in his near-perfect comatose world.

Alex leaned back and looked past Jennifer and Lenny. "You've suddenly gone quiet, buddy. Are you okay?"

"Yeah. Mostly," George replied.

"Define 'mostly'?" Jennifer asked.

"Just memory flashes—still having trouble separating the real world from the one I dreamed up. I came very close to asking why Bubba wasn't here."

"Wow," Lenny said, "that is strange."

George sat on the empty stool next to Lenny. "It's not as strange as how I envisioned your dad in that world of my own making. Want to hear it, Len?"

Lenny sighed. "Sure. Why not? I still miss him. No one deserves to have their life snuffed out like that. I did love the old fart." Lenny dropped his chin onto his open palm. "Tell your story."

"In that world, I had Alex's job at the tractor dealership. That armed meth-head that attempted to rob us only wounded Buck and he saved me from taking the fatal bullet. Here's the kicker, there was no way that bullet could have missed me. The muzzle of the pistol was firmly against my stomach, yet, it missed striking me, while still putting a hole in the wall directly behind me."

"It sounds like your subconscious was telling you that that bullet was never meant for you," Lenny said.

George's eyes drifted toward the window over the kitchen sink as he contemplated Lenny's accidental wisdom. "Yeah. There's no other explanation," George replied.

The room fell silent for a couple of seconds. Alex sprang to his feet. "Okay, guys, let's not let the party get gloomy. I refuse to let it go there. George, do you want a beer or maybe something with a bit more kick?"

"Don't give him a choice," Jennifer said, topping Alex's question. "He needs kicking."

George pulled a wry grin. "I'm not sure I like how you said that."

Jennifer held up her mostly empty glass. "Again, I say, cheers." She turned to Alex. "While you're up getting George's jet fuel, how about a refill?" The four of them laughed.

The evening continued light and happy, but eventually alcohol consumption and the lateness of the hour pulled everyone down to quieter, more pensive moods. They relocated to comfortable seating in the living room. Jennifer sat on the sofa between George and Lenny, while Alex claimed squatter's rights on a recliner. George glanced sideways. He nudged Jennifer with his shoulder. "I see the wheels of your mind turning. What're ya thinkin' about?"

"I may have a problem, but I can't be certain yet," she replied.

Alex sat up straight. "Anything we can help with?"

"I don't think so," she replied. Her response was halting.

George attempted reading her expression. What he saw beyond uncertainty was worry and that was bothersome. "You'll never know if we can help you or not, if we don't know what the problem is," he offered.

"I worked for a man by the name of Michael Lassiter, an attorney in Abilene—"

"Oh, him," George said, his voice sinking."

"Yeah, him," she continued. "Michael was the only man I've dated since Sean died. It was a mistake—no, not simply a mistake—a major screw up that I've regretted every day since. I don't believe I consciously decided to date him, just went along with it. There was a lengthy period of mourning over the loss of Sean that, in the moment, I didn't recognize my actions as a byproduct of grief. I was numb emotionally. Anyhow, once my head cleared and I descended back to earth, so to speak, I tried to break it off with Michael, but he wouldn't let it go. Part of the reason I moved back here was to get away from him. And, lo and behold, it didn't work. He has insinuated himself into a partnership with Dwayne Brewster on an implied promise of a huge payday as the result of a Sweetwater lawsuit taken on contingency by Michael and his Abilene firm." She paused and downed the last swallow of her drink. "Would you like to guess the name of the paralegal that worked on that lawsuit while employed at Lassiter's firm?"

"I'll have to go with Jennifer Andrews as the answer," Lenny said with a smirk.

Jennifer snickered. "Ooh, Len. You're good. Ever thought of becoming a private investigator?"

"Let me see," Lenny said, holding his hands palms up as if balancing scales, "selling cars or private investigator? Options. How cool is that?"

"Anyhow, Michael has worked it out with Dwayne that I'll be traveling alone to Sweetwater for occasional overnights with him to work on the case. Now, you know why I'm uncertain if it'll be a problem or not. Surely, it will not be any worse than it was when I worked for him, but I don't know, because at his office there were always other people around to temper his sexually charged aggression. Plus, now that I don't see him every day, he may feel pressure to make his move and do it forcefully."

"If you need the three of us to kick Lassiter's ass all the way back to Abilene, let us know. That's what friends are for," Alex said.

"I'm with Alex," George quickly added.

"Aw, hell yeah," Lenny chimed in.

"You guys are great," she replied.

George sat back as Alex, Lenny, and Jennifer continued talking over her dilemma. He contributed little to the conversation, sinking into jealousy that she dated anyone after Sean's passing. After a time, possessiveness became tinged with anger, but he couldn't tell if he was mad at Lassiter for re-inserting himself into her life or angry with Jennifer for not stopping it before it started, or himself for allowing a guy she admittedly didn't like to make him feel this way. At the surface, he felt silly. Deeper down, covetous anger threatened to bubble up, and he didn't know how to rein it in.

Chapter 23 ~ A Good Idea

Jennifer kept her head down and did the best work for Dwayne Brewster's law office that she could. She owed him for the opportunity and spent the week following the party by soliciting clients. Although the week's successes were small, she believed the time had been well spent. She secured an agriculture seed wholesaler, a family owned grocery chain that had six stores in nearby rural towns, and even managed to poach a small privately-owned oilfield pipe company away from Michael Lassiter's firm. She was proud of that one. She and Brewster would have to prove their value as legal counsel to retain the account, but that was true of them all.

By late Friday afternoon, the hard week had taken its toll. Sharpness of mind yielded to daydreaming and her physical energy had become equally precarious. Since five straight days were spent working alone, only talking to prospective clients, she craved company that didn't require deep thought, clever comebacks, or negotiating skills of any kind. George Waller was on her mind and had been for several days. Long dormant feelings for the man were never far from the surface.

As she sped north up the highway toward Smithtown, she snatched her cell phone from its perch on the dash and hit George's speed dial number.

The reply came quickly. "Hello."

"George? Jennifer. How's your week been?"

"Busy. I've been searching for a piece of property suitable for a car lot and trying to take care of business at the lot in Lubbock by phone. How about you and your week?"

As George spoke, Jennifer heard brightness in his voice, excited by what he was doing. It was infectious. "Let me make a suggestion. I'll preface by saying that due to my current pay structure with Dwayne, I can't offer to pay, but how about we go out to dinner and I'll tell you all about my week."

George chuckled. "Finances a bit tight right now?"

"Yeah," she drawled. "It'll be that way for a while. What do you say . . . you and me, dinner?"

"Let me put it this way: the story of your week is worth paying for. I'll meet you at the Village Diner," he said with no hint of hesitation.

"Give me fifteen minutes. I'm in the car heading that direction as we speak."

"You got it, kid." He ended the call.

Jennifer let the phone dangle from her fingertips still as an affection induced tingle spread over her. That brief conversation had her feeling like a teenager again, excited about spending time with George all to herself. After a few moments of a sparkling mood, a familiar murmur surfaced: *Enjoy his company, Jennifer, but be careful—very careful.* The trust bugaboo may have taken a positive step forward, but still had hold of her. George had no qualms about their relationship and where he planned on taking it. How could he? Part of him still believed they were married. He seemed to be biding his time until she came around and left his abandonment of her in the past where it belonged. Jennifer wanted to begin writing new chapters, but coming to terms with the backstory was difficult. Now that they both had returned to Smithtown to stay, maybe—just maybe—trust would have a chance to blossom. Her love for him was real, but so was lingering distrust.

The final miles went by in a blink, and she soon steered into the gravel parking lot of the most popular eatery in town. She parked next to George's car and saw him through the large window in the same corner booth where they had shared breakfast a couple of weeks ago. He was talking to the waitress and hadn't noticed her. She bounded out of the car, stepped up onto the sidewalk fronting the diner, and knocked on the window. He turned and offered a bright smile. She hurried inside and straight to the booth where he sat. "I hope you haven't been waiting long. Have you?"

His head tipped thoughtfully. "Haven't you figured out yet that even if I had to sit here for hours, the wait would be worth it?"

"Gosh . . ." Heat of embarrassment flushed her cheeks. She slid into the booth opposite him.

"Okay, Jen, tell me about your week."

"It was good," she said as the waitress placed a glass of ice water in front of her. "Picked up a few new clients. That puts me a little closer to earning an income. That's the good news."

"You say that like there's a downside."

"Sort of. Michael Lassiter wants me to meet him in Sweetwater Monday for a nine o'clock dinner meeting with our shared clients," she said, unable and unwilling to hide the dread in her voice.

"Nine O'clock in the evening?"

"Afraid so."

Why so late?"

"I suspect it was on purpose so he could make it an overnight thing. Dwayne told me that he reserved me a motel room for the night since the meeting would likely not conclude until around midnight." As she spoke, Jennifer watched the joy drain from George's face.

"If the bastard tries anything that you don't want him to, I'll break his face," he said through clenched teeth.

Jennifer smiled but said nothing more, realizing it was something she shouldn't have shared. She snaked her hand across the table and placed it over his. "I don't think it's anything I have to worry about. I can handle him. Don't worry, but thanks for the offer. You're a good friend." She patted his hand and then pulled it back to lift the menu. "Let's order. I'm hungry."

* * *

Although well intentioned, it hurt George when Jennifer referred to him simply as a good friend. The word "friend" should only be one of many that described their relationship.

He kept a close eye on Jennifer through dinner, trying to determine if her self-proclaimed dread might better be described as fear of Lassiter and his suspected intentions. She changed the subject and steered the conversation to lighter fare. Although he rolled with her into less dour territory, he committed to learning more about the man. George developed a nagging sense of concern about Lassiter's potential anger issues.

"How's your search for property going?" she asked.

"I have a couple of prospects, but both require considerable demolition and renovation," he said. "I've spent too much time getting bids on both and have yet to decide on anything."

"I've given it some thought, too."

"You have?"

"Sure. When I got home from work yesterday, I fixed myself a salad and, since the weather was mild outside about sunset, I sat on the edge of the front porch of my little rent house to eat and watch cars go by. So—"

"The Hovel, right?"

Jennifer chuckled. "Yeah. The Hovel. As I sat there eating, I envisioned two or even three rows of used vehicles between the house and the highway. It's a deep lot, you know, with good frontage. Of course, The Hovel sort of mars the appearance of the lot, but it might be useful."

"Hmm, that place never crossed my mind. Is it for sale?"

"The day I rented the house, the owner pulled up a sign that said: For Lease *or* Sale. So, yeah, I believe he'd entertain an offer," she replied, and then smiled shyly. "I have a feeling that you could work out something with the current lessee, if the owner bites on an offer. I understand she's easy to talk to and quite agreeable."

"Funny girl. But, seriously, you may have a good idea." George stroked his neck beneath his chin with the backs of his fingertips as he thought about it.

"All you'd need to do is grade the display area and then put down gravel, or pave it, or get fancy and concrete it," she said. "The old house needs remodeling desperately, but the structure is solid enough. It's about the right size and would make a good office. That done, all that would remain is putting up a sign out by the highway and voilà! You'd have a car lot."

George felt the heaviness of indecision leaving him as intention firmed to follow through on Jen's idea. He smiled at her and nodded affirmation. "I'm going to do it," he said, and maybe we—"

Jen jerked her head around and looked through the front window of the diner out onto the parking lot. "Oh shit," she hissed."

George's eyes followed. A man sat in an expensive looking black sedan staring at them.

"Let me guess, Michael Lassiter?"

Jennifer dropped her head. When she lifted it, he saw disgust. She slid out of the booth. "George, just sit. I'll go out and see what he wants and then tell him to be on his way. It probably has something to do with that Monday night meeting in Sweetwater." She marched out into the parking lot as Lassiter got out of his car.

George sipped his ice tea but kept a watchful eye on Jennifer through the diner window. She came to stand in front of Lassiter next to his car. It was clear that she lectured him about something. Her hand gestures were sharp and angry. She poked him repeatedly on the chest. Lassiter's demeanor changed. His face reddened as anger clearly ratcheted to increasing highs.

Finally, Lassiter grabbed Jennifer's wrist and yanked her finger off his chest.

Jennifer attempted to wrench it loose.

Lassiter twisted her arm up and away.

She grimaced and spoke loud enough to get the attention of others in the diner. All heads turned toward the spectacle.

Jennifer slapped Lassiter across the face.

George leaped up and jogged out of the diner to the parking lot.

It appeared Lassiter was on the verge of losing control. His fist was doubled. He shouted, babbling bullshit about being led-on and something about deserving her affection and a few other idiotic things.

George saw that in another second or two, the guy would likely hit Jennifer with a clenched fist. He shouted, "If you hit her, you son-of-a-bitch, be prepared to take a bath in your own blood!"

Lassiter finally noticed George and forcefully threw Jennifer's arm back down to her side. She backed away massaging her wrist.

George didn't slow until he came to stand between them, facing Lassiter. Lassiter was a big man, three to four inches taller than George, broader in the shoulders and likely outweighed him by twenty or more pounds. George's anger and need to defend Jennifer overshadowed hesitance over the disparity. He glared up at Lassiter as he rolled both hands into tight fists. "I suggest you sheathe your sword, get back in your fancy car, and drive on out of our little town," he said, his voice seethed with hate, even though it was the first time he had ever seen Lassiter.

Lassiter looked over George's shoulder to Jennifer. He pointed an accusing finger at her. "This isn't over," he shouted.

George took an aggressive step toward Lassiter. "Oh yes, it is, you arrogant bastard," he snarled.

Jennifer grabbed George's arm and pulled him away before Lassiter redirected that anger. "He's not worth it."

Lassiter finally yielded and flung open his car door. "I'm outa here."

As Lassiter dropped into the driver's seat and started the car, only then did George notice that most of the customers in the diner had joined them in the parking lot. Lassiter sprayed gravel, screeching onto the blacktop, heading south toward Abilene.

Jennifer pulled George around to face her and pulled him into a thankful embrace, pressing her cheek to his chest.

The small crowd applauded.

George's anger drained away almost as fast as it came up. "Are you okay?"

She looked up at him. "I'm fine. I guess I overplayed it. I told him straight out that I'd be driving back to Smithtown Monday night and not staying overnight. I think the way I chose to state it made him mad." She smiled sheepishly.

George chuckled. "Ya think?"

Jennifer returned her cheek to his chest and squeezed him tight. "Shut up and hold me," she whispered.

George stroked the back of her head. He didn't want the moment to end, but Jennifer gave a final hug, growled affectionately and then backed away. "I have part of a bottle of bourbon at the house. Care to follow me to my place for a drink?"

"I'm glad you asked. Otherwise, I'd have to stalk you back to your place without invitation."

Chapter 24 ~ An Evening to Forget

Jennifer checked her rearview mirror repeatedly, making sure George was keeping his promise to follow her home. She needed this and she needed it with him. Although it was only supposed to be for a drink and some company, her need for this companionship went deeper than a few laughs while buzzed. A yearning for the closeness of a man, but not any man. It had to be the guy she watched in flicking glances in her rearview mirror. She had developed a tingling sense of desperation. It was hard to define, but she was certain that George was the key and not simply the need for some random guy. She shook off misgivings and chuckled at her concern. She didn't know why she worried. George was committed to her from the moment he woke in the hospital. It was her own fear of abandonment that wedged a wrench in the gears.

As she dwelt on that, the humor of it sagged away. *Damn it, Jennifer!* She slapped her thigh hard enough to sting. *You know you love him. You can't stay away from him. For God's sake, moving to Smithtown to get away from Michael was the excuse, getting closer to George was the reason. Hell, girl, moving here hadn't crossed your mind until George talked about it. Why can't you accept that? You have to stop dipping your toes in. Take the leap!*

Jennifer had become so lost in thought she almost missed the turn into her own driveway. She braked hard and went into the turn simultaneously. George pulled up beside her as she was getting out of her car. He was laughing. "What's so funny?" she asked, as he got out and slammed his door behind him.

"Were you in a hurry to get home?"

She smiled. "I suppose it looked that way." She whirled around and headed for the front door of her house and waved him on. "There's a bourbon bottle in there with our name on it." She attempted to open the rickety screen door wider for better access to the main door, but it drooped onto buckled tongue-and-groove wood planks of the porch and wedged tightly. About halfway open was as far as it was going. "One of the first things I need to do is remove the screen door. It serves no purpose and it's ugly." She playfully kicked at the disengaged corner of the door.

He gave the whole house a cursory look. "The place doesn't have an abundance of curb appeal."

"Hey, dude, this is my home you're talking about. Be kind."

As she unlocked the door and gestured for George to come in, he hesitated at the large rusting novelty thermometer nailed to the outside door jamb trim board with an ad for a local feed and seed store on it.

The store had gone out of business years ago. An odd expression came over him. He gently ran his fingertips over its severely aged surface.

"What are you doing?" she asked.

The question jolted him back to the moment. "Sorry," he blurted, and then continued the almost mesmerized examination of the instrument. "Like I told you, this old house was our first home in—you know, that other life. This old thermometer was an abrupt reminder."

"I remember," she whispered as she took his other hand into hers.

He sighed. "This rusty and dented old piece of stamped tin reminds me of a cold winter day when you told me that you were pregnant with Rachel Irissa."

It occurred to Jennifer that George had only spoken of that imaginary life in bits and pieces. She had been steering him away from the subject. It had been subtle, but she would only allow him to quickly relate remembered scenarios in the broadest sense. If he happened to dwell on any single event of that dream life, she'd cut him off and change the subject. She had been fearful of pressing him for details. The excuse was to prevent upsetting his mental stability, but also for selfish reasons. She had her own tipping point. If she fell, it would be into a love of no return. But now, suddenly, she craved knowing all there was to be known about how he had envisioned their married life. The man had lived sixteen years within a one-week coma. He had to have hundreds of stories if it was as real as he repeatedly said it had been. She wanted to hear them all. She wanted details—to know everything. Over drinks seemed like the best way to begin learning what George Waller wanted to recreate with her in this life—in this world, the real one. She tugged on his arm. "Come on in and sit. I'll get the bottle and a couple of glasses."

As George entered, she noticed a tangible sense of déjà vu come over him. He stopped just inside the front door and slowly scanned all within view. She thought she noticed him shudder.

Hesitating, giving him the moment, she finally asked, "Have you actually ever been inside this house?"

He slowly shook his head. "Uh-uh. Oddly though, the layout is pretty much like what I had envisioned. Although, as small as this place is, it couldn't have very many different floor plan options. The furniture is a lot nicer now."

She continued to the kitchen. "Well, we *were* newlyweds, after all."

"Right. I was terrified about having enough money to support a family," he called out through the kitchen wall, as he sat on the sofa.

Jennifer came back into the room. "I want to know more. Start at the beginning. I want to know every detail you remember, starting with waking up in the church on our wedding day until that day you submitted to hypnosis by Doctor Levenson, or whatever you thought his other name was, that brought you out of the coma." She set the glasses on a coffee table fronting the sofa and poured each about half full.

"Are you sure? It's a long story. We're talking epic."

"Well," she said, raising her glass. "We have plenty of bourbon and I have nowhere to go, if you don't." She sat on the opposite end of the sofa and made a show of becoming comfortable.

"All right, but remember you asked for it."

George began by explaining floating in the tepid river that he now understood was likely a mental bridge between that imaginary world and the real one. He then recounted highly detailed stories with Sweet Jen, hitting only highlights of less interesting times. Still, he told her everything he could remember of that sixteen-year marriage that never was. Jennifer interrupted occasionally, but only for clarification. Otherwise, George spoke for two hours. The bourbon ran out about the same time the story ended. The exhausting day of client solicitation and alcohol had taken a toll. Jennifer's eyes were red and her lids heavy. She yawned. "I'm sorry. I guess I'm a little sleepy."

George stood. "I'd better get on back to the motel and let you get some rest, but I'll see you again soon. We can talk more about this place becoming a pre-owned auto dealership."

"Sure." Jennifer sprang to her feet, but stumbled sideways a step.

George came around the coffee table in a rush to grab her arm.

"Oops," she said, snickering. "That bourbon affected me more than I thought."

He slid his hand down her arm into her hand and squeezed it. "You okay?"

"Yeah." She looked up and her eyes locked onto his. In fact, better than okay," she cooed.

His examination of her clearly sought more than her level of sobriety. He took a step closer, pulling her into him and then placed her arms around his waist and held them there. He leaned in to kiss her.

She began pulling her face away, but then stopped. She wanted this. She deeply wanted this. *Oh, what the hell . . .* She met his advance. As their lips came together, she took the initiative, forcing her tongue between his lips, exploring. It may have been exhaustion or the alcohol, or perhaps just the deep need for the touch, smell, and feel of this man. She didn't know and didn't care, throwing a full measure of desire into the moment. The need was mutual. George cupped her cheeks between his palms as she slid her hands behind his head and grabbed his hair. She held onto to him desperately, as the urgency for closeness escalated.

Jennifer broke away, grabbed George's arm, and took him in tow to the bedroom. At the foot of the bed, they roughly removed one another's clothes. There was no talk and no need for it. The urge was as old as humanity itself and nothing would get in its way or stop it now.

George slowed the pace and guided Jennifer down onto her back on the bed. He slid on his side up to where he had easy access to her lips. He gently pressed his onto hers. She took his lower lip between her teeth and bit down, but only a little, and then sucked his lip between hers. He submissively allowed whatever her heart desired. She desired it all.

George pressed his body against her. His fingers traveled down between her breasts.

She shivered.

With the flat of his hand, he rubbed soft circles on her stomach and, with each revolution, inching farther down.

Jennifer grabbed his wrist and stopped the motion. She pulled her lips away from his and whispered into his mouth, "If you keep that up, this'll be over before it starts."

He smiled and positioned himself over her as their bodies came together.

She wanted it to be slow and sweet, but it simply could not be. The sexual drought they both had endured caught up with them. It was urgent and hot, coming to a blissful and mutual end all too soon.

George rolled off and snuggled his face into the side of Jennifer's head. After only a moment, he began drifting off to sleep and whispered into her ear, "Oh, Marie, I love you so much."

When that name came out of his mouth, it was as if a blistering hot stone had replaced her heart. She was paralyzed and couldn't move, suddenly aware of the mistake she had made. Sobriety was equally sudden. Modesty came back. She pulled away from him as he snored softly. She covered herself with the sheet and tucked a cloth wall between them, wondering if she should even stay in the same bed.

It was too soon to be doing this, if ever. George's mind remained intertwined between two worlds. She had given herself a conundrum. She wondered if she had gone so far as to be incapable of turning back. Was her love for George as deep as her simple need for sexual contact? Could she confine herself to this one time, or had the floodgates come down? George was not the only one caught between two worlds. Sean's name could have just as easily slipped out.

She rolled away from him, pulled her knees up high, clutched the sheet like a child scared of the dark, and she cried.

Chapter 25 ~ Just Business

Jennifer slept little Friday night. She quietly slid out of bed and left George sleeping, having no heart for a confrontation over his slip of the tongue that he likely didn't remember. *How could I have allowed the bourbon to do my thinking for me?* She rolled her eyes. *But, that's exactly what I did.*

She dressed and sat in a chair in a corner of the bedroom, pulling her knees up, planting her heels on the edge of the worn wingback chair's seat and then surrounding them with circled arms. Brooding, she watched George breathing deep and even as he slept. She contemplated the complications of their shared situation. Sullenness pressed her shoulders into a slump.

It was awkward. If the evening had been anywhere but in her own house, she would've left seconds after the name "Marie" cleared George's lips and fallen asleep. She had nowhere to go. Besides, she had no right to be angry. Marie was his dead wife—not enough time had passed. His wounds of loss were raw. She thought about her own loss and remembered how difficult the struggle had been. It could be no less for George. He had to have been in the midst of a fight against allowing that loss, as heart-wrenching as it was, to control his future. The poor guy had the added problem of separating real from unreal. His head must swirl with memories he still sorted—genuine from imagined. His problem had become her problem. Feelings for this man lying asleep on her bed intensified at an alarming rate. The whispered refrain, "I love you, Marie," played over and over in her mind. Fresh tears threatened to spill. She twirled hair dangling over her cheek with her thumb and forefinger and, as a sudden spark of anger at herself struck, she grabbed the dark auburn strands and pulled, wanting the pain. With quivering lip and clenched teeth, she thought, *God damn it!* Her thoughts remained selfish despite good intentions. She simply couldn't abide being made love to with another woman's name upon her lover's lips. The battle within was turning into a tornadic vortex of jealousy, altruism, good intentions, friendship and, of course, love.

After a few moments, her mind settled. She forced her breathing back to within calm limits, realizing that her love for this man transcended the hitch. It should only be a speed bump in the relationship. She pondered that word. George Waller was not, and may never be, a hundred-percent hers. Welling tears finally rolled from her eyes and ran in rivulets down to form bulging drops on her jaw.

In a few more minutes, he'd wake. She had to, somehow, get him out of the house without alerting him to her fear-filled thoughts. She needed time alone to work on getting past the ache that the utterance of that one word—that name—had drilled painfully into her heart.

George drew a sudden breath and snorted. He licked his lips and swirled his tongue.

Jennifer hurriedly dropped her feet to the floor, swept tears from her cheeks, and came to her feet.

His lids parted, and his eyes moved around, scoping the room, possibly having forgotten where he was. But after only a couple of seconds scanning the area, George's eyes locked onto her with laser-like efficiency. "Good morning," he said in a low gravelly voice. "Have you been up long?"

She bounced a fast smile but could not hold it. "Only a few minutes. Did you sleep well?"

George didn't immediately answer. His smile broadened. "Afterwards, I slept very well."

"Why don't you get up and put your clothes on while I make coffee?" she replied, refusing to acknowledge the intimate implication. She spun and marched out of the bedroom. Once clear of the door, she stepped laterally and leaned back against the wall. Her immediate goal was to reestablish even breathing and swallow an overpowering urge to cry because one question crossed her mind when he alluded to the lovemaking: *Did he close his eyes and see Marie while making love to me last night, or was it truly an unintended slip? I have to know.*

Over coffee, George attempted conversation. Jennifer fought a near uncontrollable urge to allow hurt feelings to shade her demeanor, although primed and ready to spew from her at any moment. She worked so hard at the neutral facade that she offered little beyond single syllable responses. It didn't go unnoticed.

"Are you okay?" he asked.

"I'm just being a worry-wart. Nothing for you to worry about. I need time alone to work through some stuff to get my new life here in order and settle in." She gestured, sweeping an arm in a wide arc toward stacked boxes. She forced a grin. "As you can tell, I'm some time away from making that happen. I'm developing a to-do-list in my head for the weekend. That's all. I apologize for not giving you full attention."

"Anything I can help with?"

"No," she blurted, and then became embarrassed by the abruptness of her answer. "I mean, not right now." She smiled. "Thanks for the offer, though."

"Your mouth is smiling but your eyes aren't."

"I'll be okay." She turned her mug up and downed the final swallow of tepid coffee then flipped a finger casually toward the boxes. "I don't mean to be a bad hostess, but I have housekeeping to set up and want to get it done today—all of it. Then, I can put it behind me and get on to other things."

"Sorry, I didn't mean to hold you up. I don't have anything on my agenda for the day. So, I've been in no hurry, but I'll leave and let you get on with it." He rose and headed for the front door. She followed. He opened the door and then turned to face her. He leaned in for a kiss. She turned her lips away, presenting her cheek. He hesitated, but then kissed it, lingering momentarily. "I could help you with those boxes, if you like."

"No, no. It's not necessary. The work requires no concentration and will allow me time to think through some things. See you next week," she said, sweeping him out of the house with the closing door, just as a formation of Sandhill cranes passed high overhead, flying south, trilling their migratory song. Jennifer leaned back against the door. *That's what I should do. Pack up and fly away.*

* * *

Jennifer spent the weekend numbed by George's unintentional slip. It's not like she was not aware that Marie had been the love of his life for sixteen years—real years—not coma fabricated years. She wondered if her near future should include George in a romantic way. Her muddled mind could not decide—confusion all-consuming.

Jennifer perfunctorily unloaded moving boxes, did laundry, bought groceries, and ran errands. By Sunday night, she retained little memory of having done those things. Monday at work was no improvement. It was a good thing that Friday's client solicitation trip had gone so well. It was a measure of comfort when she chose to delve into busy work requiring little attention to detail and did nothing to advance her cause with Brewster's law practice. Powers of concentration were at a premium.

After noon, her thoughts turned to the trip to Sweetwater to meet with Michael Lassiter and their shared clients later that evening—much later—far too late for a business meeting. She wondered how the clients felt about such a late meeting. Then she remembered how persuasive Michael could be when there was something he wanted. In this case it was her. The clients had little to do with it, but everything to do with the proximity of Sweetwater to where she now resided. She wondered what cock and bull story he fed the clients to get them to agree to a meeting so late in the evening.

Anger welled as her train of thought took side tracks off in the wrong direction, having latched onto Michael's lecherous nature. She realized that she needed to shake off personal problems and put together a plan for the meeting and what her contribution to it would be on behalf of The Brewster Law Firm. She forced aside dogged thoughts of relationships. Fear of failure, working on Brewster's behalf took center stage, sharpening her mind. The upcoming meeting was a matter of taking a breath and getting on with it. It was just business.

A semblance of the clever and witty Jennifer returned by departure. She looked forward to alone time during the drive to Sweetwater. Of course, that treasured time of solitude and ease would end abruptly upon arrival at the motel in Sweetwater. She answered a series of concerned questions from Brewster with panache and patiently listened to his worried advice. In the end she advised him, "Go home and be with your sweet wife. Don't worry so much. I'll represent us well. Promise. If I encounter something I shouldn't be handling on my own as a paralegal, take comfort that you are only a phone call away. I will not dispense legal advice beyond prepared paperwork." Her affection for this man was growing fast. Pleasing him was important to her.

Brewster smiled. He slid back in his chair. His body language settled. He began rocking gently, chair squeaking, while lacing his fingers together over his protruding belly. "You're a treasure. Did you know that?"

Jennifer chuckled. "No, but, please, don't ever stop saying it."

Darkness descended over Smithtown. Jennifer didn't at all like how short the daylight hours were this time of year. Not only did it get dark early, she now had to contend with an arctic front sweeping through, driving gusty north winds. The temperature was dropping fast. She tried outrunning a chill to her car. She didn't win the race and shivered mightily, fumbling to get the key into the ignition. The engine turned, slowly at first, but then cranked and eased into a fast idle. She looked skyward and sent up a silent prayer: *Please, God, no car trouble—not tonight.*

About an hour and a half later, good fortune was with Jennifer as she took the designated exit off the Interstate into Sweetwater. She pulled into the parking lot of the Hampton Inn where Michael had reserved a meeting room. She took a moment to steel herself for what would be a confrontation with Michael's expected pleas for her to stay the night. It didn't take clairvoyance to know it was coming. The man didn't give up easily. He was conquest oriented—always had been. Romance was never his thing. Whenever he attempted showing a romantic side, it came off shallow and artificial. She saw Michael Lassiter for what he truly was—a spoiled rich kid that had grown into an adult version, getting what he wanted and damn well felt he deserved it. He was never thankful to anyone or anything, always self-centered and self-serving.

Easing through the parking lot searching for an open slot she noticed Michael's BMW. A parking spot was open next to it. She passed it by, choosing one in another row farther back in the lot and a few more steps she'd have to run for the warmth waiting beyond the lobby door. She gathered her purse and a satchel crammed tight and bulging with information about the lawsuit that she had reviewed. She prepared for the blast of frigid air she was about to encounter. She threw open the car door, bounded out, and raced for the entrance to the hotel, again trying to outrun a shiver. The blustery north wind seemed to be stronger in Sweetwater than it was in Smithtown—colder, too. As she crossed the threshold into the lobby and the automatic sliding doors closed behind her, she blew warm breath into her cupped hands and then chuckled at a thought. *It's not colder here. I'm dreading being near Michael. That's enough to make anyone shiver.* It was absurd, but humorous. A smile was still on her lips as she approached the clerk at the front desk.

The young man behind the counter matched her smile. "It's a cold one out there this evening."

Jennifer shivered once for his benefit. "Sure is. Could you point me toward the conference room? I'm late for a meeting."

Finger extended, the young man replied, "Take that corridor to the left. It's the fifth door on the right. You can't miss it."

She was already on the move as she said over her shoulder. "Thanks."

"I hope your meeting goes well," the young man said to her back.

She hurried from the lobby, turning left into a long corridor as instructed. A mirror caught her attention and she took a moment to check her appearance. She finger combed her long dark hair that had been whipped by the frigid wind. She patted it into a better shape, turning her head this way then that, searching for even the tiniest imperfection in her makeup that might be a distraction during a business meeting. She saw nothing objectionable and continued her march down the hall, stopping at the designated door. A small engraved brass placard on the wall next to it indicated that this was indeed the conference room. She took drew a breath and opened the door.

Seven men ranging in age from mid-fifties to seventy, plus a couple of spouses sat on one side and the ends of the long table. Michael sat alone in the center on the other side. As she approached him, he stood. "Gentleman . . . and ladies, of course …," he smiled condescendingly at the women, " I'd like you to meet Jennifer Andrews. She worked with our firm while we were building the case on your behalf. She is now with the Brewster Law Office in Smithtown. She, and her new firm, will be collaborating with my firm on your case so that we might not allow any stone to remain unturned or any detail, no matter how minor, to go unnoticed. The collaboration of Dwayne Brewster's office will be of invaluable benefit to that end."

The men stood, quick to smile, extending friendly hands across the table and offered words of welcome. Jennifer was instantly comfortable with these salt of the earth country people. As pleasantries were exchanged, Michael pulled out the chair next to him for her. She didn't reference the gesture, ignoring it entirely. She pulled out the chair next to it and sat. She had quickly determined that the empty seat between them would serve as a necessary buffer from pawing hands. It had happened before in other meetings in Abilene and she didn't want even the possibility of a repeat here.

The meeting went well, for the most part. There was only one contentious moment. Michael made a reference to the two of them working shoulder to shoulder, whatever it took—even pulling all-nighters to get the job done. Michael's inflection made it clear that the remark was meant as humorous. But it was not at all funny to Jennifer. She remained stoic. All it took was a sideways smirk from Michael for Jennifer to shut him down with the fast retort, "Long hours, maybe. All-nighters? Never." It was enough to elicit exchanged glances from the folks across the table, especially the two wives, who seemed no more amused by the suggestive remark than Jennifer was. Michael's quick smile went to a frown just as quickly. An uncomfortable period of silence ensued around the table.

One of the wives queried, "I did hear it correctly, didn't I? You two are working *together* on our case. Right?"

Jennifer became embarrassed. "Of course. Both our firms will be working together on your behalf."

"Whew, for a moment, I thought we misunderstood and that you are the opposing counsel," she quipped, as the other plaintiffs grinned and chuckled.

The meeting came to an end after eleven o'clock and the clients filed toward the door of the conference room. Jennifer heard one of the wives whisper to her husband, "If you agree to another meeting this late, I'm divorcing you, Harvey."

"Yes dear," he replied.

"Now, let's get home. I'm exhausted," his wife quickly added.

All went suddenly ear-ringing quiet when the door closed behind the couple. Jennifer found herself alone with Michael, knowing that time was now of the essence to get out of there and on her way back to

Smithtown before he had a chance to play his game. She gathered papers together and unceremoniously stuffed them back inside her satchel. "It's time for me to hit the highway home."

Michael approached her and attempted reaching for her hand.

She pulled away, not allowing him to even touch it. "No, Michael. Don't start."

"Come on, Jenny. It's cold outside and late. I have that room reserved for you. Why don't you stay the night and get an early start in the morning?"

"If I could keep you out of my room, I would. But I can't, so I won't."

"We were good together, once upon a time. Would it be so bad now?" he asked, attempting the soft approach. As talented as Michael was in arguing cases before a jury, this was one area he was an abject failure. The guy simply could not convey romantic feelings. It was a thin mask that couldn't hide the conceit of his true self.

Her mouth fell open. She shot him a hard look. "Michael," she whined, "how many times do I have to say it? I have no feelings for you and the attraction I did have was born of not wanting to be alone after a traumatic episode in my life. I've tried to be nice but you're forcing me to say it, it was a huge mistake. There is no *we*. Please stop trying to recreate something that never was." Her own word choice shocked her into thoughtful silence because that was exactly what George was attempting to do with her. She shook it off. This was different—very different.

The lines of his face hardened. "You're telling me that what we had was a mistake—that I'm a mistake?"

Although her comment had plainly angered him, she didn't care. His contrived emotional states were of no concern, but suddenly laughable. He ran through a litany of them in less than a couple of minutes, throwing them at her to see what might stick. She smiled. She tipped her head and snickered.

His face reddened, and the veins stood proud on his temples. He took an aggressive step toward her. "You think it's funny?" His lips pulled into a hard, straight line.

"I'm glad you finally are seeing yourself for what you are, a mistake." She chuckled.

The red on his face took a darker turn as he moved toward explosive rage.

Jennifer's quick assessment told her that she probably screwed up by driving a humorous knife deep into his ego, which could only be matched by his arrogance, refusing to fail at anything ever. She pumped an open palm at him. "Calm down, Michael." She suddenly regretted making light of his proposition.

"You bitch," he shouted and then swung a hard backhand into her cheek.

The force sent her spinning over a chair, stumbling to the floor as the chair crashed to it its side. She quickly sat up. She swiped hair away from her eyes so as not to lose sight of what he might do next. Jamming alternating heels into the floor, she pushed herself backwards until the wall stopped her retreat. Her skirt had risen to her waist, obscenely exposing everything beneath. She was terrified that his volatile anger might not have run its course. She had never seen him this angry before. She turned her injured face away and covered it with both arms.

He took a long single step and stopped next to her.

Without looking up, she shouted, "Please, Michael! Stop it! I'm sorry, I'm sorry. No more, please!" Hearing no response, she peeked up at him over her elbows. What she saw shocked her. The expression on his face, this time, was sheer terror.

"Oh God, Jenny. I'm the one that's sorry, so sorry. I didn't mean it." He attempted to help her up.

Jennifer refused his hand and rolled over onto hands and knees. She crawled a short way and then came to her feet while still on the move. "Stay away from me," she shouted. She snatched her purse and satchel from the table and hurried for the door. "You son of a bitch," she growled, and then her face screwed down tight and she exploded in tears.

She flung the door open to see the night clerk, alerted by the commotion. "Is everything okay in here?" he asked.

"No," she blurted, "Not in the slightest." She hurried past the young man, avoiding his examining gaze. Engulfed in fear and anger, she ran down the hall, turning into the lobby and sprinted for the exit, sobbing all the way.

Jennifer sat in her car attempting to recompose before getting on the highway. Her face stung. A burning pain localized high on her cheekbone near her eye. *Now I have to deal with a black eye and a lot of unwanted questions. Crap!* She looked into the cold night sky through the windshield and saw streaming clouds obscure the moon. Her eyes followed them. This time, the cold held no sway as she looked toward heaven. *What next, God? What next? There must be a better life out there somewhere. Where is it? Will I ever see it?* After a moment of searching the sky for truth, she began to realize that no answers were forthcoming. Even if there was an answer out there somewhere, she wouldn't find it tonight. Loneliness weighted her head onto the steering wheel, wishing for less reasons to cry.

Chapter 26 ~ In Need of Advice

Tuesday morning Jennifer stood before the bathroom mirror, dancing fingertips over the damage done by the back of Michael's hand. The painful red mark the night before had darkened into a mostly purple and bluish bruise on her left cheekbone, radiating laterally to beneath her eye. It was puffy and sensitive to even the gentlest pressure. Discoloration would be difficult to conceal with makeup, maybe impossible, for a day or two.

Jennifer finally gave up experimenting with various cosmetic applications, having reached the point that the makeup itself gave her face a mannequin-like appearance. Maybe in a couple of days the bruise might be camouflaged, but not now. She leaned against the bathroom vanity, supporting her weight with both hands, as she attempted fabricating a story to tell Dwayne about what happened to cause such an injury. It was so obviously not the result of an accident, but she had to think of something. She didn't want the sweet old guy to walk away from collaboration on the lawsuit defending her honor. Her problem with Michael was hers, not Dwayne's. She didn't know, but figured the lawsuit might be the biggest case the old man had ever been part of. No suitable explanation for the injury came to her.

Jennifer stepped out of the bathroom and picked up her watch from the small table next to her bed. It was after eight o'clock. Dwayne would be expecting her at work by eight-thirty and there she stood in her preferred sleeping attire—oversized sweat bottoms and a floppy t-shirt. Even beyond the injury, she looked like hell, having arrived home after midnight and then lying awake for hours.

Jennifer's world abruptly came crashing in. Her lip quivered. Life and indecision were becoming too much to bear. Her burdens were exhausting, and she was alone in bearing them. Her personal life was screwed up. It seemed her career was now heading in the same direction. She collapsed onto the bed. It had become almost normal for tears to flow freely and suddenly. Remaining in control was unimportant. She needed this—sobbing loudly, growling, and squealing. Her face buried in a pillow, pounding it with clenched fists. There was no one around, and she was not certain it would have mattered if there had been.

After a time, she came down from the angry emotional high and decided that going to work was out of the question, at least for today. Even before her diaphragm had ceased to spasm from the crying, she dialed Dwayne at home.

"Hello. Brewster here."

"Dwayne, if it's okay with you, I think I'll attempt another client solicitation day today. So, I'll be on the highway and out of town most of the day. Are you okay with that?"

"After the day you had Friday, how could I possibly not be okay with it?" he asked with a cheerful sparkle in his reply.

"In that case, I'll be back in the office tomorrow and begin the task of writing thank you letters with retainer contracts attached, confirming in writing the attorney/client relationships. How about that for a plan?"

"Excellent. I'll expect you back in the office tomorrow morning. By the way, thank you so much for taking the job as seriously as you do."

Jennifer cringed at the compliment. It wasn't that she didn't take her job seriously. It was of supreme importance to her. She had just lied to him, but she couldn't think of any other choice if she wanted to protect his law practice and her employment at the same time. She ended the call feeling badly about the concocted story, having no intention of making a client solicitation trip. The list of lies to her new boss was growing alarmingly long. For today, her goal was time to allow swelling to go down in her cheek and, hopefully, the gruesome rainbow of colors would fade to a concealable shade. Alternating ice packs were her only true plan and one would be against her cheek most of the day. It also gave her a day to think of a good excuse that would be a spin on the truth, not a lie. She also had to find a positive perspective. She couldn't be sneaking off to cry all the time. She frowned, but thoughtfully so. This final goal for today was likely beyond her reach. And then there was George—her favorite problem that crossed her mind. She smiled.

Like a flash in her face, it came to her. Maybe there was something she could do about the spiraling mess she was in. The first step would be to talk it out with a trusted confidant—someone to bounce the problem off and maybe get helpful hints in the process. She snatched the phone back up and pecked in the number for Alex Burton. It only rang once. "Alex? Jennifer. Are you at work already?"

"Yeah. What's up?"

"What are you doing for lunch?"

"The usual . . . burger, fries and a soda from the drive-in. Why?"

"I have chicken breasts in the fridge and a couple of nice size potatoes. How about you come to my house for lunch? I'll roast the chicken, bake the potatoes and then heat up green beans to go with it."

"Is your lunch break long enough to do all that?" he asked.

"I'm not going to the office today."

"Oh?"

"Today, I need a friend and you're it."

* * *

"Shit, Jennifer. What's that on your face?" Alex asked as soon as she answered his knock at the door.

"That's what I need to talk to you about. But it's only one of several things in my life that are reeling out of control."

"I suppose it partially answers the question of why you didn't go to work today, but I gotta tell ya, kid, you certainly have my curiosity up. You have my full attention."

Jennifer grabbed his hand. "Come on, let's have lunch first. If we start talking about all the crap going on with me, the food will get cold and possibly not eaten at all. I promised to feed you, and that's what I'm going to do."

Although always aware of this little house on the highway, it was the first time Alex had ever been inside. It badly needed remodeling. The floor in the front room was laid in linoleum with a pattern that hearkened to life in the fifties. Areas of it had worn entirely through. The walls were papered with a water-stained, puckered and peeling floral print in a faded lilac. Alex bounced on his toes a couple of times. "The old house seems solid enough," he observed.

Without breaking stride, Jennifer glanced over her shoulder. "That's the nicest thing you can say about my hovel, huh?"

He grinned. "It's never good to lie to a friend."

Jennifer jerked a smile. "It just so happens that that comment goes right to the heart of why I invited you over for lunch today."

It was obvious that Jennifer wasn't in a mood to buy into his jokes. He could read Jennifer well, always could. Alex figured that he'd have to control his happy-go-lucky side, but it wouldn't be easy. He was a jokester—always had been. He needed to listen and support whatever came out of his friend's mouth. Her dour expression kicked his curiosity up yet another notch.

It may have been Jennifer's plan to finish eating before getting to the point, but Alex was impatient and couldn't set it aside. He talked around mouthfuls of chicken and potatoes, getting the low-down on the Michael Lassiter assault. "You know, Jen, George and I were not joking when we told you that we'd be happy to drive to Abilene and put a few bruises on that guy's face for you. I bet we could decorate that perfect skin of his better than he did yours. Us country boys don't take kindly to strange men treatin' our women-folk that way," he drawled.

"No!" Jennifer blurted, wagging a stern finger at him. "That's not funny. Get that notion out of your head. Physical violence is not an option—not on my behalf." She then flipped up a warning palm and waved it in his face. "By the way, I'm trusting you not to tell George about what happened in Sweetwater. He's the other half of my problem."

Alex stopped chewing. Surprise froze his expression as he forced down the food in his mouth. He had a faint grin, still not taking her concerns all that seriously. "Are you telling me that I need to bruise George a little for you, too?"

Jennifer rolled her eyes. "Surely, you're joking."

Without taking his eyes from hers, he replied, "I hope I am. Am I?"

"Oh, shut up."

Alex smiled at her and forked another piece of chicken, shoving it into his mouth and then said around, "Shootfire, girl. You know me well enough to realize that I wouldn't hurt George, but I might talk harshly to him for ya." He kept smiling, unable to resist levity.

Jennifer didn't respond to the flippancy. He wanted to keep her from getting too moody. It wasn't working as well as he would have hoped. Her expression darkened. "Look, I love George—always have. Even throughout my marriage to Sean, George was never far from my thoughts. Although he had been a teenage ass to me. It took years to get over my anger for his sudden departure the day before our wedding all those years ago. But now that both our lives have taken dramatic turns, my feelings for him are back in a big way and, frankly, it's scaring hell out of me."

Alex ran a napkin across his mouth and shoved his plate back. "That, you didn't need to tell me, but I don't see the problem. It's no secret that ol' George loves you just as much, maybe more—*a lot* more, considering his sixteen-year imagined life with you."

"Don't you see," she implored. "That's exactly the problem."

Alex sat straight and ran fingers over his receding hairline. "You're even more confusing to talk to than my wife." He belched. "By the way, thanks for lunch."

She finally smiled. "You always were good at not allowing me to get too glum about anything."

"Clever little devil, ain't I?" he said. "Let's pretend I'm really dense and slow witted. Spell it out for me."

"Pretend?" She lifted one eyebrow and tipped her head.

"That's the Jennifer I know, sarcastic on her darkest days. Now, tell me again what your problem is and, this time, make it sound like a problem."

Jennifer drew an exaggerated breath and huffed it away. "Okay. I have abandonment issues I can't get over, around, or through. George leaves me before our wedding and then years later I lose a husband without adequate time to prepare for the traumatic absence from my life. Now, I can pick up the pieces and move on with George.

Unfortunately, each time I find myself getting comfortable, he says or does something that reminds me that he's not far enough along in his healing process, regardless how often he says he wants to be with me. I know he wants me, but I'm having a helluva time believing it's for durable reasons. I have doubts that I can live up to his idealized version of me. I know he loves me, but does it have depth, or would I simply be filling a void in his life that he'd come to regret when he realizes that I'm *not* the Sweet Jen he thinks I am?" As she spoke, Jennifer's eyes glossed with renewed emotion. "And, now, I have Michael Lassiter showing up in my life and complicating my career goals. Even after what he did to me," she caressed the injured cheek with her fingertips, "I can't afford to push him away and risk losing a client that Dwayne Brewster figuratively dances a daily jig over. If I push back too hard at Michael, I'll be directly responsible for losing the account. Mister Brewster has been good to me. I can't do that to him." She hugged herself as if suddenly chilled. Her face tightened, and she started to cry. "Alex, I don't know what to do. My life is so messed up. I can't talk to George about it. He might do felonious damage to Michael if he knew about the jerk hitting me, *or* get himself hurt . . . or, God forbid, get killed trying. And, of course, George is the other part of my problem." She covered her face, but didn't attempt to stanch free flowing tears. "Alex, what do I do? What the hell do I do?" Her voice trailed off, replaced by a ragged sob.

Alex rose and hurried around to Jennifer's side of the table and knelt beside her chair. He put an arm around her shoulders and squeezed. "Shh, it's okay, Jen. Everything will work itself out. Life has a way of finding balance. All you have to do is visualize and then internalize where you want the road ahead to take you. Once that's accomplished, you'll automatically stay on that path and the outcome will be inevitable."

Jennifer swiveled around in the chair to face him. "Oh Alex. You *are* such a dear friend." She kissed his forehead and hugged him as tight as she could.

He pushed hair away from her face. "I have my moments."

"Yeah, my own personal therapist with chicken breath." She laughed through her tears as she stared into Alex's smiling eyes.

He gently reached over her head and pulled hair on the other side of her face away from the bruise on her cheek for a better look at its size. *I still wish she'd let me give that Lassiter guy an ass-whoopin'.*

She swiped away tears, clearly wanting to put on a happy face. "Well, my day is set in stone and it revolves around bruise management. I'll be intimately attached to an ice pack all day."

Alex kissed his own finger and touched her forehead with it. "As your friend, I'm guaranteeing you that when the smoke clears from your current situation, you'll have exactly what you want and it'll last as long as you want it to last."

Chapter 27 ~ Don't Tell George

"Let me guess. You quit your job at the Cottonseed Delinting Plant, bought a farm, and now you want to buy a tractor," Alex inquired of Lenny as he came through the door of the John Deere dealership. "At least I sure hope that's the case. I need a commission check this week."

"Sorry, man. I can't afford to buy a bag of potting soil, much less a farm—or a tractor, for that matter."

"In that case, I won't ask you to buy my lunch." Alex cocked his head inquisitively. "Although, your presence here does present an interesting question. What are you doing here in the middle of a work day on a Friday?"

"Let me start by saying that your assessment of me quitting my job was not far off the mark. I got sick of that supervisor, the whiny bastard, and walked off the job." Lenny sighed, then continued, "I may not have a job Monday. I suppose I should've gone ahead and formalized it by yelling *I quit* into his face. But, I didn't. I just left."

"Ouch! Not a good move. Although, it is a good thing that you didn't tell him that you quit."

"Why?"

"You should never leave a job before you have another one lined up. Go back to work Monday and let them fire you since you didn't tell them you quit, if you think they'll be so-inclined anyhow." Alex laughed. "If he doesn't fire you, call him an asshole to his face. I bet that gets it done."

Lenny bit the inside of his cheek and scratched his head. "Why would I want to go back just so they can fire me? I want the last word."

"You'll have the last word. Believe me. You can't draw unemployment if you quit, doofus, and you have no job lined up to replace that one. You might get hungry before you find other employment."

"Oh."

"I'll help if you need it. But remember, I'm not exactly rolling in gold either." Alex paused. "That still doesn't explain why you're here."

"Oh, yeah, right. I was on my way home. When I drove by, I wondered if you might have seen George this week. I wanted to ask him if he was serious about offering me that car sales job when he gets his lot set up."

Alex didn't respond. He tugged at the loose skin under his chin and gazed over the top of Lenny's head. After a couple of quiet seconds, he simply shrugged his shoulders.

"It's a simple question, Alex. Have you seen George this week?"

"The question is simple enough," he replied in a slow calculating way. "An honest answer may sound bad."

Lenny grinned. "Now, you *have* to tell me. You can't leave me to wonder what's going on between you and Waller."

"Nothing. It's what's going on between Jennifer and me."

Lenny's eyes grew wide. "Crap! You're not sleeping with her, are you?"

"Aw, hell no," Alex blurted. "Get that thought out of your head, you pervert. It's nothing like that. I can't believe you would even think it."

"Hey, man, you're the one that made it sound that way."

Alex thought about it. "I guess I did," he said, and then paused. "Here's the deal. No, I have not seen George since last week. I've been avoiding him because I'm carrying a secret of Jennifer's that she did not want me to share with him. I've never been able to keep things from him. So, I figured the best way to handle it was to not be around him."

"This, I have got to hear." Lenny walked by Alex and sat in a chair fronting Alex's desk. "Get over here and sit," Lenny said, pointing at the chair behind the desk. "I want the story. This sounds like one worth hearing."

Alex ambled around his desk. "I'll tell you but you *cannot* tell George. Do you swear it?"

"Yeah, yeah." Lenny spun a fast finger. "Talk to me."

Alex looked around for prying eyes and ears and then rolled his chair forward until the desk stopped it. He leaned far forward and in a tone meant for secrecy, he said, "Jen has gotten herself between a rock and a hard place with that dick of a boss she tried to leave behind in Abilene. As you know, he created a partnership with Dwayne Brewster on a joint lawsuit by a few farmers and ranchers against a company over placement of wind generators—or some such thing. Anyhow, it was a thinly veiled excuse to remain close to Jennifer. After a client meeting Monday night in Sweetwater, he propositioned her and she shut him down. He got pissed and slapped her hard enough to put a big bruise on her face."

"Are you serious?"

"Very. You know how George's feelings have been since coming out of the coma. His head is still screwed up over the loss of his wife and daughter, but he had that other life with Jen and his love for her is very strong, much more than it should be because of that comatose thing he had going on with her. Jen is very afraid that if he should find out about the assault, he might do something stupid that would get him hurt, thrown in jail—maybe killed. I think she might be right. If George is sufficiently triggered to act, he might lose all reason. Jen has the added problem of not wanting to mess up the relationship between Brewster and that Lassiter guy. The lawsuit could mean big bucks for his little firm. She really likes the old man and feels that she owes Brewster for taking her on when he really couldn't afford it."

Lenny blew a breathy whistle. "What a mess. I see what you mean about that rock and hard place thing. Jennifer has some serious tap dancing to do. Are you going to help her out with the problem?"

"Nah. This is something Jen has to work out, but it is hard on her. I'll just be her ear to chew on if she needs me."

Lenny nodded approval. "She does need someone to talk to. We all do from time to time." He paused and then stabbed the air with his finger. "Speaking of needing to talk, do you mind if I use the phone? I think I'll call George and ask him about that car sales job."

"Sure." Alex handed him the receiver and grabbed Lenny's arm, not allowing him to take the phone so quickly. "Not a word about Jennifer."

"Okay, okay."

Alex punched in George's number for him.

George answered, "Hello."

"Hey, George. This is Len. I'm here with Alex and I wanted to ask you about that car sales position. Were you serious about it?"

"Sure was," George replied without hesitation. "Say, how about meeting me at that little red tack store and bar up the highway. Ya know the one?"

"Sure, I do, old man Donovan's place. When Dad was alive he spent a lot of time there. They were close."

"Donovan told me that he and Buck were on the rodeo circuit back in the day."

"They were the best of friends," Lenny said, his voice losing enthusiasm. His dad was suddenly back on his mind.

"Meet me there. I'll buy the drinks," George said. "Invite Alex along, too."

Lenny put his hand over the mouth piece and whispered to Alex, "George wants to buy us drinks at Bradley Donovan's place. Want to go?"

"Sorry. I promised the wife I'd take her out to dinner. It's our Friday evening thing. Remember?" Alex replied.

"Lenny pulled his hand away from the phone's mouthpiece. "George, it looks like it will be just you and me, compadre."

"Meet you there in an hour," George said and then ended the call.

"Don't forget, say nothing about that . . ." Alex fluttered his fingers as if the right words were not coming to him fast enough. ". . . that *thing* going on with Jennifer."

* * *

Lenny fired up his old pickup truck and gunned the engine. A cloud of gray smoke belched from the exhaust pipe. He pulled out onto the highway and looked in the rearview mirror at the receding tractor/implement dealer feeling jealous. Of his close friends, himself included, Alex was the only one that seemed to have his feet planted firmly on planet earth. He had a job he liked, a devoted wife, and two basically well-behaved sons. Whereas, he, Jennifer, and George juggled difficult problems.

Lips pursed tightly, Lenny reflected. Negativity slowly rocked his head. After his mother died, he spent his early years living with his father, Buck, never allowing himself a romantic relationship, unwilling to leave his father a loner. His dad died, leaving Lenny with no family, no wife—not even a girlfriend. Most of the girls he knew were married and had families. In a sparsely populated area like Smithtown, the choice was severely limited. The pall he didn't want his dad to suffer was now upon him. His short conversation with George put his dad back on his mind. He missed the old guy. Lenny wallowed in a generalized malaise. It was a good thing that George suggested meeting at a bar because a drink happened to be exactly what he needed.

Passing the Smithtown city limit sign, he pushed the old dented and dinged Ford pickup to a more appropriate highway speed. The rusted exhaust rumbled to a decibel level that drowned out the music from the radio. He cranked the dust-covered radio to a distorted volume—too much sound forced through a single speaker in the dash. Nonetheless, the music lifted his spirits. Lenny prided himself for the knack of shaking off sadness before it had a chance to slather over him and suffocate a good mood. He attended pity parties—never hosted them.

When he arrived at Donovan's place, George's Charger was the only vehicle parked out front—slick and shiny. He wished that it belonged to him. He parked next to it and threw open his door—hinges squawking at the sudden thrust. Lenny ran his fingers over his flat-top haircut and a grin stretched his slender face. His hair stood too tall, in need of a trim. Aside from a few deepening lines in his face, Lenny's appearance hadn't changed appreciably since childhood—tall, skinny, and walked with a gait reminiscent of an ostrich. While kicking the dust off his cowboy boots on the tire of his pickup truck, he nodded reaffirmation that drinks with a friend was what he needed. *Let's get this party started.*

Marching into the tack store, the smell of saddle leather and dust was earthy and inviting. His eyes fixed on the rear area reserved for the bar.

"Lenny Poe," Bradley Donovan called out from behind the battered and scarred bar that had clearly seen many decades of service. "Been a long time since I've laid these droopy old eyes on ya, boy. How ya doin'?" The old man held a plug of chewing tobacco inside his left cheek. A drying brown dribble decorated that corner of his lips. His eyes were droopy and faded pale blue but sparkled with enthusiasm. Lenny hadn't seen the old guy since his father's funeral and appeared to have aged considerably since that day over five years ago.

"Just fine, Mister Donovan. Thanks. Good to see you again. It has been a long while."

"Yep, it has. What can I get for you?" the old man asked.

"How about a shot of bourbon while I'm thinking about what I want to drink," Lenny said.

George, at the bar with a sweating bottle of beer in front of him, laughed. "Get on over here," he said, then pulled the stool next to his away from the bar and patted its worn surface. "Sit. Tell me about your job situation."

Before Lenny reached the bar area, he began, "Well, I'll tell ya, it seems to some that I have a problem with authority, but that's just not the case. I have a problem with assholes. As lack of luck would have it, I work for one." He held an expressionless face but sucked air through his teeth as a clear show of country punctuation.

George looked to the old man behind the bar and they traded stares for a second and then burst into peals of laughter. "Don't sugar coat it for us, boy," Donovan said, still laughing. "Tell us how you really feel." The old man set a shot glass brimming with bourbon in front of him.

"I'm serious," Lenny replied, as he slid onto the stool. He rocked until his butt found a sweet spot of comfort.

George shoved the shot glass a little closer to his buddy. "Aw, Len, you know we're just having fun with ya. Knock back a couple of these. I bet you'll be laughing with us in no time."

Lenny swiped the little glass from the bar top and downed it in a single gulp. "That's the plan," he said, and then slapped the bar. "Hit me again."

Bradley Donovan bellied closer to the backside of the bar and refilled the glass.

Lenny asked George, "I have to know. Are you telling me I can have a car sales job *just* because we're friends?" Again, he downed the shot glass full of strong spirits in a single gulp, smacked it onto the bar and was tapping the top of it for a refill. Donovan had not yet returned the bottle to the shelf on the back bar.

George reared his head. "Hell no. Yes, you are my friend—no, I didn't offer it because of that . . . not specifically anyhow."

"Care to explain?"

"It's because I know that I can trust you to do the best job you can. You've never let me down, Len."

Lenny felt an abrupt flush of affection. Bourbon had begun softening the rough edges. A lump attempted to form in his throat and he coughed to clear it. "I'm sorry, man."

"Sorry about what?"

"Trying to make my problem your problem."

"That's what friends are for."

"After all you've been through this year, George, I'd expect my situation to be a very low priority for you." He reached for the full glass, but his hand went by it, having to retract and try again.

George watched, clearly amused. "You might want to slow down on those shots," he said, and then appeared to become reflective, looking away and staring at the mirror behind the bar. "It's true. You can't prepare for the stuff I'm dealing with." He refocused on Lenny. "But, my friend, that certainly doesn't diminish what I think you deserve.

Lenny put the little glass to his lips and, this time, savored it. "Damn that's good." He stabbed the air with an unsteady finger. "Hey, I just figured out what I want to drink, Mister Donovan. Let's switch to beer. If I get any mellower, I'll liquefy and flow off this stool."

George snickered, then his smile wilted away. "Seriously, Len, I think you can be a good salesman. I want to give you that chance. You're a good man—close friend or not."

Lenny now looked at George through a liquored haze. His lip quivered, on the verge of alcohol-induced tears. "I don't deserve a friend like you, man."

"Stop that," George fired back. "I'll have the lot set up in a couple of months and we'll start selling cars."

"Where?"

"You know that little house that Jen rented just north of town?"

"Yeah. The one she calls The Hovel."

"That property is for sale and I'm in negotiations with the owner to buy it. It's a deep lot with good frontage and even that little house can be converted into an office. Jen was a sweetheart to give me the idea."

Now that Jennifer had been introduced into the conversation, the promise he'd made to Alex to keep her secret stood prominently in his thoughts. "Does Jennifer know that you're following through on her idea? Maybe she didn't really mean it—just being nice."

"Well, she knew I was going to. Why?"

Lenny said, "Well, it seems to me, that with her financial situation bein' what it is, there's probably nowhere else in town that she can afford to rent. Where would she live?"

George leaned in closer, as if sharing a secret. "It's all part of my plan." He winked at Lenny. "I want to make my imagined life with Jen a reality. I want to marry her and then move into Mom's old house together, like I thought we had. I want *that* life back—whatever it takes. I'll not give up until I make it happen. I love her so much."

Lenny listened attentively and, as he did, developed a strengthening sense of indebtedness, wanting to help George in return for all that his lifelong friend was doing for him. Lenny's good judgment slithered away. "About that. There's something I need to tell you."

George may have been looking at him, but his mind was across town with Jennifer. Lenny waved a hand in front of his face. "George? Yoo-hoo."

George flinched, appearing to have regained consciousness. "Sorry, man. Drifted away for a second. What were you saying?"

"I said that I need to tell you something. I promised not to, but . . . you know."

"No, I don't know. What are you talking about? You promised what to whom? What information has been kept from me, and why?"

"You're too good of a friend to be kept in the dark." He then mumbled, "Alex is gonna kill me and Jennifer will probably kill Alex."

"Lenny," George drawled, "what little conspiracy have y'all cooked up?"

Lenny slowly nodded, building courage to betray a trust. He took a swig of the beer, but then slapped the bar top. "Mister Donovan, I think I'll need one more shot of that bourbon."

Old man Donovan was becoming as curious as George about the secret. "Sure, sure," he quickly replied, snatching the bottle from the shelf behind him and filling. "If that doesn't get this story underway, nothing will," Donovan said. "This'll lubricate your resolve."

Lenny gulped it down and returned his attention to George. The old man propped his elbows on top of the bar and cradled his chin in his hands like a child about to hear the best story ever.

"Well?" George asked.

"You haven't seen Jennifer in a while, have you?"

"It's been a few days," George replied. "Over a week actually. But what does that have to do with anything?"

Lenny's head felt as though it was about to float up and away. He blinked back an acceptable level of lucidity. "Have you tried calling her?"

"Several times."

"She didn't answer, did she?"

"Len, you're beginning to scare me."

"Jennifer is juggling three problems—all connected like a three-legged stool—ignore one and the stool collapses. If—"

"Get to the point. If she has problems, I can help her."

"Let me finish. You're not grasping the situation yet. You see, she can't overlook any one of the three or solve only one at a time. All three problems would have to be dealt with and solved at the same time or nothing will be resolved." Lenny struggled against slurring his words.

"What are the problems?" George snapped. "I don't give a damn what they are. I want to help her any way I can."

Lenny held up his forefinger and tapped it with the other. "Problem number one is her desire to keep Dwayne Brewster happy because she loves the old guy and deeply beholding to him."

"Okay. So?"

A second finger sprang up. "Number two: her former employer has poked his nose in her business by developing a partnership on a lawsuit with Brewster and it directly involves her working closely with him not old man Brewster."

"So far, you're not telling me anything I don't already know."

"I'm just setting it up for ya, buddy. You won't appreciate the gravity of her dilemma until I get it all told."

"I watched her ream Lassiter in the parking lot at the Village Diner. I think she can manage that problem."

"And that is where the unraveling in your logic begins." He anchored his swaying body by placing one foot on the floor. "Now, for the hard part—problem number three. You."

"Me?" George blurted. "I love Jen. What makes you think I'm a problem for her?"

"She loves you, too. Quite a bit, I'd sh—say. But I can't climb inside her head with a flashlight and look around for confirmation on that." He suddenly stopped.

George frowned. "Go on. Don't stop."

"I just meant that I only know what I see. She wants to keep you from getting into trouble or getting hurt by Michael Lash—shiter." As hard as he tried, Lenny could no longer control the alcohol-induced fog rolling over him. He swooned.

George grabbed Lenny's shirt sleeve and pulled him back before falling off the stool. "Don't you pass out and leave me hanging like this."

Lenny felt as though his eyes floated independently in their sockets. With considerable effort to enunciate, he wrapped it up by saying, "Get the rest of the story . . . from . . . Jennifer." The curtain of consciousness suddenly dropped and blackened Lenny's world.

Chapter 28 ~ A Slow Boil Begins

George pulled out of the parking lot of Donovan's place onto the highway north of Smithtown, confident Lenny was in good hands. Old man Donovan said that he owed his deceased friend, Buck Poe, the favor of taking care of his only son, at least for a night, so that the boy could sleep off an over consumption of bourbon and beer. The old man's living quarters were cramped but he didn't hesitate to offer a bed at the rear of the store. It was abundantly evident in the aged cowboy's face that he saw Buck in Lenny's face and mannerisms. He may have seen Lenny as a son that he never had or as a nephew since he spoke of Buck like a brother. George simply shook the old guy's hand and told him, "You're a good man, Bradley Donovan," and then turned to leave. He glanced back to see Lenny with his eyes closed, head down on the bar, sporting a drunken grin—maybe conscious, maybe not.

Driving home, George thought about what Lenny had told him. Although, he still didn't have all the facts, there existed a bubbling unease in the pit of his stomach born of that deep sense of impotence when it came to all-things-Jennifer. It was an odd combination of fear and anger—almost as if both sought domination but in equal parts, leaving them to simmer mutually.

He replaced the unsettling imagery with thoughts of what Bradley Donovan and Buck Poe may have been like during their rodeo days in the sixties. It was easy to imagine a couple of carefree cowboys— drinking hard, laughing loud, riding dangerously, and loving the same way—always having one another's back. Those kinds of friends were rare.

Friends. He thought about that word. Flashes of Lenny, Alex, and Jennifer at different stages of their lives danced through his mind. At every age, no matter how long they may have been apart or hadn't seen one another, all it took were mere moments in their presence to again become like family. All four had endured atypical childhoods. Jennifer was raised from her prepubescent years by her aunt. Alex's dad was an alcoholic that played hardly any role in his developmental years. Lenny's mother died of cancer at an early age. And, his own father walked out on his mother while he was still in elementary school. They were truly four against the world.

But since his coma, the friendship dynamic changed. They conspired to walk and talk gently around him. *Was it really necessary?* He thought not. *I have a handle on things now. What other things might they be sharing behind my back?* Still, he believed that, if so, it was a family-like desire to protect him. Although he ached and longed for a return to the life he imagined with Jen, he felt as though he had achieved mastery of the difference between what is, what was, and what never was. Desire pricked his heart like the point of a sharp knife. He loved Jennifer so much that, if he became too lost in the fantasy, it became painful. Jennifer's life had taken a different course and, yes, she may still love him but how deeply was a question he needed to know. Regardless what Lenny had been babbling about a short while ago, George remained nervously uncertain about Jennifer's thoughts.

Now that Jennifer was firmly embedded in his alcohol-mellowed head, George had a sudden desire to drop by his childhood home, the house his mother had left him. It was now vacant. The intention to follow through on the place firmed up when he pulled into town. He headed straight for that cozy tree-lined street where he spent his childhood. He steered the Charger onto the driveway and stopped, allowing the car to idle for a moment. George scanned the roofline, shook his head and grinned, remembering the fall from that roof on a cool but sunny day in his comatose world.

That was followed by a genuine memory, yanking the smile from his face—those God-awful feelings he had when he and Jennifer had entered his home in Lubbock for the first time since waking from the coma. It had been traumatizing. He saw the Lubbock house and its memories as a painful reminder of tragic loss. Of all the random feelings he had been experiencing the past few minutes, it now focused sharply on a hollowness descending over him, as snapshots of life with Marie and his precious Louisa clicked off before his mind's eye. His eyes drifted skyward. He allowed their memories uninterrupted reverence. After a time, he brought his eyes back down to examine the home of his youth. This time, he saw it as the house he hoped, one day, to again call home with Jennifer at his side.

Whether Lenny had been spouting idiotic ramblings or not, George figured there must have been a modicum of truth to it. He wondered if Michael Lassiter had become more of a problem than even Jennifer had counted on. He wanted to think about her and his love for her, not about that arrogant guy, Lassiter. *Hell, I love her, and she loves me. All I have to do is convince her that it's real. I need to build trust, that's all.* With renewed purpose, he killed the rumbling engine and bounded out of the car.

As he unlocked the front door and pushed it open, the view filling his eyes could only be described with positives—all the many wonderful childhood memories and the various episodes that shaped his life while living with his mom. The house was void of furniture. Slight color variations on the walls where pictures and other treasures had hung over the years brought a smile, easily visualizing each wall-hanging clearly. George walked through the living room into the hall and on to the bedrooms. As he stepped into the master, small hairs came up on the back of his neck. This room was a strong reminder of his Jen and loving her on a bed that never existed. As that image flashed before him, it occurred to him that he couldn't remember a time that he and Jennifer had even stood together in this bedroom in the real world. He swallowed hard and backed out of the room right into the bedroom behind him, Rachael Irissa's, or so he had imagined. He was haunted not by them or the false memory, but by a situation he desperately wanted. There was still time for building a family, giving birth to Rachael Irissa and watching her grow up a second time.

George suddenly could no longer stand in this house without his Sweet Jen at his side. He pulled his cell phone from his pants pocket and dialed. Since he and Lenny had begun the bar visit shortly after noon, the sun was only now beginning to set, the bottom of the solar orb turning red and just touching the western horizon.

Her phone rang but voice mail picked up, "Hi, you've reached Jennifer Andrews. Leave a message."

"Jen, this is George. I'd really like to see you this evening. Have plans? Let me know." He reluctantly ended the call—slow to return the phone to his pocket, staring at it a moment longer. He thought about adding persuasiveness with another message.

He finally gave up on putting his desperate side on display, believing she'd call if she wanted to and that nothing he could add would convince her otherwise.

George continued his examination of the house, but now in a pragmatic way, thinking about furniture and appliances and what was needed. He'd be starting from square one, having sold at auction all personal possessions from the Lubbock house. That house remained unsold and still on the market. Having no need for obtaining a mortgage, it was of little concern. He went from room to room taking copious mental notes. Finally, he became confident of furnishing needs and a general idea of cost. He checked his watch. Over twenty minutes had passed since he left that message for Jennifer. Not a good sign if a spontaneous date was to happen this evening. *What harm would there be in dropping by her house—just to make sure everything is okay, of course?*

His desire to see her overrode intention to allow her time to respond to his message, now that a legitimate, although contrived, reason surfaced not to wait. It was less than two miles from the front door of this house to hers. He locked up the house and headed for his car.

As he threaded his way from the cozy neighborhood to the highway that split Smithtown down the middle, the drunken things that Lenny had spouted circled at the fringes. George was curious to know more, but the possibility of holding her in his arms warmed him and kept worry at bay.

His first hurdle was to make sure she was at home. As he approached, he noticed the older model Toyota parked near the front door. It was almost dark and there was a light glowing from inside the house through the front window. He steered into the driveway. The air seemed fresher than it did only minutes ago, probably due to stubborn lilac blossoms at the corner of the little house that refused to succumb to the erratic winter temperatures.

He knocked on the door and then looked to the big white thermometer nailed to the trim next to it. He kissed his finger and touched the rusting surface. To George, it represented so much more than what it was. It was a reminder how much he loved Jennifer—his Sweet Jen—in the here and now and his other so-called life. It represented a solid link between both worlds.

The knob turned slowly and then opened a crack with the same apparent lack of enthusiasm. Jennifer peaked around the end of the door showing only half her face. "What are you doing here?"

The question wasn't asked with any sense of anticipation. It confused him. "I, uh . . . I just wanted to see you again."

"Not a good time."

"Are you ill?"

She hesitated, as if wondering how to answer. Finally, "No—not really. I just don't think a get-together is a good idea, not tonight."

George's heart and temperament darkened. "It's been over a week since I've seen you and when someone loves a person as much as I love you, that's far too long."

He thought he saw a smile try to form at the corner of her mouth. "I love you, too, George. I really do."

"If you let me in, I promise not to attack you, or even touch you, if you don't want me to. I promise to leave you the same way I found you. What do you say?"

She stared at him. After long quiet seconds, her face disappeared from around the door, but she made no attempt to close it. George put a single finger against the door and gave it a gentle push to reveal Jennifer in a floppy t-shirt and sweat bottoms walking away toward the sofa at the opposite end of the living room. Her hair appeared to be in need of shampoo. He had already noticed that she had no makeup on and her feet were bare. He wondered if she had even gone in to work today. Tentatively, "Does this mean I can come in?" he asked.

Her back remained presented to him, but she offered a beckoning wave over her shoulder. "Come on in."

By the time she was turning to sit on the sofa, he caught up to her. They sat at the same time and, although her body was toward him, her head didn't square with him. She refused to fully face him and looked off toward the other side of the room. His eyes followed hers. "What are you looking at?"

"The wall."

"Why?"

With clear trepidation, she slowly turned her head to face him.

"What happened to you?" he asked when the black eye and radiating bruise down her cheek became visible.

She sighed. "Well . . ." She broke eye contact. Her eyes darted around the room. "I'd like to tell you that I walked into a wall, or some explanation such as that, but I'm a horrible liar. I wanted to avoid this conversation altogether."

"So, this is what Lenny was trying to tell me."

"Lenny? What does Lenny have to do with this?"

"I don't know, but it seems that he knows much more than me about what you've been going through lately. Sooo?"

"So . . . what?"

"So spill it. I want details."

Jennifer huffed frustration. "The first thing is that I need to have a heart to heart talk with Alex about abusing a confidence."

"Don't be too hard on Lenny or Alex. They just wanted to help. We're all friends, you know."

She nodded, pushed her long dark hair behind her ears and then pulled her feet beneath her at the end of the sofa. She sighed. "I know." She let her head wilt forward for a second and then whispered, "Now that you're here, would you hold me?"

George slid down the sofa and closed the gap between them. He lifted her head with a fingertip. Her eyes darted over his face. He then pulled her into full body contact. "Why didn't you trust me enough to share your problems with me?"

Jennifer pressed the side of her face into the top of his shoulder. "Because you and I have feelings for one another. I am afraid that you're too emotionally invested. So, I confided in Alex. Of course, I *am* using the word 'confided' much looser now. If he were here right now, I'd bop the boy on the noggin."

"Enough set-up. I want the whole story." As he made the demand, Jennifer pulled away and folded her arms across her chest in a clear move to defensively close her body language. "You *are* going to tell me, aren't you?"

She sat quietly. Finally, "If I tell you, you have to promise me that the information will be kept between you and me until I can resolve a fairly difficult web of circumstances. I think time and finesse will take care of it, but I can't be certain yet."

"Start by telling me how you got the shiner."

"Uh-uh. Give me your promise first. And, I don't mean keeping a secret in the Alex Burton way."

"Okay, okay, I promise."

"Not good enough. You promise what?"

"I promise what you tell me will stay between you and me." He twirled a hand, wanting her to get off the fence and start talking. "Come on, come on. What's the story?"

Her eyes only occasionally landed on him and didn't remain longer than flicking glances when they did. She nervously ringed hair behind one ear then the other. After a deafening pause, she slowly raised her eyes to meet his. "After the meeting with those farmers and ranchers in Sweetwater last week," she said, "Michael Lassiter propositioned me. I knew he would. He's very predictable that way. I became flippant in my refusal and it made him angry and . . ." Her attempt at maintaining eye contact failed. Her gaze drifted down to her hand where she picked at a thumb cuticle.

"And, what?"

"Michael backhanded me hard enough to knock me to the floor," she said quickly. "This is the result," she added, touching the bruise.

George sprang to his feet. "That bastard! I ought to knock him into next week with a baseball bat."

Pulling her feet from beneath her, she reached for and grabbed his hand. She tugged at it. "Calm down." She pulled him back down. "I'm certainly not happy about it, either, but I have to react in a smart way. First of all, I have to take at least a little of the blame for—"

"The hell you do!"

"Yeah, I do. I took a humorous jab at what he obviously believed to be a serious proposal. I know how big his ego is. I shouldn't have taunted him." She dropped her hands back into her lap and scooted closer to him. "Look, I don't care at all about Michael and I would like to avenge his treatment of me somehow, someday, but those are lesser points. I don't want to involve Dwayne Brewster in this at all, thus my desire to keep it all a secret from him, if possible. He has been very good to me and I don't want to jeopardize a potential windfall payday from that Sweetwater lawsuit, even though I'm sure he'd be a gentleman and walk away from it if he ever discovered what happened. I didn't want you to find out either. Judging by your anger, it was the right decision."

He eliminated the final inches between them. Their knees touched. He took both her hands into his, shook them gently, and growled. "Why do you have to always make so much sense?"

She smiled. "I don't—not always."

"How else should I have reacted?"

"You reacted in the most wonderfully gallant way imaginable." She kissed him lightly on the lips. "I would've been upset if you had shown indifference. She quickly kissed him again.

"I love you far too much to ever be indifferent when it comes to your safety or about anything that's important to you," he said. "I'll always do whatever I can to better your world because, someday, I want your world and my world to become *our* world."

She touched her forehead to his. "Oh, George. I love you so much." She pulled her hands from his grasp and slid backwards. "But I'm not there yet. I have trust issues. You know that. I still haven't gotten over our history, but I'm working on it."

"I understand. But, please, don't push me away. Let me help."

"For now, I have to maintain some aloofness while I work through everything."

"Help me to see it. Help me to understand you—everything about you."

She straightened, gathering thoughts. "It won't be easy, but I'll try." She sighed. "You see me as your Sweet Jen and I love that," she began. "The problem is, Sweet Jen existed in a different world. I'm Jennifer Andrews with baggage that your Sweet Jen simply didn't have."

"But—"

"Let me finish. I know what you want to say, that she and I are the same person. We aren't. You believe that you and I were married for sixteen years. We weren't. That doesn't lessen my love for you. I may even love you just as much as your imagined Sweet Jen. I don't know. It happens to come in a familiar wrapping to you but, George, I'm a totally different package." She paused. "Is any of this making sense?"

George was the one who now couldn't maintain eye contact. In a whisper, "Yes."

"I don't mean to drag you down, but for the sake of this conversation, I have to say something else that I've considered never sharing with you at all, but I must—to make a strong point," she said. "When we slept together a couple of weeks ago—"

He looked up from his feet. "It was wonderful."

"It was *beyond* wonderful. As you were drifting off to sleep, you told me that you loved me."

His smile grew wider.

"My heart soared when you said it. And then you called me Marie."

His pleasant expression melted away. "I did?" He began to babble, "I didn't mean it. I was drunk. I would have never made that mistake sober. I'm so sorry. Please forgive—"

"Stop it," she blurted. "It's okay. I was not fishing for an apology. I only mentioned it to point out that when Marie and Louisa are thrown into this mix of problems, I have to believe that more time has to pass before you and I are truly on the same page when it comes to a long-term relationship."

George suddenly realized the steep uphill battle that Jennifer had been struggling with, all the while trying to spare him anguish. There was nothing left to be said. What could he say? She was right. There remained bridges to be crossed in his recovery—bridges that he had been refusing to acknowledge. She simply couldn't trust that he might see her as a replacement for Marie. On top of that, he had left her once before without explanation. She was clearly afraid that someday he might come to realize that she couldn't replace his dead wife and would walk away again

"George?"

He reconnected with her gaze.

"I'm done talking." She held her arms out for him. "All I want now, is for you to hold me . . . all night."

Chapter 29 ~ Jennifer's Problem to Solve

Morning came too soon. Jennifer wanted to lie in George's arms forever. *Forever? Really?* She thought about that simple word—forever. The implication was far from simple. Although, it had a comforting romantic ring to it. She smiled and cuddled closer, pulling tighter and placing her head on his chest. She relished the rhythmic rise and fall of his breathing—the sound of his strong heart further seducing her.

To remain snuggled under warm blankets on a day of dropping temperatures outside seemed a reasonable goal—only slightly selfish. Wind howled, rattling windows, and buzzing weather stripping around the ill-fitting front door. A blue norther raced through overnight and ushered in the new season in a new world. *Brand new world?* Interesting thought. She tilted her head up and looked into George's sleeping face, feeling his warm breath sweep over her. A fresh start, a new world is exactly what she yearned for, but only if George was in it permanently and no longer harboring confused romantic feelings that pitted her against his dead wife.

Jennifer's world, her perfect world, had to be just so, like the one he had described to her while in a coma—a world in which there was absolutely no confusion and no other woman. It was an existence Jennifer thought about often, rolling it over and over in her mind. Every nuance George had ever shared with her about that fantasy life was like a puzzle piece neatly fitted into a picture of her own life under construction. The image was almost complete in her mind, but not quite. As hopeful as she was, she wondered if that kind of wedded bliss was possible when translated into this world—the real world. *Maybe.* She thought.

George smacked his lips and rolled over onto his side away from her. She scooted closer and spooned him. She kissed the back of his neck. He roused and moaned lightly—the sound of contentment. He rolled over to face her. Their foreheads touched. "Good morning," he whispered.

"Mornin'."

George put a finger beneath her chin and pushed her face up to square with his. He kissed her on the lips."

When their lips parted, she smiled and said, "You're a brave man to kiss me first thing in the morning." She grinned mischievously. "My breath has to smell like the skin of a rodeo goat."

He chuckled. "Maybe. But it's my kind of goat." He stared into her eyes for a moment. "I sure do love you, Jennifer Andrews," he said, over-enunciating her full name.

"I'm sorry if I made you uncomfortable last night."

"I'm just being silly," he said. After a silent second of gazing into her eyes, he snapped his wristwatch to his face. "Crap. It's seven-forty-five."

"What's the matter?"

"I promised to meet old man Buford at eight this morning."

"Buford? Are you talking about Virgil Buford, the guy who owns this place?"

"Yeah. We're going to try and come to terms on a price for this house and lot. I have every intention of buying this property and turning it into a used car lot. Of course, I credit you with the idea and it was a great one." He lifted an eyebrow and shot her an evil grin. "If all goes well, I'll become your personal slum lord. Pretty cool, huh?" He tossed the covers off and sprang out of bed. He rubbed his arms. "Good grief! It's cold in here."

Jennifer grinned. "Is that what cold does to you?"

He looked down his naked front. "Uh, no, that's what you do to me."

She lifted her head from the pillow. "Are you blushing?"

"I suppose that's what this heat in my face is." He turned his back to her. "As you can tell, I'm certainly no player or man of the world. There is a smidgen of modesty left in me."

She drew a ragged breath and then cooed, "I think it's endearing and, frankly, a turn on."

He faced her.

She lifted the covers to reveal her own nakedness. "Let's be rude to old Mister Buford and make him wait a while longer. What do you say?"

George stood holding his boxers for less than a second before dropping them back onto the floor, accepting the suggestive invitation.

As soon as their bodies came together under the blankets, Jennifer's tongue began exploring his lips. The fever of love came on suddenly, raising her temperature to the level of the night before. Her breathing deepened in direct proportion to escalating lust. After he pulled back from the passionate kiss. She watched his eyes travel over her face. She was going in for another kiss when she noticed his eyes lock onto the bruise under her eye. His dreamy smile drooped. She detected a slight hardening of expression as he stared at the injury in the light of day. "Whatever you're thinking, don't let it ruin the moment," she whispered.

His smile returned. "Never." He kissed her again as his urgently seeking hands explored her body. "But I think I know how to prove how much I love you."

Jennifer didn't break the magic of the moment, but George had planted a bothersome seed, . . . *prove how much I love you. What does that mean?* She needed clarification, but later. "I don't need proof later," she murmured while their lips still touched. "I just need you to shut up and love me now."

* * *

A day of cuddling in bed was not to be as Jennifer watched George virtually sprint out the front door for his meeting with Virgil Buford. She followed him and stood at the front door in her sweat bottoms and t-shirt, holding herself against the blustery chill.

As he climbed into his car, he offered a quick wave. He, too, was affected by the sudden onslaught of winter and didn't linger outside the vehicle. He wore no coat. Yesterday evening, it hadn't been necessary. Now it was.

Jennifer closed the door and leaned back against it, basking in the afterglow of love making. She drew a long, deep breath and sighed. It was marvelous. The feeling that she had at this very moment was what she wanted for the remainder of her life. Her smile grew so wide that the bruise on her cheek sent out a reminder that it had not yet healed. She massaged it lightly. The pain wasn't bad, but noticeable. She recalled George's comment earlier after examining the bruise, ". . . I think I know how to prove how much I love you," she wondered aloud. She thought about it for a moment but dismissed it. *I'll get him to explain it later.* She had no more time to think about it, having her own day to prepare for. She came away from the front door and headed for the bathroom to get ready to go to work. It would take extra time and extra makeup to make the injury less noticeable. Hopefully, she could get through this day without offering Dwayne Brewster a clear look at her cheek. She might get away without having to lie to him.

Like George, she found herself in a rush to get ready. It was almost eight-thirty. She should have already been at the office and had no intention of calling in sick again. So, the race was on to at least be there before nine. There was no time for extraneous contemplations. All her mental energy must go into dressing and makeup.

After achieving the best look possible, she grabbed her warmest coat and headed out the door.

During the drive into town, her mind settled. She relived the time she had shared with George. It was wonderful. For the first time, a wedded life with him took a hopeful step—a plan in the making. Confidence soared. She hummed a tune and smiled. All the while, recalling stories George had shared over the previous weeks of that wonderful world of his imagination—a married life in perfect harmony.

When she walked into the law office across the street from the courthouse, she was still humming. Clarice Beatty, Dwayne's loyal secretary of many years looked at Jennifer with a questioning stare. "Well, aren't you a little ray of sunshine this morning?"

"I guess I am."

Clarice's desk was front and center in the office. Dwayne's office door was situated in the rear of this reception area. "I take it you're feeling better today," the elderly lady said, tipping her head and raising an eyebrow.

On that comment, it occurred to Jennifer that she had taken a sick day yesterday and now realized that appearing chipper might appear suspicious, as if taking advantage of the company. Although Jennifer never socialized with Clarice because of difference in ages, Jennifer had known her most of her life and respected the older woman. In a town as small as Smithtown, it was difficult, even for the most unobservant person, to not know almost every permanent resident. Clarice had served Mister Brewster well for many years. The silver haired woman had also distinguished herself by doing charity work for her church and other organizations around town. She was a grandmotherly type. Jennifer couldn't remember a time that Clarice hadn't had that silvery white hair, perfectly coiffed, or dressed in anything other than a springy floral dress that flattered her portly stature. The elderly woman held herself and everyone in her presence to a high moral standard. Jennifer was a new hire and didn't want to disrespect the secretary by lying to her. Jennifer looked to Dwayne's closed office door. "Is Dwayne in this morning?" she asked, whispering while stabbing the air surreptitiously with a pointing finger toward his office door.

"He'll be in later. Had his annual checkup with the doctor scheduled this morning." The elderly woman smiled slightly. "At our ages, we cannot miss those appointments."

Jennifer pulled one of the two chairs in front of the secretary's desk in closer and sat. "Can I trust you to keep a secret?"

"From Dwayne?"

"Especially Dwayne."

Clarice stiffened. "Oh no. I don't know what kind of intrigue you have on your mind, but if it hurts Dwayne or his practice, or affects either in any way, I can't make that promise." She lifted her nose to an indignant angle. "I *won't* make that promise."

"It's not intrigue, Clarice. Honestly. I want to *protect* Dwayne from his own good nature and sense of chivalry that could *hurt* the business."

The old lady's negative headshake suddenly froze on that statement, now offering a quizzical look. "I don't understand what you could possibly be referring to," she finally said, "but you do have my curiosity piqued. You want to help Dwayne?"

"I can't think of strong enough words to tell you how much I want to help him. He's been kind to me and gone far out on a limb to help me. I love the man and will do everything in my power to help this company prosper. Does that address your concern?"

Clarice settled back into her chair. "I suppose it does." She thought quietly for a few more seconds. Jennifer didn't interrupt the woman's decision making process. Finally, Clarice leaned forward and put her elbows on her desk. She waggled a warning finger. "Okay, but if I determine what you have to say is hurtful in any way, I'll not be keeping a promise to remain quiet about it."

"Understood."

"Let me have it," the elderly lady said. "What's the secret?"

"I've noticed you looking at the discoloration on my cheek and beneath my eye."

"I couldn't determine if it was a shadow, misapplied makeup, or something else. If it is indeed something else, I figured it's none of my business."

"Oh, it's your business all right . . . and Dwayne's. Yet, it must stay between you and I until all this plays out."

"Until all *what* plays out? What are you talking about, child."

Jennifer took a breath and huffed it away. "It's a bruise that I can't quite hide with makeup. It goes to the heart of the reason why what I'm about to tell you should remain between the two of us, why I took a sick day yesterday, and why I can't let Dwayne find out about it." She paused.

"Keep talking, child," Clarice said with an edge, tiring of the wait for answers.

Jennifer spent the next fifteen minutes detailing why Michael Lassiter forged a partnership with Dwayne's firm on the Sweetwater lawsuit and why it would have never happened if Jennifer hadn't come to work for this firm in Smithtown. At first, Jennifer had to convince Clarice that she wasn't bragging and why it was not entirely a good thing. Although, it meant money, potentially lots of money, for this firm. Jennifer described her brief affair with Lassiter that culminated in the confrontation after the client meeting at the hotel in Sweetwater. "I simply cannot allow Dwayne's good nature to kick in and make him feel forced to intervene on my behalf," Jennifer pleaded. "It wouldn't be fair to him, you, this company or me—if he should do what he believes to be the right thing. I don't doubt that he would. Clarice, I have to handle this on my own until this lawsuit is settled."

"I promise I won't say anything to Dwayne but, dear, now I'm very worried about you."

"Don't be. Please. I brought this on myself. I may not have meant to, but I provoked Michael and this bruise is the result."

"Sweetheart, every abused woman says things like that. It does not make a hill o' beans difference what you told Lassiter. It was *not* your fault."

"I understand," Jennifer said, "but that logic only holds true for women who can't let go of their love for the abuser. I don't like Michael. I can't stand the son-of-a-bitch. Pardon the language."

"No apology necessary. That is the right terminology for the man. In fact, I can think of a few other words to describe a man like that," she added with righteous indignation.

"I did provoke him by making fun of what he considered a serious proposal. His ego couldn't handle it. I knew that before I opened my big mouth, yet tossed out a flippant response anyhow. Yeah, Clarice, in this case it was my fault. I can handle Michael. I really can."

"Well, you should at least turn it over to the Sheriff. It is assault with definite intent to harm, ya know."

"I thought about that. But, you've lived in Smithtown all your life. You know what it's like. Shortly after reporting it to the authorities, everyone in town would know about it. In half a day, or less, Dwayne would know about it. I have no choice but to let the episode slide."

"Okay," Clarice drawled. "I hope you know what you're doing."

"I think I know what I'm doing." Jennifer smiled. "Then again, I always *think* I know what I'm doing."

"You can trust me entirely, dear. Just tell me what you need and I'll try my best to get it done."

"The first thing is to help me keep this bruise hidden from Dwayne until it fades so I might be able to hide it entirely with makeup. It wouldn't be fair to take any more sick days. I have to consolidate and work those new clients I signed, or we may lose them. Their signatures will mean nothing if I can't deliver on ideas I promised would be forthcoming to ease their legal problems." Jennifer sighed relief over the simple act of sharing the information with Clarice, now confident that this day may prove productive after all.

Jennifer called all the newly solicited clients and went over ideas with them, endearing herself and the value of the firm to each. All the problems of two days ago now seemed manageable.

Jennifer walked out of the law office after five and the jaunty spring in her step that had been missing for a while was back. Neither the injury on her face, nor Michael Lassiter seemed like insurmountable problems.

She slid into her old Toyota and slammed the door, rattling every loose screw on its body from headlights to trunk lid. She rarely paid attention to such faults anymore, as long as the little car transported her there and back. She had learned to love it like a member of the family and had considered giving it a name. That's normally what people did with old vehicles that had remained in possession for years. She smiled and stabbed the key into the ignition switch and turned it. The engine rolled over slowly and then backfired. Even the sound of it seemed cute—sounding more of a dainty sneeze than a cannon shot. She glanced up at the rearview mirror in time to see a belch of grayish-white smoke billow from the exhaust and then drift away in the breeze. *Come on, Little Sweetie. Don't act this way.* She tried again. This time the engine spun energetically, and the car started. *Ah, so you like the name Little Sweetie, huh? Well, all righty then. You are now Little Sweetie for the remainder of your days.* She grinned and rolled her eyes. *However long that might be.*

As she drove around the courthouse square in the center of Smithtown's main shopping area, she was about to turn onto the street that would connect with the highway to her house when she had a thought. She drove on around to a street that headed east out of town and would turn into a Farm to Market highway just beyond the city limit. She suddenly didn't want to sit in her little house and watch television, not yet anyhow, but had nowhere else to go, until she remembered Mesa Park. It was not a long drive, fifteen minutes perhaps, and it had been years since she had been out there. It was not much of a park, more of a roadside rest area. Still, it was situated at the edge of the Caprock, providing a breathtaking vista into the distant lowlands beyond that were uninhabited for several miles. Standing on the high ground, looking across it all, it was easy to envision life in this area hundreds of years ago. Plus, the view had always reminded her of Christmas because besides stunted mesquite bushes, the only other vegetation of any size were cacti and cedar bushes scattered across the countryside with the reddest soil in the world. It looked like the inverse of giant Christmas trees, green balls on red trees.

The drive was pleasant. The only other vehicle in sight in either direction was a car over an eighth of a mile behind her. After a leisurely drive, she steered into the small parking area just off the highway. The park had not changed at all. This stretch of road was mostly used by

185

local farmers and ranchers because it only extended a few more miles and then curved into another, more heavily traveled road.

Jennifer got out of the car and breathed the crisp air. The sun had done a reasonable job earlier but was losing its grasp on the day and the evening chill had begun settling in. She zipped her heavy parka and scanned the horizon beyond the breaks. Behind her the sun was little more than an orange lump spreading fading flamingo wings across the western sky. *I wish George was here. He'd enjoy this.* She suddenly wondered where he might be and how his conversation with Virgil Buford had turned out. She pulled out her cell phone and hit his speed dial number, but the phone was dead, no bars showing on the phone's display pad. *Oh well.*

Jennifer walked beyond a couple of concrete picnic tables to where the earth fell away, providing the vista she sought. She noticed a descending and well-trodden path between two cedar bushes. It didn't appear steep or perilous, so she decided to see where it led.

Enjoying what was left of the day, she played a mental game of comparing herself with what she believed George's Sweet Jen to be like. For over a week such contemplations had become an obsession. She prodded him frequently for more information, unable to satisfy an insatiable need for details. He readily shared and she had done a credible job of creating the perfect story arc. George and Sweet Jen had been fifty-one years old by the time he woke up from his coma. He came back with intricate details of how they looked, lived, and loved.

Jennifer had been watching the trail at her feet but suddenly realized that the light of day was dimming fast. She livened her pace on the return trip up the hill to the picnic area. It had been a pleasant experience and worth the trip.

As Jennifer rounded the last cedar bush and the concrete tables and benches reappeared just above her, she saw Michael's car parked next to her Toyota. He was leaning back against it—arms folded across his chest and legs crossed at the ankles, waiting. *What the hell . . .?*

"I was wondering when you were going to reappear," Michael called out. "It's getting darker and colder fast."

"What are you doing here, Michael? Surely you didn't come for the fresh air."

"I felt like I needed to come and give you a better apology for my conduct the other day in Sweetwater."

"I would've preferred you just forgot about it, so I could. How did you know where I was?"

"I followed you."

"That was your car behind me?" Jennifer asked as she continued closing the gap between them.

"Yeah. I was going to talk with old man Brewster when I saw you back out of the parking space in front of his office and then head out of town."

"Whatever. You came a long way for nothing. I've already forgiven you. It's the only way I can put it behind me and move on." She came to stand before him and thought about what she needed to say next and, this time, it certainly didn't include flippancy. "Look, Michael, your presence here is sort of disturbing to me because it indicates that you believe there's still hope for reconstructing a romantic relationship. There isn't," she said, almost apologetically. "I want to have a good working relationship with you, but that's all. That's all there ever will be. Please, try to understand that?"

Michael straightened. "Sorry. I can't believe that." He stepped toward her until Jennifer could feel his warm breath on her. "I won't believe that," he added.

She stepped back, maintaining a buffer between them. She kept her demeanor low-key and said softly, "I'm sorry, but you have to believe it. I won't be changing my mind."

"Oh, Jenny, you are so lovely," he said reaching for her.

"No, Michael, please don't."

He grabbed her arms and pulled their bodies together. "Stop it, Michael." Her voice pushed into a higher range as she turned her head to the side, attempting to avoid a kiss.

He clutched a handful of hair at the back of her head to hold it steady. "It's okay, Jen. We'll both enjoy this."

"Damn it, Michael! Stop!" She squirmed, trying to break his embrace around her waist. He was too strong.

He slung her around and pinned her against the side of his car, forcing his mouth against hers. He pressed his body into hers. She felt the swell below his waist. There was no one around—no one she could call out to for help. She was alone and now beginning to panic.

His hand around her waist had already found the side zipper of her pants and shoved it down.

Jennifer's panic turned to anger as she struggled. She managed to pull her mouth away from his long enough to scream, "Get your goddamn hands off me!"

The harsh language had the opposite of desired effect. Michael squeezed her tighter and pulled her pants down so violently that the seam below the zipper ripped.

Oh my God! Oh my God! He's going to rape me.

* * *

Alex finished up a bit of paperwork before heading home for the day. As he wrapped up a formal bid on a shiny new green John Deere combine, he thought of George and figured his friend might like home cooking instead of another trip to the Village Diner. He tossed the triplicate bid form in a basket at the front corner of his desk and then his hand flew smoothly on over to the phone. He dialed George's cell.

"Hello."

"Hey George, I thought I'd call and see if you'd like to eat with me, Patricia, and the boys tonight instead of at the diner again. Their food is good, but it must get tiresome. Whaddaya say?"

"I appreciate the offer, but I'm in Lubbock right now. It might take a couple of hours before I make it back to Smithtown."

"Not a problem. I'll tell Patricia to go ahead and feed the boys and send them to bed. It'll be easier to carry on a conversation without the constant chatter of those little guys. That should make dinner more pleasant and peaceful. The offer still stands. Why are you in Lubbock?"

"I'm following through on putting in a satellite dealership there in Smithtown. I talked with old man Buford this morning about buying the property where Jennifer is renting." He paused and snickered. "I thought the old guy was going to kiss me on the lips when I told him I wanted to buy the place." He laughed.

"So, he's going to sell it to you?"

George was still laughing. "Buford came close to accepting an offer I hadn't made yet. We hadn't discussed price, but he was ready to hand over the deed right then and there. Can you believe it?"

"Why, yes . . . yes I can. Do you know how long he's had a for sale sign stuck in the ground out by that mailbox at the highway?"

"No."

"Well . . . I don't either exactly. But I'm pretty sure it has been multiple years. So, you got a good deal on it, did ya?"

"Sure did. About twenty percent below appraised value."

"I'm impressed."

"I'm gung-ho now about getting all this done and start selling cars in Smithtown. That's what I was doing in Lubbock today, talking to Bernie Moore, my lot manager here, about financing and timing on ordering vehicles for a start-up.

"Okay. But, what about Jennifer?"

Clearly lighthearted, George quipped, "Well, she'll have a choice to make—marry me and then we'll move into Mom's old house together, or she can live in a refrigerator box."

"You sure seem confident about the direction of things."

"I really am. I haven't felt this good since . . . well, since I woke up."

"Excellent. Now pile your butt into that slick old Dodge of yours and get back to Smithtown. I'm sure I'll be starving by the time you get here."

"I'm walking out the door right now. What's for supper?"

"Heck if I know. It's always a surprise."

There was a second of quiet on the line. "You did tell Patricia I was coming, right?"

"I'll tell her when I get home."

"What are you trying to do, destroy my reputation with your wife? She's going to hate me for showing up with such little notice."

"Nah, she loves you."

"Okay," George replied, drawing out the word, "but remember, if she says anything negative to me about it, anything at all, my finger will be pointing at you, and then I'm throwing you under the bus."

"You've got a deal." Alex ended the call.

* * *

Within minutes he was in his car heading south out of Lubbock. His head swirled with the way he wanted the balance of his life to turn out, Jennifer's part in it, the renovation of his childhood home, the car lot, and other things that blew into and out of his thoughts. None of it unimportant, but some of it certainly of lesser importance.

It occurred to him that twice today he had thought of Marie and Louisa, but instead of shading his mood, he remembered them fondly with love, eliciting a warm smile. His state of mind continued to improve. He coped and compartmentalized their memories in a special place in his heart in such a way that it now didn't superimpose over a vision of a future with Jennifer. He still had a hill to climb with Jennifer, though. He had to convince her that he saw her as a real person and not as Sweet Jen—that he loved her for who she was in the here and now.

It crossed his mind that he had a notion how to do that and had even mentioned it to Jennifer without details. Although she didn't want to make a fuss about the assault by Lassiter, George figured someone still needed to come to her defense. She shouldn't have to bear that burden alone. The fledgling idea had suddenly become conviction. He popped the top of the steering wheel with a fist. *I'm going to do it!*

George patted his coat until he remembered which inside pocket held his cellphone and retrieved it. He dialed Alex.

"Hello," Alex replied.

"Alex? George."

"Hey George, we have the kiddos fed and in their bedroom so we can eat in peace. How far out are you?"

"I hate to drop this on you at the last minute, but there is something I've got to do, so I won't be stopping in Smithtown. I'll just be passing through without stopping."

"Passing through? What possible business do you have to deal with south of here?"

"Just something I have to do to prove a point to Jennifer."

"Oh crap. You're not heading for Abilene, are ya?"

"I'll explain everything tomorrow."

Alex growled and then grunted. "I'm going to kill Lenny, if that's where you're going. He had no business telling you what that guy did to Jennifer."

"It's not Len's fault. He was trying to be a friend. It was entirely the fault of that prick, Lassiter." George ended the call.

* * *

"George? Hello, George?" Alex let the phone dangle from a limp wrist between his fingers while he thought about the conversation.

"How long will it be before George gets here?" came the question from Alex's wife, Patricia.

"He's not."

Patricia came around the kitchen door into the living room, wiping her hands on a cup towel. "Did I hear you right? He's not coming?"

"Nope," he replied as he chewed on the inside corner of his cheek. He was wondering whether he should do anything. If George was indeed heading for Abilene, Alex believed there were several ways things could go wrong if he confronted Lassiter. "I need to call Jennifer," he finally said and punched in her one button quick dial on his phone. All he received was a recorded message that her phone was either turned off or beyond the service area.

"What's going on, Alex?" Patricia asked.

"Not sure, hon. But I'm afraid George is in the process of doing something stupid."

Alex repeated the effort to reach Jennifer over the next fifteen minutes with the same result. Finally, on the eighth attempt, she answered.

"Alex," Jennifer said, her voice clearly strained.

"Hey Jen. Are you crying?"

"Oh, Alex," she said, sniffing. "It has all gone totally out of control."

"What are you talking about? What's going on?"

"I drove out to Mesa Park for a little *me* time. Michael was pulling into Smithtown as I was leaving town and he followed me. I went for a long walk and when I got back to my car, he was waiting for me. He . .

. he raped me, Alex," she said and then added more forcefully, "That sonofabitch raped me!"

"Oh crap. Where'd he go, back to Abilene?"

"Hell, I don't know. Probably."

"This is bad, very bad."

"Are we still talking about the rape?"

"Yeah. That and the earlier assault on you. I, uh, had a very strange and abbreviated conversation with George. That's why I've been trying to call you."

"Oh?"

"I can't guarantee it, but I think he might be heading to Abilene to confront Lassiter about that earlier assault. I bet Lassiter will think it's about what happened this evening. It won't take George long to put two and two together to figure out that it's now about much more than a slap."

"Did George tell you that he was going to Abilene?"

"Not directly. I guessed it and he did not deny it."

"Then I need to stop him before he learns the whole story," Alex said.

"No," she blurted. "It's getting late and Michael will probably be home by now. You don't know where he lives. I do."

"Point taken. But how would George know where he lives?"

"I think that's what George was trying to tell me—a way to prove his love for me. He's probably already looked it up and mapped how to get there."

"Are you going to follow him?"

"I have to. If George figures out that Michael raped me, George will kill him, or try. I'm still in my car. He doesn't have that much of a head start on me. Maybe I can intervene before George gets himself thrown in jail, injured, or worse yet, killed. He's no match for Michael in size, strength, or volatile temperament."

"Drop by the house and we'll go together. I'm sure as hell a match in size and strength. I'll twist Lassiter's head right off his shoulders, if need be."

"Uh-uh. No way."

"Why not? George is my friend, too."

"Exactly. You're not the coolest head around. You'll dive in and start throwing fists as quickly as Michael will. Sorry, but you'd be worse than George about staying cool. And you can't raise a family from a jail cell. I think I can diffuse the situation. With you at my side, that becomes a much more difficult thing to do."

The comment deflated him. "You don't trust me?"

"Trust you? No, not in this situation, but love you—absolutely. You're the dearest friend a person could have, and always have been. I will treasure you for the rest of my life. Don't worry. I can take care of it."

An ego busting comment had suddenly transformed into something endearing. He became emotional. "Right back at you, Jen."

"All I want you to do is tuck your boys into bed and then hold that sweet wife of yours."

"Okay, but keep your phone handy and if you run into trouble, any whatsoever, call me and I'll come running."

"I know you will. I'll definitely call if things go sideways." Jennifer ended the call.

"Well?" Patricia asked. Alex didn't respond quickly enough to suit her. She grabbed and shook his arm. "Don't keep me in suspense, Babe. What's the deal?"

He was suddenly shaken from his thoughts. "Huh? Oh. Jennifer wants to handle it alone."

"Can she?"

"That's what I was just wondering."

* * *

Jennifer reached the intersection of the highway to Abilene as she ended the call with Alex. She turned left and accelerated south out of town toward the area of Texas known as the Big Country.

She was supremely confident, but had to be there before George discovered that she had been raped. If late, even by seconds, all hell would break loose. George would be all-in before good sense could clue him that he didn't have a chance against Michael in a fist fight. She had never seen him in a fight, but she had seen George in altercations when they were in high school. He didn't fare well. But one thing she was certain of—George had not had a good year. He was ripe for sadness and anger to collide in a violent way. That scared hell out of her. As various scenarios streamed through Jennifer's reeling mind, tears squeezed from anxiety-riddled eyes.

The worst-case scenario involved Michael's penchant for violent outbursts. She stroked the bruise on her cheek. He had that explosive side. He could and would react dangerously before thinking. It was not beyond believability that Michael could kill George and be justified, regardless of the rape. Michael was a talented attorney and knew the law inside and out.

That was enough self-instilled fear to push her speed up.

Damn it, George! I love you—you fool. We can have what you thought we had. I can be your Sweet Jen.

She topped eighty miles per hour and the speedometer continued climbing. Her fear that she might not get there in time to prevent calamity also escalated.

As Jennifer approached the exit to the Abilene suburb of Tye, the red heat indicator on the instrument panel flickered, then stopped winking and stayed on. She slammed the top of the steering wheel with a clenched fist. "Crap! Not now!" She drew in a large volume of air and exhaled slowly, forcing calm. She patted the dashboard. "Come on Little Sweetie, just a little farther. After everything we've been through, don't let me down now."

Jennifer took the exit off Interstate 20 and headed south on the highway that would take her to the upscale neighborhood where Michael Lassiter lived. As she passed the barbed-wire topped chain-link fence of Dyess Air Force Base, her car began to intermittently sputter. The glowing red heat indicator light seemed to pulse even brighter. *Damn it!*

* * *

Alex sat fidgeting in his recliner, but the blaring television couldn't hold his attention. All he could think about were possibilities for George and for Jennifer before this night was over. None of those potentialities were appealing and would possibly be dangerous. He shoved the footrest down on the recliner and sat straight, snatching his cell phone from the short table next to his chair.

"Who are you calling, Babe?" asked Patricia, as she came into the living room from the kitchen.

"I know I promised that I'd let Jennifer handle the situation, but I can't sit on my butt and do nothing. I'm calling George."

"Wait a minute. You're not going to tell him that she was raped by that jackass, are you?"

"No, no. Whomever Jennifer chooses to share that information with is entirely her business. I do hope she presses charges against that sonofabitch though, and I'll be encouraging it. I know she wants to preserve the legal collaboration for old man Brewster's sake, but this is way over the top. As her friend, I won't allow her to ignore it. I thought I'd try talking George out of confronting the guy, though. At the moment George thinks it's only about a slap in the face and Lassiter's persistent interference in her life. He has a cockeyed notion that standing up to the guy on her behalf will prove to Jennifer how much he cares for her. If Lassiter thinks George knows about the rape, all hell will break loose. So, no, I'm not going to give away any information about the more serious offense. All I want right now is for George to come home before something bad happens to him."

Patricia stepped closer to Alex and gave his shoulder a gentle pat. "You're a good friend."

"Jennifer, George, Lenny, and I—we all had our problems. All our families were broken in one fashion or another, but we had each other. It never mattered that we drifted apart for a time." He covered her hand with his own and looked up at her. "You and the boys are my family. I love y'all beyond words, but those three people, my crew, are also my family . . . always have been."

She smiled. "I know. Make your call."

Alex punched a single digit speed dial on the phone. As he waited for a response, he looked up at his wife and said, "You and me, later, our bedroom."

Her smile broadened. "I'll be there."

He watched his wife walk away just as George finally responded. "Alex, what's up?"

"I've been thinking about you confronting Lassiter over his assault on Jennifer. I think you're making a huge mistake."

"What makes you think that's what I'm doing?"

"Come on, George. Don't play this game with me."

"Okay, okay. That is what I'm doing."

"I know. It's a mistake."

"Why?"

"Jennifer wanted to handle this situation herself. Is it not reasonable to assume that she will see what you're doing as interference? She'll be royally pissed, Brother."

"I didn't consider it from that angle," he slowly replied, and then went silent.

"The point I'm making, George, is I think you should turn around and come home. You and I can figure out something you can do to Lassiter, but with Jennifer's knowledge and approval. Whaddaya say?"

"But I'm approaching his house now. I've come too far to turn back now." George paused for a second. "How about I soft-peddle it by knocking on his door and telling him that I was in Abilene anyhow and thought I'd look him up. And then simply ask him to not bother Jennifer anymore and let her get on with her life. I might as well tell the guy something since I came all this way. How about that? Soft enough for ya?"

"I—I'm not sure even a low-key approach is a good idea. How about—"

"Oops, sorry, got to go, pal. His house is just ahead." George abruptly ended the call.

"Oh George," Alex mumbled to himself, "I sure hope you don't find out about the rape."

Two sudden knocks on the front door sat Alex straight. Patricia was already on her way before he could get out of his chair. When she opened the door, there stood Lenny. "What brings you out after dark?" she asked.

"I came to beg forgiveness," Lenny replied.

Alex stood and gestured to the sofa. "Sit. Talk to me."

Lenny shuffled over and lowered himself slowly onto the sofa as if he had been called into the principal's office, which he had been many times in his younger years. "I think I may have screwed up by telling George about that Lassiter fella hitting Jennifer."

Alex raised an eyebrow. "Friend, stop thinking it and start owning it. You may have tipped the first domino."

Lenny's eyes widened. "Shit! Really?"

"Afraid so," Alex said. "George was supposed to come over for dinner but after stewing on it for a day, he decided to blow right on through town and head for Abilene to confront Lassiter."

"I messed up in a big way."

"Don't feel too bad, Len. It's not all your fault. I shouldn't have told you what Jennifer shared with me in confidence." Alex paused and pulled a half-smile. "I've known for years that you and secrets didn't play well together. You were always trying to get rid of them as quickly as you could—usually, right after you were told not to tell anyone." He chuckled.

Lenny smirked. "Thanks a lot."

"Seriously, Len—and it is much more serious than you're aware— this evening Lassiter drove into Smithtown and followed Jennifer out to Mesa Park. She just wanted to be alone and go for a walk. He waited in the parking lot for her and raped her."

Lenny snapped to stiff attention. "Is she okay?"

"Physically, I think she's fine. But her concern is that George will find out during his conversation with Lassiter and do something impulsive that will not end well. Jennifer is racing down there right now, hoping to get between them before that can happen."

"Why didn't you go with her?"

"I tried. She didn't want me to. She thinks I'm more of a hothead than George is."

Lenny nodded. "Inability to keep a secret is my curse. Yours is holding your temper. But I think you should have forced the issue."

Alex ran his fingers through his thinning hair, frustrated. "You're right. I should have." He slapped his knees, feeling a renewed surge of commitment. "Now that you're here, there's no reason that you and I shouldn't hop in the car and go right now."

Lenny sprang to his feet. "Let's do it. Can we take your vehicle? My old truck only knows how to get home. Your car has GPS."

"Honey," Alex said to Patricia, "I've got to do something."

"Somehow, I already knew that." She snapped up a warning finger. "But you and Len be careful. Don't you boys get caught up in something that gets y'all hurt or thrown in jail . . . or both."

As she spoke, Alex was already marching toward a short bookcase near the front door where his car keys lay, "Don't worry about us. If you must worry, do it for George. He has no idea what he may be getting himself into."

Lenny came to stand next to Alex. "Is it even possible to get down there before something happens?"

Alex puffed his cheeks tight with air, shook his head slowly, and then blew it out in a huff. "No. But the four of us have always been there for one another and this time should be no different. Even if all we can do is bail George out of jail or, God forbid, sit with him while he's unconscious in a hospital emergency room while holding and consoling Jennifer, then that's what we'll do, be there . . . for them both."

* * *

Wisps of steam escaped from both sides of Jennifer's hood and swept back over the windshield, the engine clattered. Her eyes darted nervously from that prophetic hint of impending failure to the intersection ahead as she approached the street she remembered so well. The street that would take her to Lassiter's home in a prime neighborhood in northwest Abilene. The old Toyota she had put so much faith in was on the verge of failing. Base intuition told her that she approached the most important moment of her life. Although, specific reasoning for that assumption escaped her.

She took a hard turn onto the winding street, squealing the tires. Carelessness was of no consequence. Her goal was single-minded. She had trouble regaining control—almost going into a sideways skid, but she continued. She remembered two sharp curves ahead and then Lassiter's house should come into view after rounding the second on the left. The car engine had now progressed to misfiring, becoming sluggish and unresponsive to the accelerator. Even to the mechanically challenged, it was clear that the overheated engine was about to seize.

Going into the first curve on this street the car abruptly died, leaving her to coast to near the second curve.

Jennifer whimpered, imagining the worst—a violent physical altercation between Lassiter and George. *Oh George. I hope you have enough sense to walk away.*

The car was now quietly coasting. Jennifer couldn't bear the slowing pace and slammed on the brakes. She threw open the door and began running. The night was chilly, but she scarcely noticed and certainly didn't care. Huffing the chilled air, her lungs began to burn from exertion.

Much more slowly than desired, she rounded the curve. Although running as fast as she could, it wasn't fast enough. The house came into view. She saw George's car parked out front. Her eyes went directly to the porch light above the front door on a portico befitting a home of such size and obvious expense. What she saw pushed her to ignore her winded condition and to run even faster. George, standing in front of Lassiter, took an exaggerated step toward the bigger man—clearly an aggressive move to invade Lassiter's personal space and to antagonize him.

Peripherally, she heard the rumble and roar of an engine over-accelerating. It must have just turned off the highway onto this winding residential street behind her. The noise scantly registered in her consciousness. She was convinced that the two men were headed toward a violent showdown that George would lose. Lassiter countered the move to get in his face by planting a hand on George's chest, disallowing him to come any closer.

* * *

"Get away from me," Lassiter bellowed. "I'll be damned if I let you assault me in front of my own home."

"Assault? That wasn't the plan. All I want you to do is leave Jennifer Andrews alone. She has enough adversity going on in her life without you throwing your crap into that mix. You two working together is one thing, but I'm asking you to stay out of her personal life."

Lassiter squinted, and then frowned, cocking his head to the side.

George paused, wondering what brought on the sudden odd look. "What?" George asked, becoming frustrated.

"You don't know, do you?" Lassiter replied.

George's aggravation clicked up a notch, confused by the question. He tossed his hands into the air in a clear display of frustration. "What sort of damn guessing game are you playing? What is it that I don't know?"

"George! Don't!" came an imploring scream from across the street, almost canceled out by the roar of an older model pickup truck just then coming into view behind her.

George's eyes darted between the truck and Jennifer. He spun away from Lassiter. He began walking toward her.

She came off the sidewalk with clear intent to keep running across the street.

George broke into a sprint. "Jen! Look out," he shouted as loud as he could.

Party expressions of the driver and his passenger vanished and went terror stricken in an instant. They both saw at the same time what was about to happen. All four of the big tires squealed like a banshee as the driver locked the brakes.

"Jen, get back!" George screamed, waving his hands.

His warning came too late, falling on ears deafened by a loud engine and screeching tires. The right end of the highly polished chrome truck bumper hit Jennifer with such force that it lifted her into the air and threw her spinning back onto the grassy easement between the curb and the sidewalk.

George's appeals went from high-pitched warning cries to guttural anguish. "Oh no—oh God." He collapsed onto his knees next to her. She moaned and attempted to move. The pain on her face tore at his heart. A trickle of blood oozed from a cut on her scalp and from another on the opposite cheek. He placed a hand on the less injured side of her face. "Don't move. Lie still."

She opened her eyes. They swam in their sockets for a couple of seconds until locking onto his face. Miraculously, the pain so clearly present seconds ago melted into a dreamy smile.

Michael Lassiter came to stand over them. George snapped a hard look up at him. "For God's sake, man, don't just stand there gawking. Call 911."

The young men in the truck came toward them. The driver shuffled forward tentatively, rubbing the sides of his jeans with flattened palms, as if scared to see the damage he had done. He was in tears, babbling, "I'm sorry. I didn't see her. She darted in front of me." Both the boys were young—high schoolers.

George barely took note, glancing up and nodding at the young man, knowing that the boy spoke the truth. His eyes went to Lassiter who gave details to the dispatcher about the nature of the emergency. George felt helpless.

Jennifer continued smiling up at him. She snaked a hand across the grass with obvious difficulty and covered his other hand upon the ground. "Hold me, George," she whispered. "It's so cold."

He carefully slid a hand beneath her head and the other hand around her shoulders. He leaned into her, offering the only thing he could—his warmth. They were cheek to cheek.

"Tell me that I'm your Sweet Jen," she breathed into his ear.

George drew a ragged breath. "Oh, God, yes you are. You *are* my Sweet Jen . . . always have been, always will be."

Just as the name was clearing his lips, she lost consciousness and went limp in his arms. George lost control, soaking the grass beneath his face with his tears.

* * *

George stood outside the treatment room looking through the emergency room window and watching a team of doctors and nurses working in unison on Jennifer—a dance of professionals—hands flying but none overlapping. Each had a task and knew exactly what to do and when.

George had impressed upon the emergency medical tech that she be taken to the best hospital in Abilene. It was that EMT who suggested Waters Emergency Care Center as the only level three trauma center in the area. From the moment that Jennifer was wheeled through the automatic doors, he saw that the level of care was good. Still, he didn't relax. Jennifer's face had lost the blush of health—now a disheartening grayish blue. She hadn't regained consciousness.

Fresh tears filled his eyes. Although he sought only thoughts of a positive outcome, pessimism nipped at him. Tears spilled and took the same track as those shed earlier. He slowly bumped his head against the glass of the large window that offered a view of Jennifer's treatment room.

After an agonizing few minutes, George felt hands come to rest on each of his shoulders. He looked up and saw Alex on one side and Lenny on the other—brothers in life. That was all it took for George to crumble. He openly wept, pulling them both into an embrace at the same time.

"What's the word on our gal?" Lenny asked in a low calm tone.

George sniffed and swept away tears. "From what I can hear, it's nothing good. They can't get her vitals stabilized. The only thing they can determine definitively is a broken hip and a couple of ribs, but I heard one of the doctors say that the bones were of little concern compared to an undetermined number of likely internal injuries." His face screwed down tight. "Guys, she's torn up inside real bad," he said, forcing the words through sobs.

Alex squeezed George a little tighter. "Keep it together, brother. Jennifer is tough. That girl is a fighter. You know that."

"He's right, George," Lenny offered.

George nodded. "How did y'all know to come here?"

"When we pulled up to Michael Lassiter's house, he was standing in the front yard talking to a neighbor. Apparently, we just missed the ambulance. He told us where they took her. That asshole said he was about to leave and come here, too. Of course, I felt it necessary to impress upon him that that was not going to happen and that he was forbidden to ever see Jennifer again. Of course, he became testy. So, I punctuated my statement with a nice tight fist to the side of his fool head. I just wasn't in a mood to debate it."

Lenny nodded. "Yep. It happened just that way. And, here we are."

"You guys are the greatest," George said, as he turned his attention back the other side of the window. The frenzied level of activity over Jennifer continued unabated. He, Alex, and Lenny looked on quietly, but it was clear that prayers were being sent up by his pals, just as he was doing. The clock, suspended outward from the wall down the corridor, seemed to slow. After a few minutes, one of the doctors placed a hand on the forearm of the nurse next to him, causing her to cease what she was doing. That's when George saw it—the doctor's almost imperceptible negative shake of the head.

Chapter 30 ~ The Way It Is

Jennifer heard a voice, but thought that it was born of her imagination. Or worse, possibly of evil origins inhabiting this present darkness that she wanted no more to do with. She remained trapped in a nightmare, swimming in a soup of indecision, fear, and despair, struggling mightily to find a way out, yet not realizing that the voice she heard sought only to help. "Wake up," the voice repeated down through murky depths to reach her. Someone was shaking her by the shoulders. She changed directions and swam toward the voice and emerged from the bottomless depths of a frightening dream. The suffocating heat turned to a chill as she navigated upward toward an awakened state. Her eyes popped open and then darted about frantically. She saw that a comforter and sheet had been shoved aside and mounded between her body and the warm body at her back on the bed.

Strong hands gently pulled her over onto her back. Her eyes settled on the man—the love of her life, George. She shivered in the open air of the cool bedroom on her exposed body, covered only in an over-sized t-shirt. Jennifer took a deep breath and smiled. "It's so cold in here. Please, hold me."

"Welcome back, Sweet Jen," George whispered, pulling her into his arms as he closed the gap between them.

She had trouble believing that the dreaded gloom holding her prisoner inside the dream hadn't followed her. All it took was an eye-to-eye connection with George for the dreary weight of her nighttime prison to take flight. Memories, wonderful memories, flooded her mind. She realized, once again, just how wonderful her life with this man was, and had been all the way back to their prepubescent years, especially the past sixteen years, the day of their wedding.

George suspended his body on his elbows facing her. "Bad dream? It sure must've been."

Jennifer's breathing evened out. She closed her eyes and pressed the heels of her hands into them. "Oh, George, it was horrible." She shivered. "Hold me tighter and don't ever let me go again."

"Again?" he asked, as he arranged the disheveled covers and pulled them back over her, and then lowered his upper torso onto her to add his own warmth. "What do you mean by 'again'? I've never gone anywhere."

"Sorry. I don't know why that word slipped out. Forgive me?"

George put his mouth to her ear and kissed it. He whispered, "It's the very least I can do for my Sweet Jen." He lifted his head and then kissed her softly and sweetly on the lips. "The dream? What was it about?" he asked, breathing the questions into her face.

"It was horrible, George. I dreamt that we . . . I mean that you . . . I honestly can't remember. All I do remember is a feeling of impending doom and loss. Deep in my heart I felt like I was losing you, and that it wasn't the first time."

George smiled. "Never." He kissed her again—this time slowly, nibbling on one lip then the other.

When he pulled back, he traced her face with his eyes, running his fingers through her short dark hair.

Jennifer did no less, looking into the face of the man she had loved with all her heart since childhood. He wore his fifty-one years well. He was as handsome as ever with a smattering of gray at the temples and his only wrinkles were those adorable smile lines around his eyes.

"Getting warmer now?" he asked.

She smiled and snuggled deeper under the comforter. "Oh yes. Thank you for being here when I woke."

"Where else would I be?"

"I-I don't know." She thought for a moment, but then smiled. "Let's blame that stupid dream."

George grinned. "Yeah. Stupid dream." He chuckled.

Her smile faded. "George, that scenario you made up about the hierarchy at John Deere sending you on a business trip and the plane going down in the ocean, leaving you stranded and out of touch with the world—"

"I feel silly about that now," he said. "I was just scared about the hypnosis session with Doctor Levine. But it worked. All the strange visions and headaches are gone."

"I know," she said, "but that's not why I brought it up."

"Oh?"

"You wondered if our love was strong enough that I'd know you were still alive and could sense that you were trying to find a way back to me."

"I just wasn't sure what hypnosis would do to my mind. That's all."

"I understand. But the reason I brought it up has to do with the horrible dream I had last night."

"Similarities, maybe?"

"Kind of. I had the most profound feeling that we were apart, but it was me that was lost, trying to find my way back to you. Unfortunately, I can't explain it beyond that."

"Jen, I can't imagine you ever having such dismal thoughts, even in your worst nightmares. You and Rachael Irissa are the lights of my life."

Tears brightened her eyes. "Make love to me."

George hesitated with a smile fixed. "We are living the dream, you know."

Jennifer reached for the back of his head and began pulling it closer. Just before their lips came together, her breathing deepened and she whispered, "If this is a dream, I don't ever, ever want to wake up."

About the Author

A lifelong Texan, Daniel Lance Wright is a freelance fiction writer and novelist born in Lubbock, Texas now residing in Clifton, Texas. He lives with Rickie, wife of 46 years. He is the proud father of two and grandfather of four.

Having spent the first nineteen years of his life on a cotton farm on the South Plains of Texas and the next thirty-two in the television industry, he has seen the world from two distinctly different angles.

Daniel has received recognition for writing skills from The Oklahoma Writers Federation in 2005, 2006, 2010, and 2011; from Art Affair in 2008; from Frontiers in Writing in 2004; from Canis Latran of Weatherford College in 2011; and from The Indie Excellence Book Awards in 2013. Also from ATTMPress, *"Annie's World: Jake's Legacy"/soft science fiction/print, ebook, & audiobook*